CROSS ROADS

Other Books by Karel Čapek
from Catbird Press

CROSS ROADS

By Karel Čapek

Translated from the Czech and
With an Introduction by Norma Comrada

Illustrated by Paul Hoffman

CATBIRD PRESS
A Garrigue Book

Translation of *Boží muka* (1917) and *Trapné povídky* (1921)

First English-language edition

CATBIRD PRESS
16 Windsor Road, North Haven, CT 06473
800-360-2391; catbird@pipeline.com
www.catbirdpress.com

Our books are distributed to the trade by Independent Publishers Group

This book is a work of fiction, and the characters and events in it are
fictitious. Any similarity to real persons, living or dead, is coincidental and
not intended by the author.

Library of Congress Cataloging-in-Publication Data

Čapek, Karel, 1890-1938.
 [Boží muka. English]
 Cross roads / by Karel Čapek ; translated from the Czech and
introduction by Norma Comrada ; illustrated by Paul Hoffman.
 Contains two collections: Wayside crosses, and Painful tales.
 "A Garrigue Book."
 ISBN 0-945774-54-0 (trade paperback : alk. paper) -- ISBN
0-945774-55-9 (hardcover : alk. paper)
 1. Čapek, Karel, 1890-1938--Translations into English. I. Čapek, Karel,
1890-1938. Trapné povídky. English. II. Comrada, Norma. III.
Title.
 PG5038.C3 A23 2002
 891.8'6352--dc21
                                 2002001282

CONTENTS

Czech Pronunciation Guide

b, d, f, m, n, s, t, v, z - like in English

c - like ts in oats

č - like ch in child - Čapek = Chop'-ek

ch - one letter; something like ch in loch

d' - soft, like d in duty (see ě below)

g - always hard

h - like h in have, but more open

j - like y in you

l - like l in leave

ň - like n in new (see ě below)

p - like our p, but without aspiration

r - rolled

ř - pronounce r with tip of tongue vibrating against upper teeth, usually approximated by English speakers by combining r with s in pleasure

š - like sh in ship

t' - soft, like t in tuesday (see ě below)

ž - like s in pleasure

a - like u in cup, but more open - Karel = Kah'-rehl

á - hold it longer

e - like e in set, but more open

é - hold it longer

ě - after b, m, n, p: usually approximated by English speakers by saying the consonant plus yeah; after d and t, soften the consonant by placing tongue at tip of upper teeth

i, y - like i in sit, but more closed

í, ý - hold it longer, like ea in seat

o - like o in not, but less open

ó - hold it longer, like aw in lawn

u - like oo in book

ú, ů - hold it longer, like oo in stool

ou, au, and eu are Czech dipthongs

Rule No. 1 - Always place accent on the first syllable of a word.

Rule No. 2 - Pronounce all letters.

Introduction

Cross Roads brings together two early volumes of short stories by Karel Čapek, *Wayside Crosses* (1917) and *Painful Tales* (1921). Although he had been publishing numerous stories, columns, reviews, and other works since 1904, many in collaboration with his brother, Josef, but these were the first story collections Karel had produced on his own. These two books are thus an important milestone in Karel Čapek's literary career, and the second came out at another critical turning point, just after the premiere of the play that would make the young Czech author internationally known: *R.U.R. (Rossum's Universal Robots)*. After this success, Čapek's literary attention turned from stories to plays and novels; it would be eight years before he would publish another story collection, *Tales from Two Pockets*. And he rarely wrote with his brother again, although they remained close and Josef often illustrated Karel's books.

The original titles of these two collections convey more meaning than do their traditional translations into English. In the case of *Wayside Crosses*, the original title, *Boži muka*, literally means "God's torment," or "Calvary" (however, it is people who are tormented in both these collections), and it is also the Czech term for the small roadside shrines common in Europe, often found precisely where the protagonists in both collections tend to find themselves – at a crossroads. *Painful Tales* in Czech is *Trapné povídky*; the word "painful" is inadequate to all the senses of *trapné*: the sense of awkwardness, of embarrassment, of frustration – much like the feelings of the characters in these tales, not to mention those of the reader.

Wayside Crosses

Some critics deem these metaphysical tales to be among Čapek's best work; others see their value more as a starting point for some of the themes Čapek continued to address: the nature of miracles and the absolute, of faith and reason, of truth and intuition, of illness and time. Čapek had just completed his doctoral studies in philosophy, with a dissertation on "Objective Methods in Aesthetics," influenced primarily by the work of the French philosopher Henri Bergson and the American pragmatists. Other significant influences on the stories include the delicate state of his health – especially a debilitating spinal condition – and the First World War with its senseless killing, the seemingly endless waiting, desolation, and despair. In Čapek's own words: "The motivations behind *Wayside Crosses* were the war and the expectation of a miracle, meaning that it would end favorably for us, and – based on a mistaken diagnosis – a supposedly fatal illness and thus, to a certain extent, a coming to terms with life and death…"

Wayside Crosses was also a starting point for some of Čapek's literary techniques, most significantly his literary cubism. In his excellent book *Karel Čapek,* William E. Harkins calls this "perspectivism," the construction of a cumulative series of viewpoints, each of which contributes something to the entire picture. As his brother Josef experimented with planes in his cubist paintings, so Karel experimented with viewpoints and impressions in these stories (especially "Temptation" and "Reflections") and in many of his later works (most notably *Three Novels*).

For all their variety of style and circumstance, these stories have some common elements. One is the theme of searching, whether for a specific person or solution, or for truth and redemption. The searches are necessarily limited by the characters' all too human shortcomings and their varied perceptions of reality. These stories are also pervaded by a sense of mystery, and while Čapek referred to them later as a failed early attempt at detective fiction, the mysteries here tend to be far more enigmatic and elusive than what that genre usually offers; the mysteries are as elusive as what the characters strive but fail to find.

All this searching and mystery led some critics to wonder whether the book represented a religious conversion. Čapek's reply was, "In a certain sense it is a conversion: not to faith, but to sympathy. I continued this in *Painful Tales*."

Painful Tales

Despite their expression of sympathy, *Painful Tales*, written during the four years following the publication of *Wayside Crosses*, bears scant resemblance to the earlier book. To begin with, Čapek employed more conventional structures and fuller characterizations. The dilemmas these characters face are on a much more down-to-earth, everyday level. They too are searching, but for practical solutions, for ways of coping with the predicaments they find themselves in, or for escaping from an unbearable situation. These are stories in the tradition of Maupassant and Chekhov. The element of mystery is gone.

The shared element in these collections is the recognition and acknowledgment of human frailty and human limitations. The characters in *Painful Tales* are all too human. They are full of self-doubt, and of dubious, often conflicting motives. They torment themselves, they yearn for meaning and resolution, love and understanding, in a world filled with disappointment, discord, banality, vulgarity, and misunderstanding. Often they cannot (or will not) express their true feelings, creating a dichotomy between what is said or done and what was intended. Their limited emotional resources hinder their attempts to contend with a variety of troublesome situations and choices.

Čapek's intent was to depict people with all their faults, yet without – and this was critical to him – degrading their worth and value. And as B. R. Bradbrook points out in her fine book *Karel Čapek: In Pursuit of Truth, Tolerance, and Trust,* despite the sadness that pervades these stories, this collection is more optimistic than the first, because it takes the philosophical position that "truth is recognizable after all, be it only through some painful, unpleasant experience."

It is difficult to make moral judgments about the characters in the stories – greedy, frustrated, obsessed as they may be. The stories show how difficult it is for anyone to judge anyone fairly. Čapek wrote of the book: "People act wrongly, cowardly, cruelly or weakly, in a word, painfully; and the whole point is that you cannot judge any of them; you can't throw stones at anyone ... there is no one to blame."

The pain we feel in reading these stories is offset by the compassion Čapek encourages us to have for their characters, for each other.

Acknowledgments

Without Rob Wechsler and Peter Kussi, there would be no book. Wechsler not only proposed the idea but pushed and pulled it through to completion. Kussi, le bon Bohème, offered fine, funny, and thoughtful advice throughout. Anything slipping through the cracks is purely the fault of the translator.

Norma Comrada

Wayside Crosses

The Footprint

PEACEFULLY, ENDLESSLY, SNOW kept falling over the frozen countryside. Silence always falls along with snow, thought Boura, sheltered in a cabin of sorts. His mood was both festive and melancholy, for he felt isolated in the vastness of the landscape. Before his eyes the world was becoming simplified, blending and expanding, piling up in white waves, undisturbed by any confusing traces of life. Eventually the dance of snowflakes, the only motion in that glorious silence, thinned and stopped altogether.

Walking outside, Boura hesitantly sinks his feet into the untouched snow and finds it curious that, with his long line of footprints, he is the first to leave his stamp on the countryside. But coming towards him on the road is someone dressed in black and covered with snow; two lines of footprints will run next to one another and then cross, introducing the first human disorder onto the tabula rasa.

The antipode, however, pauses; he has snow on his beard and is staring intently at something not far from the side of the road. Boura slows his pace and looks in the direction of the other man's eyes; the rows of footprints meet and come to a halt next to one another.

"You see that footprint over there?" said the snow-decked man, and he pointed at an imprint perhaps six yards from the side of the road.

"I see it: it's a man's footprint."

"Yes, but how did it get there?" Someone was walking there, Boura started to say, but he held back, puzzled: the footprint was alone in the midst of a field, and neither before nor behind it was there a trace of other footsteps. The print was quite clear and distinct against the white, but it was solitary: nothing led either to it or away. "How could it have gotten there?" he marveled, and he began to move toward it.

"Wait!" The other stopped him. "Make any more footprints around it and you spoil everything. This calls for an explanation," he added irritably. "It won't work for there to be nothing but a single footprint. Let's suppose someone jumped from here into the field; then there wouldn't be any imprints in front of it. But who could have jumped so far, and how could he have landed on just one foot? He'd be sure to have lost his balance and to have set his other foot down somewhere; I expect he'd have had to keep on running a bit, the way one jumps from a moving streetcar. But the second foot isn't here."

"Nonsense," said Boura. "If he'd jumped from here, he would have left footprints behind him on the road, and there's nothing on the road but our footprints. No one was here before us."

"On the contrary, the heel of that print is facing the road; whoever made it was coming from this direction. If he were going to the village, he'd have had to go to the right; there's nothing but fields on this side, and what the hell would someone be looking for in the fields at this time of year?"

"I beg your pardon, but whoever put his foot down in the snow over there would have had to continue on somehow; but I'm telling you that he didn't go anywhere at all, because he didn't take any further steps. It's clear. No one passed this way. There has to be some other explanation for the footprint." Boura pondered the matter with utmost concentration. "Perhaps there was a natural depression in the ground over there, or a footprint left in mud that froze, and snow fell into it. Or else,

wait a minute, perhaps a cast-off boot was standing there and a bird carried it away when the snow stopped falling. In either case there would be a snow-free spot similar to a footprint. We must look for *natural* causes."

"If a boot had stood there before the storm, there'd be black earth left under it; but all I see is snow."

"Perhaps the bird carried away the boot while it was still snowing, or in mid-flight he dropped it into the fresh snow and then carried it off again. It simply cannot be a footprint."

"Tell me, can this bird of yours eat boots? Or build a nest in one? A small bird can't pick up a boot, and a big one couldn't fit inside of it. We need to solve this on general principles. I think that it *is* a footprint, and since it didn't come up out of the earth, it must have come from above. You fancy that it was carried off by a bird, but it's possible that it might have fallen from – – from a balloon. Maybe someone was hanging from a balloon and placed his foot down into the snow just to make fools of us all. Don't laugh, it's embarrassing to try to account for this in such a far-fetched way, but – I'd prefer it not to be a footprint." And both of them walked over to it.

The situation couldn't have been more clear. Rising gently from the ditch along the side of the road was an unploughed, snow-covered field, in the field was the footprint, and just beyond the footprint stood a medium-sized tree thickly blanketed in snow. The stretch between the road and the print was virginal, without the slightest sign of having been touched; nowhere was the surface of the snow broken or disturbed. The snow was soft and pliable, not powdery as after a heavy frost.

It was indeed a footprint. It was the imprint of a large American-style boot with a very wide sole and five large hobnails in the heel. Since the snow was cleanly and smoothly packed, and there were no loose, untrampled flakes on its surface, the footprint could not have come into existence until after the snow had stopped falling. The imprint was deep, and the weight that had borne down on the sole must have been much greater than that of either of the two men leaning over it. The bird-and-boot theory vanished without a word being spoken.

Directly above the footprint hung the outer branches of the tree: they were slender and enveloped in snow, with no sign of having been knocked against or shaken. A light tap on a branch would have made the snow drop off in clumps. The hypothesis "from above" failed utterly. It wasn't possible to do anything from above without shaking snow from the tree. The existence of the footprint took on a harsh, naked clarity.

They climbed the slope beyond the pristine, snowy field and walked along the top of the hill; another white, untouched slope dipped down, far down, and beyond that a new slope rose, more vast and whiter still. There was no sign of a second footprint for kilometers.

They turned back and came upon their double rows of footprints, neat and regular, as if they'd been made on purpose. But between the rows, in the center of a well-trodden circle, was the imprint of an other, more impressive foot, cynical in its isolation; something held them back from trampling it and disposing of it in silent collusion.

Exhausted and perplexed, Boura sat down on a milestone at the side of the road. "Someone's had a good laugh on us." "It's disgraceful," said the other, "it's an incredibly stupid trick, but – Damn, there are such things as physical limits. It's completely impossible – – Listen," he burst out, practically in anguish, "since there's only a single footprint here, couldn't it have been made by a man with only one leg? Don't laugh, I know it's idiotic, but there *must* be some sort of explanation. I mean, it's a matter of common sense, it's an assault on – I'm completely baffled. Either both of us are fools, or I'm asleep in my bed with a fever, or there *must* be a natural explanation."

"Both of us are fools," Boura offered, as if having given it some thought. "We keep searching for a 'natural' explanation; we'll snatch at the most complicated, most nonsensical, most contrived cause, so long as it's 'natural.' But perhaps it would be far simpler – – and more natural – if we just said that it's a miracle. If we simply marveled at it and calmly went our ways – – Without any confusion. Perhaps even content."

"But I wouldn't be content. If the footprint made something great happen – – if it brought some good to someone, I would get down on my knees and cry out, 'Miracle!' But that footprint, it's, well, painfully embarrassing; it seems awfully petty to leave just a single print behind when one could have left the customary row of them."

"If someone were to bring a dead girl back to life right here before your eyes, you would kneel down and humble yourself; but before the snow on your knees had melted, you'd be thinking that her death had been merely an illusion. What we have here isn't a matter of illusions; what we have here, let's admit it, is a miracle performed under the simplest of conditions, as if it were a physics experiment."

"I might not believe even such a resurrection. But I too want to be saved, and I'm ready for a miracle – – for something to come and turn my life around. The footprint neither saves nor converts me, nor does it disabuse me of any notions; it only torments and obsesses me, and I can't get it out of my mind. And yet I don't believe in it: a miracle might reassure me, make me feel content, but this footprint is the first step towards doubt. It would be better if I'd never seen it."

For a long time neither of them spoke. It began to snow again, more thick and heavy. "I'm reminded of reading in Hume," Boura began, "about a solitary footprint in the sand. This one isn't the first. I imagine there are thousands of footprints just like it, vast numbers of them that wouldn't strike us as anything unusual because we're accustomed to fixed, natural laws. Another person might not have noticed this footprint; it wouldn't have occurred to him that it's unique, that there are things in the world that have no bearing on anything else. You see, our own footprints are alike, but the solitary one is larger and deeper than ours. And when I think about my life, it seems that I must acknowledge that there are – footsteps in it that come from nowhere and lead nowhere. It's terribly mistaken to think of everything I've lived through as no more than a chain that begins at one link and ends at another. Suddenly you see or feel something comparable to nothing, nothing that came before, and nothing the least like it can ever occur again. There are things that have nothing in common with anything else, that are merely evidence of their own solitariness, wherever they are. I know of things from which nothing flows, which bring salvation to nothing and no one, and yet – Things have happened which led nowhere, offered no help in living, and yet were perhaps the most important things in life. Didn't it strike you that this footprint is far more beautiful than any you've seen before?"

"And I'm reminded," the other replied, "of seven-league boots. It may be that some people come across such footprints and don't know any other way to explain them. Who knows, maybe the footprints preceding this one are near Pardubice or Kolín and the next one is all the way over in Rakovník. Likewise, I can imagine the next step landing not in snow but perhaps in the midst of people, in the midst of some sort of goings-on, where something just happened or is about to happen; and that our footprint here is a link in a continuous chain of footprints. Imagine a chain of wonders in which our footprint has its natural place. If we had perfectly well-informed newspapers, we might be able to locate the rest of the footsteps in one of the dailies and follow this or that person's route. Perhaps some sort of deity is proceeding along his own route; he takes it, one step at a time, without a break. Perhaps his route is some sort of lead that we should follow; then we could walk step by step in the footprints of a deity. Perhaps it's the road to salvation. Anything is possible – And it's appalling to have before us one surely *certain* step on this route that lies before us and not be able to follow it further."

Boura shook himself and rose. It went on snowing more thickly, more steadily, and the trampled field with the large footprint, right in the midst of the others, was disappearing under a new layer of snow. "I won't let go of it," said the snow-covered man. "The footprint that is no more and will not be," Boura finished the thought, and they set off on their separate routes, in opposite directions.

Elegy
(Footprint II)

THAT EVENING Boura was giving a lecture to the Aristotelian Society. He felt exhausted and had trouble concentrating; he realized that he had not won over the small audience, and that he would be obliged to enter into a discussion, which he found vaguely repugnant. For a moment he listened to his own voice; it seemed thick and indistinct, its cadences heavy and its stresses unnatural. He made a futile attempt to adjust it, to bring it under control, and then he simply listened to himself with displeasure.

Moreover, his audience disheartened him. It seemed as if they were on the opposite side, at an immense remove, and he resented having to share his ideas with them. All of the faces seemed uniform and boring; they were so lifeless that he lost his confidence in reality and fumbled in something of a void, which he was unable to conquer by filling it with words. He forced himself to observe individual faces; he distinguished those of his friends, but he felt estranged from them and was somewhat surprised by the innumerable details he now noticed for the very first time. What on earth is the matter, he asked himself while summarizing his deductions, why is it that I am so indifferent to what I'm saying? He felt securely confident in the organization of his lecture and spoke without hesitation or doubt; he was presenting a position he had long held, which had come to him once in a moment of transport and had since become a conviction. But now, as he listened to himself in this unaccustomed silence, it all seemed alien and outlandish. But it's all true, he felt, it's truth so bald and explicit that it's no longer mine; I am merely presenting facts that have nothing to do with me. He remembered how personally, how intimately *his* these ideas had seemed when they had first occurred to him in the form of inspiration. Accordingly, he suffered when he wavered and rejoiced at each new piece of evidence, as if it were a personal achievement; accordingly, these ideas had become a part of his inner life. But today they were merely truth, external and impersonal, bearing no relation to him in any way; they were so lifeless that he unwittingly raced through his material in order to be over and done with it. The more he hurried, however, the more his words tormented him: they were alien and abstract, utterly different from what he had once believed, and yet each word and each turn of phrase had been familiar to him for ages. Now these words bore the hollow, painfully embarrassing sound of repetition. Now all he could think about was the ending; with each word he aimed toward it, unswervingly, ever closer: if only it were all over! The auditorium was hanging on his words. I've done it, I've laid it out for them; now come the fundamental points. Please, God, no faltering, no weakness! And then suddenly Boura skipped his line of reasoning and the lecture came to a sudden stop.

The Aristotelians were dissatisfied; several of the rhetoricians rose with questions and objections. Boura only half followed them; when he heard his ideas from other mouths, they struck him as even more alien and self-evident. Why should I defend them, he thought with insensible sadness. After all, not one of these ideas has anything to do with me, they're pure truth, the truth and nothing more; they have no connection with me whatsoever. He had difficulty speaking and had to force himself to concentrate, yet he sensed that he was winning them over, that he was once again "making his case." – But then, he reminded himself in wonderment, it is not, in point of fact, my case.

A new adversary stepped forward, a man whose hair, brushed straight up, struck Boura as uncommonly wild. "Please tell us, if you will, how you define the word 'truth'?" he asked in an antagonistic voice.

"I said nothing in my lecture about epistemology," Boura objected.

"Nevertheless." The speaker smiled sarcastically. "It would be of great interest to me."

"You are going off on a tangent from the debate," grumbled a few of the Aristotelians.

"Please, I beg you to excuse me," said the wildly tufted man, smiling victoriously, "but the question does pertain to the matter at hand."

"It does not," the Society roared.

"It does," Boura suddenly declared.

"Then please give us your response," said his adversary.

Boura stood up. "Please, I should like to end the discussion period."

The Aristotelians were astonished. "It would be better to address this question," said the president. "I speak in support of Societal precedent. But we would not, of course, compel you to do so."

"I have nothing to add to my lecture," said Boura obdurately. The Aristotelians laughed, and the lecture foundered. There was nothing for the president to do but bring the meeting to a close "with regret, since we were prepared to enjoy a most engaging discussion."

At length Boura escaped outside, with a parched throat and an empty head. The winter evening air was soft, as if it were about to snow; even the streetcars clanged softly, as if muffled in cotton. Boura heard someone running behind him and he slipped behind a tree. The man came to a stop, breathing heavily.

"I'm Holeček," he blurted out. "I recognized you at the lecture. Do you remember me?"

"No," Boura replied with some uncertainty.

"Think back: last year, that footprint in the snow–"

"Aha!" said Boura, delighted. "That was you! I am truly glad ... I think of you often. So, have you found any further footprints?"

"No, but of course I've been looking. – Why didn't you answer that last question?"

"I don't know. – I didn't feel like it."

"Listen, I have to say that, really, you very nearly won me over. It was all so clear, what you said! When that hairy beast asked you that idiotic question, I wanted to jump up and say: What? For an entire hour, sir, you listened to the truth, and now you are asking what truth is? You heard the evidence, which it is impossible to contradict. There were no gaps in the argument, and no mistakes. Nothing was said that wasn't rational from head to toe. Why didn't you answer him?"

"Why didn't I answer him?" Boura repeated despondently. "I don't know what truth is. I know that everything I said was self-evident, logical, correct, whatever you like. But it was not so self-evident, so logical, when it first came into my head. At the time, those notions were so bizarre that I often found myself laughing at them. I thought I was crazy. It made me extremely happy to be so fortunate. And yet there was no rhyme nor reason to any of it. I don't know where it came to me from, so pointless, so purely haphazard."

"A footprint that comes from nowhere and leads nowhere," Holeček suddenly recalled.

"Yes. And now I've turned it into a system or, perhaps, a truth; everything in it is logical and clear. But at the time – I don't know how to say this – it was so strange, more beautiful, more miraculous. – Nothing came of it then, it was of no use for anything. I knew that it is possible to have countless other, even contradictory ideas that are equally beautiful and preter-natural. I was conscious of a boundless freedom. Nothing per-fect can be refuted. But when I began to turn it into a truth, it seemed to me as if it all materialized. I had to refute a great deal in order for it to remain one single truth; I had to prove, persuade, be logical. But today, when I was giving my lecture, I suddenly understood: at the time, yes, at the time, I was closer to something different, something more perfect. And when that raging bull asked me what truth is, I had it right on the tip of my tongue: truth makes no difference."

"Better left unsaid," was Holeček's prudent opinion.

"It is something more than truth, something that does not bind, but releases. There were days when I lived as if in ecstasy; I was so free then. – Nothing seemed to me more natural than miracles. They're simply occurrences that are more freeing than others and, above all, more perfect; they are simply felicitous incidents among thousands of failures and coincidences. How close that footprint was to me at the time! But later, from the standpoint of truth, I hated it. Tell me, did we really see it?"

"We did."

"I'm so happy I ran into you," Boura rejoiced. "I was expecting you, actually. Let's go somewhere, wherever you like; lecturing at the institute made me dry as droppings on pavement. If you can believe it, at times I actually *saw* myself speaking, as if I were sitting out there in the audience."

They came to a wine cellar, walked downstairs, and went inside. Quite excited, Boura talked at great length and poked fun at the Aristotelians, while Holeček merely twirled the stem of his glass between his fingers. So, he thought, eyeing Boura, you troubled man, what is it, exactly, that you're searching for? You saw a miracle, but it didn't save you. You recognized truth, but you didn't surrender to it. You had a great inspiration, but it failed to enlighten your life. – Oh, if only I had your wings!

Wingèd spirit, were those feathers given you only that you might abandon everything? So that nowhere would you find sleep or some small corner of your own? So that you might fly up into the void and there amuse yourself in space, or rest in nothingness? Had it been I who recognized the miracle, I would have found redemption; had it been I who found the truth, how would I not have seized it with all my might! And had there flown to me no more than a single spark of God, would I not be like a chapel with an eternal light? Should the burning bush itself speak to you, it would not be your salvation. Yet your eyes are impassioned and you would recognize God in a bush, even in stinging nettles, whereas I am blind and corporeal and unable to see a miracle.

All you lack, so that you might be redeemed by faith, is a captivity in Egypt; but who could fetter you, fleeting and godless spirit?

"Remember," Boura said, leaning toward Holeček, "last year, when we were standing over the footprint? You said that perhaps some sort of god had passed by here, and that it would be possible to follow him."

"Oh, no." Holeček frowned. "It's not possible to search for God using the methods of a detective."

"How, then?"

"There is no way. You can only wait till God's axe severs your roots: then you will understand that you are here only through a miracle, and you will remain fixed forever in wonderment and equilibrium."

"The axe has already lopped yours?"

"No."

From a table in the corner a man rose and approached them. Tall and powerfully built, with red hair and a broad, open face, deep in thought, he stood with his head to one side and contemplated Boura as if from a distance.

"What is it?" said Boura, a bit taken aback.

The man did not reply, but it seemed as if his eyes were coming closer, ever more attentive, narrowed, searching. "Aren't you Mr. Boura?" he suddenly said.

Boura stood up. "I am. And you?"

"Didn't you have a brother?"

"I have a brother – abroad somewhere. What do you want with him?"

The man sat down at their table. "That's it," he said enigmatically, then suddenly he raised his eyes and said: "You see, I am your brother."

Boura was overjoyed and at a loss. "You! Are you really you?"

"I am," said the man. "How are you prospering?"

"I'm – why are you speaking so formally?"

"I'm out of practice," said the man, and he attempted a smile, but his expression was one of fixed watchfulness. "Exactly like Mamma," he said, tracing the shape of Boura's head with his finger.

"I wouldn't have recognized you," Boura said warmly. "My God, after so many years! Let me look at you! You take after Father, after Father."

"Possibly."

"What a coincidence," Boura enthused. "It was sheer chance that brought us here, me and – my friend Holeček."

"My pleasure," the man said gravely, offering Holeček his large, warm hand.

"But what about you?" Boura asked with some uncertainty.

"Nothing much, I'm here on business. I have something to take care of down south, an industrial matter. I wanted to get used to being home."

"I haven't been home ... since our parents died," Boura confessed.

"They've razed our building. What's there now is a school or something, an ugly brick structure. I went inside, and they came up to me and asked me what I wanted there. They were so stupid, they didn't know anything. But across the street is that little house, the same as before, only about this high," he said, indicating with his hand.

"I don't know, I don't remember." Boura was fumbling for words.

The redheaded man leaned toward him, his eyes narrowing in concentration as he strained to remember. "It was the house of – the house of – Hanousek!" he cried with sudden glee. "Hanousek, the beggar, lived there."

"And his daughters!" Boura was beaming.

"Yes. Their eyes were always red, with painful-looking rings around them. And I used to go there sometimes to eat with them."

"I didn't know that," said Boura.

"I did. They toasted bread for me on the stove top – anything the old man got from begging: leftovers and bread-crusts, peas, awful things; I ate everything they put in front of me. Then I'd lie down on the beggar's bed and let his lice feast."

"No wonder we called you in vain," said Boura, with a smile.

"No, when you called me, I was up on the hillside, in the high grass – this high. No one knew the place, and there I had my little hole, like a rabbit, and I could look down on our building. I could see very well when Mamma ran out calling me, searching for me, crying with fear and love. I found it ago-nizing, and terribly sweet, but I wouldn't have called out for anything in the world. I was afraid she'd see me and that I'd wave to her. I did want to show myself to her a little, but just the tiniest bit, so she wouldn't recognize me."

"She often searched for you," Boura recalled.

"Yes, often. I only wanted to see if she would search for me; I'd sit there holding my breath, waiting to see if she'd come. She called, she searched, but she didn't cry anymore. And then one day she didn't even go out looking. That day I waited until evening, although I was afraid to be up there by myself. But she never came, and I didn't go up on the hillside again. I began to roam farther and farther."

"Where are you living now?"

"In Africa. I didn't think they loved me, and that's why I roamed around so much. I wanted to try and see if something would happen to me. I liked that feeling. Well, no one at home spoke to me, and so I'd go talk with the roadworkers on their piles of gravel. Old Hanousek never said a word, except to curse a bit, but his daughters talked a lot, very softly."

"What did you do next?" Boura asked almost shyly.

"Never mind –" The redheaded man was lost in thought.

Boura waited expectantly. Perhaps he will say something about himself. There is so much time and distance between us that scarcely any number of words would bridge the gap. But look, brother, we can sit together like this for years, making small talk about insignificant, everyday things, about everything we know; it's possible that vast numbers of trivialities are necessary for people to become closer, to understand each other.

But his big brother only smoked, spat, and looked at the floor. Boura was moved by a feeling from his childhood: it was him, his older brother, who could do what he wished and have his own secrets. I'd like to know everything he's doing, but he isn't telling me anything. I'd like to tell him everything I'm doing, but he isn't asking me. I'll never understand him!

How often, how often I would see you coming from somewhere, looking preoccupied, secretive, sated like a cat who with savagery and delight has devoured a sparrow and come back with a begrimed face, a criminal with gleaming eyes! How often did I go to the place you had abandoned, to search, to discover something you had hidden there; and turning every-thing upside down, disappointed and distressed, I found nothing but the cobwebby underside of things. And even now you have that face I know so well; you have returned from somewhere as secretively as you did then, like the cat who at one and the same time remembers and anticipates the delight of its next campaign.

"Never mind," his big brother suddenly said, with something rather like relief. "I'm going. I'm very, very glad I saw you."

Once again at a loss, Boura rose. "I too am glad. – But please, stay a while! It's been so many years since we've seen each other!"

His big brother put on his coat. "True, many years. Many, many years. Life is too long." Both brothers stood there embarrassed, not knowing how to part. The big brother turned his head as if he were looking for something, some better, clearer words; he forced a smile and moved his lips. – "Do you want any money?" he finally blurted out. "I have more than enough."

"No, no." Refusing, Boura suddenly felt happy, and touched beyond measure. "No, please, it isn't necessary; but thank you, you are kind. God be with you."

"Why not?" the older brother mumbled, and then he hesitated. "I don't need it myself. Well, as you like. Goodbye then."

He walked out, tall and erect, except that he carried his head a little to one side. Holeček followed him with his eyes all the way to the door, where he saw him give a wave of his hand and leave.

Boura stared at the floor.

"He left his walking stick," Holeček called out, and he ran after the man, brandishing the stick; he was glad that he could leave Boura alone for a moment.

On the stairs he heard footsteps above him.

"Hey! Mister!"

In two jumps he was up in the entryway. But the street was empty as far as he could see. Wet snow was falling, and it melted as soon as it touched the ground.

Puzzled, he looked back at the entryway. There was nothing but the stairs going down. Two figures separated themselves from the wall. Police.

"Did you see someone just run out of here?" Holeček asked. "What did he steal?"

"Nothing. Which way did he go?"

"We didn't see anyone," said one of the officers. "No one's come out of the wine cellar since we've been here."

"And we've been here at least ten minutes," the other added.

"Perhaps he's still downstairs."

"He's not," countered Holeček, dumbfounded. "He was a few steps ahead of me. He left his walking stick."

"His stick," the officer repeated, thinking it over. "No, nobody came out of here."

"But he couldn't simply have vanished," Holeček bellowed, suddenly angry.

"That he couldn't," the officer agreed in a soothing voice.

"Go downstairs, sir," the other advised. "We're starting to get a real snowstorm out here."

They think I'm drunk, Holeček realized, and I've had less than a glass of wine. What's happened this time? "He was walking a few steps ahead of me," he explained, exasperated. "After all, he couldn't have just disappeared like that, but if he had gone out, you would have seen him, right?"

The officer took out his pad: "What is this man's name?"

"Nonsense," said Holeček. "What do you want with him?"

"Who knows what's happened to him. Perhaps an accident or –"

Holeček's lips twitched with the wild anger he was feeling. "If it were only that," he shouted and, slamming his way through the door, he rushed downstairs.

Boura was sitting over his wine, besotted with regret. He had scarcely noticed Holeček's absence. "Your brother vanished," Holeček announced, trembling with cold and confusion.

"Just like him," Boura commented, shaking his head.

"I beg your pardon," Holeček said impatiently, "but he was going upstairs and suddenly he vanished. He didn't go outside, it's as if the earth had swallowed him up."

"Exactly like that, yes." Boura nodded. "As if the earth had swallowed him up. He was always doing that. He'd run off and no one knew where; later he'd return, an odd look on his face, absorbed in his thoughts, as if he'd seen more than it's possible to comprehend."

"Dammit, listen to what I'm saying: he didn't run away, he vanished. Of course it's absurd. He vanished at the top of the stairs; two police officers were standing right by the entry and they didn't see him leave."

"A character, a genuine character. As a child he was already so – – yes, unfathomable, a loner, terribly mercurial, hard, designing. You barely know him."

"But you don't seem to understand." Holeček was seriously upset. "He vanished like a ghost, as if he'd gone right through the wall."

"I understand. He was so intemperate in everything he did, so volatile. He never troubled about what he could or couldn't do; it's as if he had neither conscience nor limits. So often, so often did he astonish us!"

"But can a man simply disappear?"

"I don't know. My brother didn't go to school, he hadn't the slightest understanding of the sciences; he had no idea at all what is possible and what is not. In fact, he had extraordinary contempt for all learning."

Holeček banged on the table. "But that doesn't make any difference!"

"Then what does?" said Boura, raising his eyes.

"No one can disappear. You understand, there are–"

"–physical limits. I know. You said that already, back at the footprint. Physical limits! As if they made such a difference to you! Look, I've seen all sorts of things and read a lot more, but there's nothing I've understood better than the resurrection of the daughter of Jairus. I saw the dead girl. – – Well, according to mechanistics, that atrocious doctrine, the only truly natural thing would be: a miracle. The only thing that would answer man's deepest questions –"

"Miracles, yes," said Holeček. "To save people, to cure the sick, and above all to resurrect those who died young. But what was the point of what I just saw, and who could have been helped by that? If there are miracles, why are they so pointless? Nothing flows from a miracle, nothing."

"Even if it isn't of any use to anyone, it's still a miracle! In us too there are such events and occurrences, which may have no purpose ... other than their own perfection. Sudden moments of freedom. – Even if they're only moments! If things came to pass in a way that was natural for our souls, *miracles would happen.*"

Time Stands Still

WHY IS HE, the one I'm thinking about, who is leaning over a writing table, why is he so motionless, why does he wait and listen for something to happen outside of himself; how could anything give him instruction in sorrow or bring an end to the endless succession of doubts moving through him? All around him are mere routines of veiled melancholy; and the opposite side of the street, in its formless silence, wears an expression so uncommonly empty and so unpleasant that in his suffering he gratefully seizes on the rattle of a carriage on the paving stones as the point of departure from this moment to the next.

The clop-clop of hooves amidst the rattling, the drawn-out rhythmic progression and clatter turn the corner, ringing off the paving stones; the sound rolls on like a ball of yarn, at a distance now, ever softer, an extended ticking like a slender, elongated thread, so slender that perhaps it is no longer, perhaps now it is no longer anything more than elongated distance, an impossible length, then silence.

The silences within and without are fused together like two unruffled, utterly homogenous surfaces. Everything is utterly homogenous, like a surface that is taut, motionless. The man at the desk holds his breath and his heart lies still, like a surface. The silence is stretched taut like a canvas, and all is silent, all things are bits of silence ironed into a smooth, motionless plane. The desk and the walls, all things around him are like a drawing on a smoothed sheet, clear, without foreshortening or shadow. They are stretched taut on the area of the plane, on which there are neither creases nor irregularities; everything is incorporated into the incorporeal plane like straws frozen in ice.

Nor is the man at the desk outside of it: he is there, motionless, in the vast surface of things, and he cannot break free from it; were he to move even slightly, he senses it would bring about the disarrangement, the warping of all its parts, a terrible corrugation of the taut planes. Without awe, without time, without within. An anguish that might be death, departure, effacement. To not feel is the positive feeling of non-existence and the powerful suffering of non-existence; the motionless conflict of non-awareness of thought, and of pressure at the edges of the void. Surface everywhere, with its sad, dead planes. What is standing still is time; if it were possible to move it even slightly, time would shatter instantly into thousands of seconds, which would fall downward, dead, like dust. But the man at the desk is afraid to move; with his multitude of anxieties and infirmities he is embedded in silence like an insect in transparent amber; he is utterly stopped.

And then footsteps on the sidewalk, fine, loud, regular. The world on the motionless plane falls to pieces in unvoiced explosion; out of the bursting rise things angular and massive, the man at his desk is sent flying in all the directions of space, feeling how abundantly he branches, how his movements thrust out into the world. The edges and angles of all things make themselves heard in the jagged buzz of space: quickly, quickly they go in their directions, with self-assurance and rigidity. The man's heart takes up its old pain with powerful, powerful beats; the one I'm thinking about stands up, so that he may bear the weight of his grief, and the great wheel of existence turns in ever wider, ever faster circles.

Story Without Words

DEEP IS THE FOREST AT NIGHT, like a bottomless pond, and you stare in silence at the star over Melatín, thinking of the beasts that sleep in the depths of the forest, of the deep slumber of all, and of all within you that never sleeps. Long and endless are the tenebrous days; how many times you have walked in the woods on days like this. Ah, the countless footsteps and memories, and never did you reach the end of those footsteps or those memories: that vast, and that deep, is the forest above Melatín.

But now it is a blazing August afternoon – burning paths beneath the crowns of trees, sickles of light combing through the thick forest. So clear is the day that the deep forest seems thinned and parted before the sun. The parching heat drains away my memories, and I could easily drift off to sleep, whether from delight or fatigue I know not as I rock with the white umbels that sway above my head. –

On a day just like this, Ježek was walking in the forest, content to be thinking of nothing and to be incapable of thought. The heat radiated around and among the trees. A fir cone broke free – it had forgotten to hold on, so still was the air; the treetops stirred and the light trembled. Oh, what a fine, beautiful day! How the quivering blades of grass glinted with silver! Appeased with pleasure, or ennui, Ježek listened to the buzzing of the heat in the woods.

Dazzled, he stood at the edge of a clearing where the searing heat inaudibly vibrated. What is this lying here? A man. He is lying motionless, face to the ground. Flies graze on his outstretched hands, which do nothing to shoo them away. Is he dead?

Reverently, yet with dread, Ježek bent over the hands that tightly held an old slouch hat. The flies did not dart away. On the hat's faded lining, a few letters were still legible ... ERTA EL SOL. Puerta del Sol, flashed through Ježek's mind, and he drew nearer to the dead man's face. But at that very moment the man opened his eyes and said: "Could you give me a cigarette?"

"Gladly." Ježek released his breath with considerable relief and fervor. The man took the cigarette, fastidiously smoothed it out, and rolled over on his side to light it. "Thanks," he said, and he became lost in thought.

He was graying, no longer young, with a broad and vague sort of face; he had somehow grown too thin for his clothes, so that they hung on him in oddly lifeless folds. And there he lay, stretched out on his side, smoking and staring at something somewhere on the ground.

Puerta del Sol, Ježek reflected, Gate of the Sun; what was he doing in Spain? He doesn't seem like the tourist type. Perhaps he isn't well, he has such solemn eyes. Puerta del Sol in Madrid.

"Have you been to Madrid?" he blurted out.

The man softly snorted in assent but didn't say a word.

He might have said who he is, Ježek speculated; one word leads to another, and you can guess the rest. – On the other hand, he might have said: Yes, I have been to Madrid, but that isn't the most distant place I've been to, and there are settings still more beautiful and lives still more strange. He might have lied about all kinds of things. Look, now he's recollecting.

The man softly waved his hand and went on staring vaguely and pensively at nothing.

Perhaps he's saying: I see by your look that you find me interesting; you mistook me for a dead man and you leaned over me in pity. I will now relate to you the story of my life. Don't interrupt me if something seems to you disconnected or extraneous. Simply read my face to see whether I lived simply and easily. That's more or less the way he'd start.

But the man just smoked, slowly and in silence, fastening his clear, unseeing eyes upon the infinite.

Surely he will have something to say, Ježek thought; it's hard to find words for the story of a life. I'll wait, then. – He rested quietly, lying on his back. The sun struck his eyes and penetrated his eyelids; red and black circles began to turn and dance searingly before his eyes. The heat radiated in long, fiery surges, and Ježek felt blissful, as if he were drifting on the rings of black and red, in a gradually welling tide of waves, in boundless and unyielding motion. And where flows this powerful yet gliding motion? Nowhere; it is merely the motion of a life in its own setting.

Suddenly he turned. A pale-hued ant was wandering across his hand, not knowing which way to go on so vast a surface. We too, little ant, thought Ježek, we too are unsettled by a world so vast: those distances, little pilgrim, the panic, the joylessness! Why do you scurry so? Wait, stay; I won't do anything to you, for all that I myself am vast. Oh, little adventurer, is it only confusion that drives you? the wild and despairing confusion of solitude? some sort of anxiety? Where is the gate through which you might escape?

Nearby, within reach of his nearby hand, a butterfly lit on a flower, its wings spread wide; it swayed on the white umbrel and waved its graceful wings, clenching and distending them with movements both bewitching and carnal, sweet to the point of intoxication. Ah, rapture, abide! Don't bewitch my heart with your endless motions of departure! Cling on, let yourself be rocked to sleep, a moment of imbalance, a vague intimation! A gracious encounter after such hardships of passage! The magical wings fluttered virginally, and suddenly, incomprehensibly, the butterfly, the moment, and the rapture vanished, as if a gate had slammed behind them.

Ježek looked up. Where had everything flown? Where do you fly to, luminous clouds, in aimless, tireless motion? Ah, to drift in just that way, to no purpose, for no reason whatsoever, other than the vastness of the firmament; to drift in just that way, for vast is space and it never ends! For vast is desire and it never ends. Comforting firmament, my soul is gentle as my eyes. But why, gentle eyes, do you search the horizon? why, most gentle soul, are you always discovering in yourself the demonic virtue of insatiability? How high the clouds sail, how dizzyingly high – as far, you could say, as the gate of the sun. Puerta del Sol! Ježek looked back at the man whom he had found. He had fallen back into sleep, and his face seemed indistinct and careworn, open and gentle. – Now Ježek rose so as not to awaken the man, and went into the hot forest, lost in thought, with no more questions, as if sated. It was as if he had overheard the story of a life, a tale with little clarity, but intimate; disconnected, but nonetheless a tale. – It was as if he had overheard the story of a life, and already it was slipping from his mind.

The Lost Way

WE'VE LOST OUR WAY!"

"Obviously."

"Where have we got to? Do you see anything? Where's the road?"

"I don't know."

"Where are we? Did you see anything at all like a heath around here?"

"No."

"But how on earth could we have lost the road? Surely we must have crossed the drainage ditch ... Listen, we did cross the ditch, didn't we?"

"I don't know."

"This is absurd. Surely a road can't get lost under our legs. Where are you?"

"I'm sitting down."

"Walking along a road is different from walking on grass. Harder and louder. And I just now heard us going down a road."

"You were making enough noise."

"There you have it! Surely this is downright unheard-of ... This is the most outlandish thing I ever ... Don't go to sleep on me, friend!"

"I'm not sleeping."

"Where exactly are we?"

It was a dark, almost starless night; only some luminous stones on the ground could be discerned, and a small, erect, motionless juniper; only the cry of an owl could be heard drilling into the stock-still darkness from an unknown distance.

"Don't laugh at me," said the standing man, "but I don't like this. We've truly lost our course. We need to find a road, no matter where it goes; a road at least says 'onward,' but roadlessness says nothing. To be without a road is somehow to taste infinity, it's around us on every side. Listen, this is an impossible situation."

"Sit down," said the other.

"I don't want to. I'll sit down somewhere on a road, in the middle, between the right- and left-hand sides, so that I know where I am. For someone traveling along a road, the world in the wings on either the left or the right is unimportant, like the walls of a long corridor, but roadlessness is like the top of a mountain: too far out into space, too open on all sides. Let's get away from here!"

"Wait a bit longer, I can't yet."

"Has something happened to you?"

"I can't go. Yes, something did happen to me. I came upon something just as we began to stray off course. Perhaps at that very moment."

"Where was that?"

"I don't know. It came to me completely out of the blue. I hadn't thought about it in years, and now it's surfaced all of its own accord. Perhaps it's precisely because we suddenly lost our way."

"A memory of some sort?"

"Not a memory. A solution. An answer. Something I've been searching for my entire life, even when I wasn't thinking about it. Oh God, is this dreadfully complicated! It's changed my entire life. – Everything relates to everything else. Do you understand this?"

"Not at all."

"Nor do I. Apparently, I had to leave the road in order to come upon it. To leave behind all that is familiar! That's why they walked in the wilderness! Even to the abandonment of their home and family. Your logic is woven from routine, and the roads you travel from thousands of bygone footsteps; and that is why you leave everything behind and begin to stray off course, so that you can search in the unknown. That is where you find what is most strange and what is furthest from routine."

"Are you saying this to me?"

"I'm saying it to myself, because I've found it. You find yourself but cannot get to know yourself; and yet, after all, it's what you've been searching for so long. My God, for so many years! And suddenly the solution: the most joyous and inexpressible feeling comes over you that here it is; it isn't yet a thought, but only a dazzling moment, a wondrous certainty. Listen, my life appears to have changed; perhaps our ways are parting, but I'm glad that I experienced this moment with you."

"If you would at least tell me – "

"I can't. Even now I can't single out any one thing. You must experience truth as a feeling before you can put it into words. You must find yourself in truth, as if it were an area leading nowhere but rather open on all sides, for thought is a road headed in one direction only, like a corridor between walls. Thought goes only onward, on one of many roads; truth alone goes nowhere and heads in no direction, for it stands like open space."

The standing man continued to listen attentively. It seemed to him that somewhere in the thousandfold silence of the vast night, a tiny, voiceless rhythm was unrolling. It seemed to be flooding the surface of the silence, but here it was and it was forcing its way resolutely along the road. Human footsteps! The distant tread of feet on the hard surface of a road! The standing man sighed with relief.

"There's the road," he said, and was immediately taken aback by his voice; it rang out so much more clearly and colorfully than before.

The seated man roused himself as if from sleep. "What? A road? Will you be heading home now?"

"You'd rather stay here, perhaps?"

"Yes. Let me explain it to you. It's extremely complicated. Wait a bit longer!"

"I'd prefer you to explain it on the way."

"If only I could write it down! Everything that's been flashing through my mind! Oh God, countless things!"

"Write it down when you get home. I'll guide you."

"Thank you. Where are we?"

"I don't know, but come. Careful, there's a deep gully here!"

"I don't see anything."

"Give me your hand! Christ, what have we got ourselves into? Careful!"

"Wait, I can't ... Let's go back!"

"Can't be done, the road lies before us. Where are you?"

"Here. Up here. And you?"

"In some water. Wait there – oh! Is anything wrong?"

"No, thanks. I'm down now."

"Then follow me. ... That's right!"

And both men stumbled to a hillside and went down the way they'd come; the ground was rugged and difficult to traverse, and a thousandfold caution was required. There was undergrowth, through which they had to force their way; there were wide, tilled tracts of land, across which they plunged as ruthlessly as boars. At last, the ditch and the road.

"Now tell me," called the one who was a bit ahead, "however could we have got way up there?"

"I don't know," the other said somewhat dispiritedly, "it's really very odd. I need to give it some thought ... I have so much to think about now!"

"Tell me, what did you come upon up there?"

"It was so curious, how we went astray! Surely I found it the moment when we lost our way. If only I were already home!"

"What was it all about?"

"About the soul..."

Now the two of them were walking at a good pace, not saying a word; they passed through a forest and hurried through a village; windows from a few houses lit the deep darkness, then once again a broad meadow opened out before them.

"What did you mean by that?"

"By what?"

"What you came across up there – the soul."

"Ah yes, right. Did I say something about the soul? Actually, it wasn't only that..."

"Listen," the other said after a fairly long pause, "what is all this about the soul? You've been terribly distracted."

"Me? On the contrary. I was thinking about it just this moment. Isn't it odd that a person is basically a stranger to himself?"

"And your solution?"

"What do you mean, solution? It's been a problem throughout the ages."

"But you had some sort of solution."

"It certainly wasn't about the soul. More likely there were other questions, about life in general ... Just this moment I was thinking how to begin."

"Begin with what first dawned on you."

"First? It was merely an inkling ... It's extremely difficult to put it into words. – I truly don't know what dawned on me first. It all happened so suddenly!"

"Then begin wherever you like."

"It's not possible. It was all of a piece ... Yes, everything was clearly related. If only I could take it all in!"

"Could you tell me some other time?"

"No, I'd rather do it now. I'll get as much as I can out of the way. But it bothers me that our footsteps are so loud."

"Let's sit down, then."

"Yes, thank you. To begin with, assume that ... When it came to me, it was all so clear. – The first thing that followed from it is how lamentable and senseless was everything that I have experienced up to now. The knowledge pierced me like a knife; I was terrified and realized that, for so many years, oh God, I had experienced nothing but unspeakable, unimagined pain. For so many years! It dawned on me exactly what I was, and how I had suffered in ignorance; how everything was futile and false, and constricting as a prison; and it was horrible to realize that my entire life had slipped by, like some newly discovered error. Oh, I could lay out still more for you. But the second thing, wait, the second – "

"The second?" his companion asked after a brief pause.

"Wait, there was indeed something about the soul – but I don't know anymore. – Yes, there was something stupendously important about the soul. God, what exactly was it?"

"In what sense was it about the soul?"

"I don't know. There weren't any words, there was simply a certainty. – It's so slippery!"

"Try to remember anyway!"

"Yes, and quickly. Something about the soul? What was it?"

"Try to think of it. I'll wait."

"Thank you. I'll come up with it in a moment."

Nighttime clung to black and formless things. But look, here is the first early bird walking along the empty road. Isn't that a cock crowing in the village? Didn't the night's silent center stir?

"Have you found it?"

"In a moment. Only something still..."

A weak illumination appeared on the horizon. The land and all its parts took on a chilly, spectral pallor; the forms kept growing whiter and sharper in outline, and then it was light.

"So what did you find?"

"I don't know ... It's slipped away. I've lost it all, and now I'll never know it."

"And nothing, absolutely nothing stayed with you?"

"Absolutely nothing, only how what dawned on me has illuminated my life."

Grafitto

PAUSING IN THE DOORWAY for a moment to catch his breath, Kvíčala felt pleased with himself: Poor ailing Matys will be glad that I've come; I'll drone on for a while by his bedside, as a diversion.

The jangle of the bell was so shrill that it gripped Kvíčala painfully; it seemed to him that the sound was blindly, alarmingly forcing its way through the now-broken silence inside, and he listened with his hand on the bell. An old woman in carpet slippers came to the door and in a hushed voice invited him in. Without knowing why, Kvíčala walked in on tiptoe and, through the open door, he caught a glimpse of Matys lying in bed, his face toward the wall as if he were sleeping.

"Who is it?" the sick man asked listlessly.

"Mr. Kvíčala," the old woman whispered, and then she went away.

Matys turned toward his friend and his eyes brightened. "How kind of you. Oh, it's nothing, just pleurisy, a bit of inflammation ... In two weeks' time I'll be up and around."

Kvíčala forced a smile. It felt oppressive in the hot room, and he became aware of the faint, drab odor of compresses, urine, tea and eggs. He was moved by Matys' bright eyes and unshaven chin; he was sorry that he had forgotten to bring a cool orange or a dewy bunch of flowers, so that he might leave it on the nightstand among the crumpled handkerchiefs, leftover food, and unread books. A vague feeling of disgust swept over him.

He tried to divert his friend; relating a few items of news, he was shocked by his thick, alien voice. He felt the eyes of the sick man watching him intently and yet at a remove; he swallowed his news items and longed to escape.

Matys asked about his friends, but Kvíčala sensed in the questions that peculiar concern of an invalid for those who are healthy, and he answered each time with difficulty. Eventually it exhausted him. At least open the window! Listen to what's happening outside! Transport at least a portion of yourself out there! Sullenly, Kvíčala avoided the absent gaze of his friend; he avoided the burning eyes and rumpled bed; he avoided the disgusting things on the nightstand and focused his eyes on the window, on the wretched, half-obscured window, on the window leading outside –

"Look at this," the sick man suddenly said, pointing his finger toward the wall at the head of his bed.

Kvíčala leaned forward. On the wall, smudged and blurry, written in pencil and underscored twice, was the word "Return." Kvíčala read it aloud.

"What's your opinion of that?" Matys asked in a hushed voice.

"Someone wrote it there. It's obviously been there for many years."

"How many years do you think?"

"I don't know. Five or ten, perhaps. – When was the room last painted?"

"I asked my mother," Matys said, eyeing the faded ceiling. "More than ten years ago. I never wanted them to paint in here for me."

Kvíčala hastily turned his eyes back to the window.

"Just take a look," the sick man urged him. "Doesn't anything about it strike you?"

Kvíčala again leaned across the bed. "It's written in a man's hand. The person who wrote it was impatient, in a state of excitement, and broke the lead right here. He dug it into the wall. In the dark. This letter is a bit odd ... These long strokes on the 'R' and 'n' look fairly resolute."

"'Return,'" Matys repeated. "Don't you have any idea what it might mean?"

"God knows, maybe some kind of resolution. To return something, for instance."

"Or to go back to something?"

"Possibly. Why do you ask?"

"Just curious. I'm wondering why it was written there."

"Perhaps someone had an idea or an inspiration and wrote down the word as a reminder, so as not to forget. Why are you so interested?"

"Because it's my handwriting. I obviously wrote it, but now I don't know, I can't remember, when or why. I keep wondering what it could mean."

"It doesn't mean anything now."

"Not now, no – but then. I came across it during my illness. I'd never noticed it before, not till now. And so for a long time I've been wondering – "

"About what?" Kvíčala said after a moment.

"I haven't thought about it for years," said Matys, his eyes closed. "What for? Everything past is so obvious. A person gets used to his past. Everything seems familiar to him. – But now I don't know what I resolved back then and I don't know what I wanted to return to or why it seemed so unbearably important to me. I don't even know when it happened. I never imagined that ... Doesn't anything from your past ever take you by surprise or disturb you?"

"No," Kvíčala said frankly.

The invalid shrugged his shoulders somewhat impatiently. "I don't know when or why I wrote it," he said after a few moments, "but I do recall many instances in which the word could have appeared to me in a dream, as some sort of deliverance. And I keep finding new moments when I might have written it. Or, rather, carried it out."

"What do you mean, carried it out?"

"I don't know. I've wondered about it for a long time, how it could have been carried out. Return, yes, but return to what? I lie here and recall all sorts of things: to which of all these do I return? I can recall much that is beautiful. There is much that I regret. A multitude of loves. Every so often an old idea flares up. And many other things, countless others, that I've forgotten, and I can no longer think about them. There is an awful lot of past. The past is dizzying."

Kvíčala sighed; the room seemed more stifling by the minute. Ah, the light, the space, the streets outside the window! The hustle and motion out there!

"The past isn't as obvious as I thought," Matys continued, as if he were by himself. "It is enormously unclear. Time and again strange and impossible things happened. It seems as if I were standing at the edge of an only half-familiar world; some things I'd already discovered, but the rest of it goes on, infinitely farther than I had supposed. I had no idea. ... It is a merciful fallacy that our pasts seem familiar to us; we know only a few things, but all the rest ... most of it remains to be lived over again in our thoughts!"

Kvíčala listened: outside, a streetcar was clanging, footsteps were proliferating, automobiles were rumbling in all directions, and the clear, thin cries of children were soaring upward. But all he could hear, disembodied, through the glass, were the insubstantial shadows of these sounds, stripped of everything close and real, an abstraction of the sounds that pressed against the window from without, a commingling with the silence.

"It's so quiet here," the sick man said, "and time goes slowly. I think about the past. It should never be overlooked. Whatever I'm thinking about now, none of it should ever be overlooked. I should live it all over again, linger, pay attention

– even the worst moments. As though I could let them all slip through my fingers, still not knowing what they were. And the most precious amongst them – ”

"You're too isolated here," said Kvíčala.

"Yes. And in two weeks I'll be back on my feet again and perhaps I won't remember that once I scrawled the word, 'Return.' Yet there it is, like graffiti on a wall. Return! Everything past is only a hint; everything remains incomplete, a suggestion, like a beginning or a vague notion ... Return! Perhaps everyone feels this way at some point and would like to go back, as if going home again – return! Ah, but it isn't a turning back to one's beginnings, to one's first steps – it is a return to endings, to closure and completion of oneself, to the final steps ... It's impossible to turn back! Never return!"

Kvíčala stood up. "Two weeks." Matys smiled. "Sorry, it's been a week since I've talked to anyone. Say hello to everyone for me." His hand was hot and dry.

Outside! Coolness, streets, people, people – And above all, "Forward!"

The Mountain

A CHILD PLAYING at the bottom of the old quarry, damming puddles left from yesterday's downpour, found beneath an outcropping of rock the corpse of a man with a shattered head. Although the child was not familiar with death, he felt a sense of dread and ran off to hide his head in his mama's lap. Now he has a cat in his arms and doesn't know why his dad has tossed his work aside and rushed out the door. Cats are better than puddles.

Anyone who stood at the top of the quarry would see the whole village as if on the palm of his hand; he would see a child screaming and sobbing as he ran off home; he would see a tiny male figure running, scurrying toward the village with the frenetic agitation of an ant. And suddenly the place is swarming with diminutive figures waving their hands and all running in the same direction, in a broken line down into the quarry. The one standing up above would laugh at this brisk stir of concentrated activity.

But if he were standing down below, in the midst of the crowd, he would feel the chill of fear and piety, and raising his eyes from the dead man, he would measure the terrible height of the cliff, all the way up to the top, to the road that runs by the low railing, dragging the gloomy sky along behind it; he would stand in silence with the rest, strangely attracted and hesitant to leave. – At that moment Slavík walked past the quarry; he felt orphaned between heaven and earth, between the hillsides and the group of cottages where he had waited out the rain. "Hey, mister!" the people called up to him, "there's been a murder." He went to have a look. –

Slavík returned home deep in thought, but once there he stood by a window and looked out at the quarry, which gaped like an open wound in the side of the mountain. It seemed horrible to him, but also intriguing.

Nothing will obliterate my image of it: the large body, the face covered with blood-stained mud, the insanely upthrust limbs, as if he wanted to leap back up, now, even now, leap up and wipe the muck off his forehead! Such a sight! The two raised hands accuse the one responsible for this hideous, broken, lifeless substance, clotted with mud – and yet, oh God, so human, those hands! Nothing will obliterate –

The dearest of faces appeared before my eyes, in a casket, eyes closed in sleep, hands crossed, and on its features an expression as if blessing me. Amidst the hours and flowers, those features slumbered with such dignity, they seemed holy. Ah, the more humane the man, the more likely to be dead, more likely than the celebrated man!

There is nothing more terrible than death, which sanctifies neither the dead nor the living. Death, with its grimace of motion, moment, chance. Death, which erases not the final traces of life. Nothing is more monstrous than the life-like gestures of the dead. Nothing more resembles desecration.

It was many long hours later that an automobile pulled up in front of the quarry, and three men hopped out. Slavík ran after them. Two of them stooped over the corpse and the third climbed along one side of the quarry.

"He fell right on his face," one of them said, adding as he rose, "all the fractures are on the ventral side. He must have died instantly. The head is completely – hm – what can I say? No one would recognize him now."

"Recognize him," the other said emphatically as he squatted over the corpse and contemplated it. "The devil himself wouldn't recognize him."

"What are you looking at?"

"Nothing, I'm just – "

"Did you find something?"

The other man also rose. "Nothing. Mine just went out, thanks," he said to Slavík, who was offering him a light. "I'm Examiner Lebeda. Yes," he said, still lost in his train of thought. – "So, doctor, how long do you think he's been lying here?"

"A day, two days perhaps – "

"Two days! Where he must be by now!"

"Who?"

"The murderer, of course," the examiner exclaimed, surprised by the question. "The one who threw this fellow down here – "

"Surely not murder!" the doctor objected. "Why – why – "

"I'm surprised that the corpse still has his hat on his head; I'm surprised it wasn't even creased or dirtied. Odd, isn't it?"

"Indeed," the doctor said with little conviction.

The examiner glared at the doctor and moved his lips as if about to burst out with something in reply. "All the dead man's monograms have been cut off."

"Cover him up," the doctor growled. Suddenly he looked at his hand with disgust. "I must wash."

"Wait," said the examiner. "Let's suppose he resisted – you know, a struggle on the edge of the cliff – but in vain. Only the hat remains up there. The murderer then picks up the hat and finds the man's initials in the lining, or the name of the firm. Look." The examiner broke off, picked up the dead man's hat, and pointed to the lining: a piece of the leather band inside the hat had been cut out with a sharp knife. "And it occurs to him that the dead man probably has similar personal markings in his underwear, on his clothes, in his pockets, and so he climbs down

with the hat in his hand – Intriguingly idiotic, isn't it; he could have simply tossed it down."

At this moment the man searching the side of the quarry called down.

"Pilbauer's found something," said the examiner. "Then down here he cuts, rips off, and takes it all with him: monograms, labels on the boots, the tailoring firm's name in the linings, papers in the pockets – everything, every indication of person or place. He didn't miss a thing. Then he places the hat on the head and goes away. This is how he left it. A nameless corpse. An identity wiped out. An enigma. A witness far too mute. What do I do now? Pilbauer, what did you find?"

"Footprints," the third man said as he descended. "Someone went bounding down into the quarry, he slipped on the wet earth."

"Yesterday afternoon, do you think?"

"Yes. He had hiking boots on, about three sizes bigger than mine."

"A big man. Hiking. Indeed," said the examiner, once again lost in thought. "A most noticeably sizeable man."

"I don't like this in the least," the doctor grumbled. "I detest murders. For heaven's sake, cover him up!"

Scowling, Slavík approached the examiner. "That's pure nonsense."

"What is?"

"That business about the monograms. Why did the murderer remove them? If he'd left them, everyone would believe that what happened was simply an accident. Not murder. Just someone falling. There would have been no incriminating evidence. Why did he do it?"

"I don't know."

"Secondly, it was stupid to pick up the hat. He obviously wasn't thinking. But once down here he certainly was – and then some. He didn't miss a thing. A good mind, apparently. – Isn't that a contradiction?"

"I don't know."

"Thirdly, you can see in here from the road and also from the village. The murderer was in mortal danger and yet he worked deliberately, slowly, downright methodically. He didn't neglect a thing. It's extremely paradoxical."

"An ugly case." The doctor was angry.

"Ugly and murky. You'll have to allow for enigmatic and extraordinary motives behind this act. Or an enigmatic, extraordinary individual who did it. The case is stranger than it seems. You're likely to have quite a job solving it; I only wanted to point out to you – "

"Thank you," the examiner said considerately. "You've given me a great deal to think about. But if you'll excuse me, you don't understand. I don't have to solve this case. I don't solve anything. I'm only an administrative executive. If it would amuse you, I could invite you to come along."

He doesn't solve anything, was going around in Slavík's mind, so what exactly does he do? – A few moments later he finally asked the question.

"I don't solve anything," said the examiner, "simply because... Look, sir, I don't take action on my own, and I cannot solve anything. I act in the name of the law, which rather than finding solutions makes decisions. The law only makes decisions about cases, and in its irrefutable procedures lies its strength. – An evidentiary judgment is a command. This is the logic of the law. No, sir, it's not a question of solutions at all."

With a look of boredom on his face, the examiner set up an inquiry. Slowly the number of people grew who, the day before, had seen an "unfamiliar person" here or there. Sometimes he was a tall, slim, bearded fellow; then again, a powerfully built outsider, redheaded and deep in thought, with shaven cheeks; or, again, an unusually large, strong-looking hiker whose face no one could see. This last one, it appeared, was literally on the run and had left behind him a confusion of horrifying footprints.

The day before the body was found, right when it was raining so hard, a certain old man driving his cart to the train station passed a large, unfamiliar man in short hiking pants. "Go sit under an awning," he called to the man. "I don't want to," the man said. The old fellow drove on, but he felt sorry for the dripping wet pedestrian and called out to him a second time. "I don't want to," the man shouted furiously, and he trotted off toward the station. It was striking, "peculiar," the driver said, "how big he was and how sorry I felt for him." (Examination of the old carter.)

A little later, this same outsized man in sports clothes arrived at the station and waited on the platform, in the rain, for the evening train to come through. The stationmaster sent him to the waiting room, but the man merely pulled up his collar. After a while, the stationmaster came to notify him that the train wasn't running today, because forty-five kilometers away, a cliff had given way during the rainstorm and rocks had buried the tracks. The huge traveler swore something awful and asked when the next train was leaving. At twenty-four hundred, said the stationmaster, and he nearly recoiled before the man's pained, wrathful eyes. "You ought to spend the night in town," he advised the man sympathetically. "Don't worry about me," was the traveler's curt response, and he left. His face was covered, which gave him a strange, "tormented" impression, "like the face of a man in mortal danger." (Testimony of the stationmaster.)

The outsider appeared that evening at the town's inn, and had them heat a room and bring him a meal. Later, the innkeeper knocked on his door. The guest opened the door and, clearly alarmed, shouted, "What is it?" "You are walking?" the innkeeper ventured. "I could recommend a good cart and driver; he's known as 'With God's Help'; perhaps, sir – " "I'll think about it," said the guest, and he slammed the door. A few moments later he called down the stairs: "Order me the cart and driver at five o'clock tomorrow morning, for the entire day." Early this morning he left; the man was dressed as a hiker, huge, terrifying, his face covered. "We were all scared of him. We were absolutely dumbfounded." (Testimony of the innkeeper.)

"He stood by the window like a statue, his head almost touching the ceiling. He didn't say a word, just made this wheezing sound. I don't know why he unnerved me so." (From the examination of the waiter.)

"What now?" Slavík asked the examiner.

The examiner shrugged his shoulders. For now he would call the wife of Mr. With God's Help and immerse himself in a map of the surrounding area. Slavík became more and more agitated. My God, he agonized, tense and somber, what a clue! How amazing! Did something extraordinary happen? Or nothing more than murder? It's incomprehensible. Senseless. Surprisingly senseless.

Meanwhile, the examiner questioned the carter's wife; she knew nothing, yet with her cautious countrywoman's instinct she sought to deny and conceal. Pilbauer calmly read through an old price list he'd found on the window sill. It's incomprehensible, appalling, Slavík said to himself, much troubled. Something incomprehensible happened. Step by step we can follow the horrifying trail of footprints. But we're only waiting. Endlessly waiting.

Dark clouds stretched endlessly above the afternoon town steeping in the stubborn, chronic rain. The examiner ran across the lifeless town square to the telegraph office. Water was drumming in the gutters, and it seemed to Slavík as if the rain were endlessly tapping out a Morse Code of its own, about strange reports and arrests. It was impossible to make it out. The case dragged on, growing hazier and more confused. Slavík was overcome by a gloomy impatience: it's late, late –

Finally the examiner came running out of the post office. He had just received a telegram from the neighboring town saying that With God's Help was at the inn there, drunk as an owl and telling people how, that very morning, he'd had this giant passenger who covered up his face in his scarf and never said a word. Halfway through the journey, the terrified carter couldn't take it anymore; he had the passenger get out and then drove off. Where the man went, the carter doesn't know.

But at least there was a direction now. As if he were sliding along the twisting ribbon of roadway, Slavík quickly drove the examiner to the neighboring town. He had no speedometer, but his blind, physical anxiety made him feel an urge to cry or vomit, feel as if the air were a fiercely cold and tangible gag thrust into his mouth and down into his chest, between his painfully palpitating lungs, compelling him to imagine that the automobile was flying along at the highest sustainable speed. Not knowing why, carried away, enrapt, with a tenacious grip on the car's paneling, he felt arising in himself two great, primitive feelings: pride and horror.

And suddenly Stop! Signaling with his scarf: Stop! "I recognized your machine," a man said hurriedly, as if he were a messenger. "I was running for a policeman; something happened in Svatá Anežka." That morning, evidently, a coach had hurtled into town behind runaway horses and without any passengers. Behind it, on foot, came a colossus and "he dropped onto a chair like a boulder." Then he had us turn the heat on in his room and he locked himself in there. In the afternoon, they knocked on his door to see if he wanted anything. He shouted that anyone who came upstairs would get thrown back down again. Nobody has the nerve to test him. He showed himself at the top of the stairs with a towel wrapped around him and threatened us with his fists. The gamekeepers had already come, but they weren't any use; the man's an unmitigated horror.

So on the automobile flew to Svatá Anežka, a tiny spa town at the foot of the tallest mountain in the region, celebrated for its miraculous year-round rainfall. But when they arrived, they heard that about an hour earlier the ogre had gone down the stairs, searched for his bill and, while nine men were discussing the situation behind locked doors, left on the path that goes to the top of the mountain. The chambermaid saw him leaving, and fled.

The nine men surrounded the examiner; they included gamekeepers, summer guests, domestics, and a tiny, bespectacled fellow who threw his arms around Slavík. This was the violinist and composer Jevíšek, who spent the summer dying of boredom in a cottage he'd inherited, the place where he was born.

"Why did you let him go?" the examiner shouted.

"We didn't have time."

"We couldn't reach an agreement."

"We were afraid of him," Jevíšek whispered confidentially.

The examiner inclined his head toward Slavík: "In short, they couldn't get organized."

The mountain at the foot of which they now stand is a steep table of rock thrusting up out of forest, accessible in only two ways: a road for vehicles and a trail for hikers. At the top is nothing but an isolated field or two and a small hut; the rest of the mountain is bare, with steeply descending rock faces. Now the mountain was simply an immense, vapor-veiled form.

The examiner walked out in front of the building and studied the huge, hazy body of the mountain, as if he were challenging it to battle.

*

Slavík became witness to events that surprised him, not only the actual incidents themselves, but the oddness of their nature. He was to find himself in the midst of goings-on in which he himself became a participant. He was present at the formation of a small, brash team that despite its military-like discipline gave him the distinct impression of senseless chaos.

Not until later did he acknowledge that it couldn't have been otherwise, but at the time the events were taking place, when he was merely a link in a search party under someone's command, he suffered unspeakably from the sheer clumsiness, the waste of time, the endless waiting and delays; he suffered equally, however, from the casual, spur-of-the-moment changes of course, the flurry of events, and the disorderly haste of the entire campaign. He thought almost with wonder of the times when he had taken action on his own, when had he found his own individual, unbroken tempo, so it was only with difficulty that he could recognize himself amidst the irrhythmic, hasty activity in which he was now taking part. He found it difficult and confusing.

In one of the worst moments of the entire sequence of events, stumbling in the night at the top of the mountain, he perceived how melancholy the situation was, and he thought about soldiers, about innumerable troops, about a short sentry waiting for orders, about the small team pursuing the criminal into the mountains, about the criminal, that odd, isolated creature who in his solitude feeds off of who knows what image of superiority, and about himself; he sat down on a rock and, unmindful of the night, wrote on a page of his notebook in a cramped, miniscule, bitter hand:

"The essence of organization: to make yourself a part of the whole. You are a unit guided by the will of another; you are one part only – and, consequently, fundamentally dependent upon the whole. Acknowledge the leader, accept his motives, his goals, his will and his decisions; nothing remains of you but a passive soul, which you sense as *suffering...*"

"Good," the examiner said at last, "we're encircling the mountain. There are twelve of us, and in addition I'm sending for the national police; that will make twenty of us altogether. Four of you will secure the vehicular road; you, sir, will lead them. Four will stay to guard the footpath; you, sir, are in charge. At night the murderer can't risk going any way other than along these two routes. I myself will climb the path to the top. Someone come with me."

"I will," Slavík volunteered.

"Good. At the same time, Detective Pilbauer will be taking the road. Some venturesome person should go with him."

"I will," Jevíšek volunteered, resolutely adjusting his glasses.

"Good. We'll meet at the hut. When the police arrive, they'll post two men down by the road as sentries. You'll climb with the rest of them to the hut at the top. – Let's go, gentlemen."

Thus was the mountain encircled.

It had already grown dark when Inspector Lebeda and Slavík reached the top of the mountain. Although the rain fell harshly and drearily, the inspector whistled to himself like a contented bird. "Well, what do you think?" he suddenly asked.

"I'm surprised," said Slavík. "I thought ... I imagined this whole business quite differently. I was interested in solving a crime; I sensed a mystery to it ... But it's hunting, that's all. An expedition for bear. The pursuit of a thief."

"What else did you expect?"

"A solution. The case is immensely cryptic. Something extraordinary happened. This nameless dead man has already — didn't you sense it immediately, as you soon as you saw him?"

"Yes, I did," the examiner said. "I don't know why exactly, but – it's enigmatic. I don't like thinking about it."

"I've agonized over this since morning," Slavík continued. "Every mystery is like an obligation, and that's why I have to involve myself in it. I'm not interested in the fact that it's a crime, but in how inexplicable it is. That's why I have to pursue it."

"Until we catch him," said the examiner.

"Yes," Slavík said, "but instead of solving the mystery, we only want to investigate it. Simply conduct an official hearing. That's exactly what I don't like. It's terribly unintelligent. Perhaps we'll catch him, but that will only be a crude point of fact. Mystery is a spiritual matter; it's as if each enigma is touched by the breath of the spirit. Only when confronted with something enigmatic does one become conscious of one's spirit – and tremble, and feel awe. *Timor Dei* ... Awe of the spirit. But what is material is without mystery. Without awe. Without the courage to feel awe. In short, I expected a more internal, spiritual solution."

"Do you perhaps have a revolver with you?" the inspector asked.

"No," said Slavík, annoyed.

"Too bad. I don't have one, either."

"Look," Slavík continued, "all this is like some romantic tale. The night! The mountains! And on top of that, a revolver! Frankly, we've lost the trail. How external everything is!"

"No, sir," the examiner gently objected. "Look, we detectives aren't philosophers. For us, this is purely a practical, professional matter. Believe me, sir, every profession seems romantic from a distance. And a revolver is only a tool, exactly like a forceps or a plow. Frankly, we haven't lost the trail."

Silently they began once again to climb the rugged path, which loomed ghostly pale under the dark trees; it seemed unreal, running on ahead of their footsteps as if by intuition.

"You wanted a more internal, spiritual solution?" the examiner suddenly said. "But in professional work there are no spiritual solutions. It might be possible to make a field fertile simply by praying, but practically speaking, it would be bad. It might be that spiritual methods are the shortest and most direct of all, but practically they are wrong. It might be possible to solve a crime by simple conjecture, but intuition is unprofessional. From a practical standpoint, all the detectives in novels do their jobs wrong. They're too personal, too inventive. Their methods are those of a criminal, not a detective. The right way is something different."

"What is it?"

"Shared routine. Organization. Look, a technique exists to bring people under control – a real technique, because it treats people as tools. There is progress in that; what was once a personal art has now become a technique. Anything we hold becomes a tool. Even people. Even you. Only the *one above* escapes us."

"God?"

"No, man. The criminal who is fleeing. And me, I am nothing more than an arm of the law. I solve nothing, I only seize and hold, and the more forcefully I apply pressure, the more I see in myself the power that is passing through me. Only an arm, true, but at least I now feel a formidable, unfailing power pulsing through me. It beats in me again today. The power of the law."

The examiner fell silent; it was competely dark now, and they stumbled with difficulty over the roots and stones beneath them. They had in fact lost the trail, and they climbed blindly up the mountainside through the sodden underbrush, their hands scrabbling, grasping at the ground. At length they came across a small shelter for storing animal fodder. It was not a pleasant spot, but at least it was possible to smoke there, half-way up the great, dripping, soughing mountain.

The rain went on pouring down through the endless expanse of night; somewhere a bough split and crashed to the ground; somewhere a boulder wrenched loose and tumbled down the slope like a gigantic foot stomping; all other noise was absorbed by the vast murmur of the rain. Listening, Slavík felt melancholic, as if lost in the extensive, impenetrable darkness of the entire world. The examiner was paralyzed, but at that moment something like a feeble electrical vibration passed through him; it came again, stronger and more prolonged, and suddenly he was seized by a spasmodic convulsion –

"What's the matter?" Slavík cried.

"Nothing," the examiner gasped, "it's nothing ... just fear ...Wait a minute! Wait a minute!"

"What's frightening you?"

"I don't know ... Just what they say about *him* ...I don't want to think about it. Don't you feel anything?"

"No. Only spiritual awe."

"That's not it. Something worse, fear ... I can't bear it!"

"We'd better get going" urged Slavík, who had begun to feel uneasy.

"At once ... You go in front. Quietly. Go on!"

Along the rocks they could only travel on all fours. Perhaps it wouldn't be possible to reach the top. "Go on!" snarled the examiner. His hands and knees chafed and sore, Slavík clawed his way upward; only when he had once again found the path did a chill of horror break over him so powerfully that it caused his feet to slip –

The examiner moved ahead of him and quickly set off toward the summit. A light was shining in the hut. The examiner tapped lightly on the door, which opened only enough to reveal a single eye. "Police," the examiner whispered, and the door burst open like sigh of relief. "Thank God," the farmer whispered, setting aside his rifle. "Thank God!"

"When did he arrive?" the examiner asked quickly.

"No more than an hour ago. He wanted to stay the night. He's in the loft."

Unexpectedly, they heard a husky, powerful voice from above. "I'm coming right down. Soon as I get dressed."

In an instant, the examiner was on the stairs, as if he had been flung there by sheer force. "In the name of the law!"

"Right away." The voice was more distant. "The thing is, I have a ... slight ... cold."

"Stand guard outside," the examiner shouted downstairs, "trap him outside! Move!"

Slavík and the farmer, holding his rifle, bolted outdoors.

Overhead, the gable window was wide open. Nothing, silence.

The examiner came out holding a glowing lantern; thus Slavík, though deciphering the old-fashioned script with difficulty, was able to make out the motto carved into the gable:

> God bless this house twas built by me
> And all within whoe'er they be.

Meanwhile, Pilbauer and Jevíšek were heading up the vehicular road. Jevíšek couldn't see a step ahead of him and was a bit afraid that they were getting lost. Detective Pilbauer, silent and undisturbed, strode on in front of him.

"Do you know this road?" Jevíšek gasped.

"I've never taken it," Pilbauer replied.

"Then how do you find your way?

"I'm following orders."

Silence again. Jevíšek started to hum a tune, but stopped: it struck him that he was with a detective, and he grew very serious. "Do you have a false moustache?" he blurted out, since he himself expected no less of the man.

"No. What for?" the large man wondered.

"You aren't wearing some kind of disguise?"

"No, I'm just me," the detective said modestly. All at once Jevíšek felt affection for the drab, quiet man. "Is it hard being a detective?" he asked.

"No. It depends on your temperament. Aren't you a musician? That's far and away an easier line of work."

"Oh, you mustn't think that," Jevíšek called ahead to him. "For instance, just recently ... I composed most of a piece, a quartet, but – To make it short, I can't get on with it. I don't know what to do. It's eluding me."

"You ought to go on a search for it," the detective advised.

"Oh, an artist is always searching. All his life. But as it is now, I'm worn out. That's why I came along with you, so I can forget about it for a while, get it off my mind."

"I think you came along out of curiosity, like that other man."

"Oh no, I really came with no particular interest. I was just looking forward to seeing something exciting, out of the ordinary. Sometimes a jolt is what's needed ... Please take me with you more often!"

"Gladly," the detective said solemnly, "if you have official authorization. But don't come without authorization. It's no good to pursue a man."

Jevíšek's conscience stirred slightly. "Well, he's a murderer," he offered in self-defense.

The detective nodded his head. "Yes, it's no good not to pursue him."

"Then what's to be done?"

"Nothing. Everything's equally no good. It's just as bad to beat as not to beat someone, to judge as to forgive. – Everything has its dark side and its faults."

Jevíšek thought for a moment. "What is it, exactly, that you do?"

"I do merely what I have to do. What's most reasonable is to obey. To comply with orders."

"What about the one giving the orders?"

"He makes blunders, sir. It's no good to give orders; the worst thing of all is losing one's way."

"And yet he has to be obeyed?"

"Of course. It wouldn't be an order if it wasn't obeyed."

Jevíšek was astounded. "You couldn't do that with art."

"No," the detective said. "Art is too spontaneous."

"No, art too has rules that must be obeyed."

"Orders?"

"No, they aren't orders."

"There you have it," Pilbauer grumbled.

Jevíšek was confused; there came into his mind every uncertainty, all the agonizing doubts he had suffered in his art; how much better it would be if some higher voice simply ordered him, told him what to do and how. – From afar, melodiously, in a higher voice, there suddenly came to him a motif. Quietly Jevíšek followed behind the large, saturnine man who, with absolute certainty, was finding his way along a dark road he'd never before traveled, while he, Jevíšek, who was on his home turf, was stumbling and making hundreds of miscalculations as he tried to determine the bends in the road that disappeared where the slightest misstep would hurl him down on the rocks.

How confident they are, he reflected: Slavík, who is full of knowledge, the examiner, who knows how to give orders – what assurance power confers on a man! – and Pilbauer, satisified with obedience; how confident they are, whereas I have no peace. – Beauty brings me no sleep, no serenity; beauty never brings certainty to anyone –

Better to be a detective, the thought swirled moodily in Jevíšek's head, and if you must search, at least search for nothing superhuman, which is *bound* to elude you! But I too am searching, it struck him – I find a footprint here or there, or I hear a voice from afar; ah, the forever receding echo of something perfect! An angel singing!

"What are you singing?" Pilbauer suddenly inquired.

Startled, Jevíšek felt his face suffuse with heat. "I – was I singing?"

"Singing. Humming. Something quite beautiful."

Jevíšek was suffused with a new, cheering surge of warmth. "Really! Thank you! I had no idea. – Actually, how did it go?"

"It was – it was – I don't know anymore. It kept changing, this way and that – I can't remember it anymore. Beautiful's what it was."

In the meantime they had reached the top of the mountain. Now Jevíšek was neither thinking nor singing. Pilbauer surely and silently led him forward. "Halt: someone's running," the detective suddenly whispered. Jevíšek strained his ears but heard only the organ tones of the mountain. "Quiet," the detective repeated.

Darting by in front of them through the rain was a huge hulk of a human body and it hurtled, leaped, and disappeared into the darkness. Jevíšek was utterly astounded and, without a word, from some primal hunter's instinct, he set out after him. Pilbauer, too, ran after him, but the figure had been swallowed up by the mist, and so he shrugged and walked toward the hut.

Meanwhile, the rain ceased and the mist descended off the summit of the mountain. The sky cleared and the moon shone through the thick mist with a milky luminosity; the broad expanse was enveloped in a soft, almost sweet silence.

Jevíšek hurried after the fleeing hulk as quickly as he could; there was a wild dodging and darting all over the crown of the mountain. Jevíšek became winded. "I can't," he gasped, and stopped.

"Nor can I," came a voice through the mist.

Jevíšek sat down on a rock, breathing hard.

"You're hunting a sick man," said the strong, hoarse voice. "You forced him out of bed and took away his shelter. Isn't that enough for you? Haven't you done enough to me?"

"You're ill?" Jevíšek called out.

"What more do you want?" the voice accused. "This is inhuman! Abhorrent! Just leave me alone!"

"You can't get away," Jevíšek said uneasily. "They'll catch you ... They've encircled the mountain."

"So many of you?" the voice spoke with great bitterness. "That's shameful! What will I do now? God, oh God, what will I do now?"

Jevíšek stiffened, painfully uncertain.

"Jesus Christ!" the voice lamented, "what will I do now? They've encircled the mountain ... Jesus Christ!"

Jevíšek's heart was filled with a luminous whiteness. "Wait," he began, trembling.

"What will I do now?" came the agitated voice out of the mist. "I'm lost! lost! lost! Oh God, how is it possible?"

"I'll help you," Jevíšek cried out.

"You'll only betray me," the voice groaned. "Our father, who art in heaven, hallowed be thy name, thy kingdom come, thy will be ... thy will... Give me a way out! God, give me a way out!"

Jevíšek felt pain, hope, horror – love and hurt, joy, tears, and impassioned courage: he rose, shaking, and said: "Come. They're only watching the roads. I'll go with you. Don't be afraid."

"Don't come near me!" the voice shouted.

"I'll go with you. Don't be afraid of me. Where are you?"

"Jesus Christ!" the voice screamed in terror. "I don't want, I don't want anything from you!"

Now Jevíšek perceived in front of him a faceless shadow, and felt a feverish breathing against his face. "Leave me alone," the voice spat out, someone's hand touched his chest, and suddenly, with an awkward bound, the shadow vanished into the mist.

The examiner stood on the doorstep of the hut, biting his nails. Slavík walked up to him. "Look," he began, "I've been thinking things over. – You've heard the witnesses; they all spoke of him in the strangest way. As if he kept getting bigger. To us, it's as if he never stops growing. An extraordinary case of suggestion."

The examiner raised his tired eyes.

"Perhaps that's his method of operation," Slavík continued. "He overwhelms people. He's a madman, a megalomaniac. That would explain everything."

The examiner shook his head and lowered his eyes.

The team of men formed a chain from the hut across the mountain's broad plateau. Ten, perhaps twenty people. They advanced slowly and wordlessly, with mechanical precision. Only occasionally did a weapon clank and break the silence.

The examiner relaxed his clenched teeth. I'm tired, too tired. I can't go on.

He leaned against a tree and closed his eyes. He felt wholly diminished by fatigue. I can't go on. "What's this? Tired already, you young rascal?" the voice of his father suddenly materialized. "Come on, hop up onto my back." Oh, there was nothing more the boy could have asked for. Papa had a back like a giant, and the boy settled himself there, as nice and high as if he'd mounted a horse. The road ran on ahead of them. His father smelled of tobacco and strength. Like a giant. Nobody was stronger. Then, aching with tenderness, the little imp pressed his small face against the damp, powerful nape of his father's neck.

The examiner wrenched himself from his reverie. I'm tired. If only I could concentrate! What, for instance, is seven times thirteen? With furrowed brow, moving his lips, he started to do the arithmetic. It's impossible to calculate. Endlessly, he repeated both numbers to himself. Somehow, they were particularly hostile, indivisible, obstinate. The worst of all possible numbers. In despair, the examiner gave up on finding a solution.

All at once he heard, clearly and articulately: what is seven times thirteen? His heart came to a frightened standstill: It's the schoolmaster. This time he's going to call on me, yes, this time … For heaven's sake, where can I hide? What can I do? Give me a way out, God! Give me a way out!"

At that moment a shot rang out.

Meanwhile, Jevíšek was wandering along the hillside, knowing neither direction nor destination. At intervals he listened, but never had the world been more silent, never more muffled; he felt a bit of pain and a bit of intoxication; he went on, without thought, not knowing where he was.

At that moment a shot rang out. From mountain to mountain the echo flew, ever more distant, ever more soft, ever more frightening. Once again silence set in, grimmer than before; only now did Jevíšek realize that he was entirely alone, aimless and insignificant here in the mountains, that he was going back home, that solicitude would continue to stream through a tiny fissure in his heart, and that imperceptibly, distressingly, an immeasurable sorrow, too, would continue to flow.

Pilbauer was trudging on through the underbrush; water was running down his neck and into his boots; with guile and hostility, he struggled, squeezed, and sidestepped along; then he abandoned all consideration for himself and attacked the underbrush like a ram.

At that moment a shot rang out. The report came from a distance of several paces in front of him. "Better watch out," the detective muttered, and he had to lean into the mountain so

as not to fall down; consequently, his knees shook beneath him.
It could already be tomorrow, he suddenly thought, it could
very well have happened! Tomorrow's here! Tomorrow's here!
It could already be tomorrow! At long last!

Slavík spotted a shadow walking jerkily, mechanically, like a
puppet. Only with difficulty did he realize that it was the
examiner, and he headed towards him. "Listen," he said, "I just
thought of something. About those initials. The whole thing's
clear. The victim was a foreigner."

It seemed to Slavík that the examiner whispered something.

"Yes," he continued, "unquestionably a foreigner. A man no
one's going to ask about. Otherwise it makes no sense. His
identity will never be known, he will never be reported as
missing. – And if the murderer escapes, there's nothing to give
him away. He isn't mad. He knew very well what he was doing.
He murdered a man's life, form, and name; perhaps what
matters more than anything is that he killed a name; oh,
perhaps the most appalling loss of all was just that, the name.
A name that would have revealed the murderer. And even if I
am never to know that name, now, now, at last, it's all clear to
me."

"Yes, yes," the examiner managed to say weakly, "yes. –
Hold your distance, there – Keep that line! March!"

Jevíšek was back home, the lamp was buzzing softly and
warmly over his unfinished quartet, where the final note,
extremely high, fluttering like a skylark, called for closure.
Hesitantly, apprehensively, Jevíšek buried himself in his work.
It was all there, just the way it had been: the bright joy of the
movement, the slow, melodious cantilena. – Nothing had
changed. Nothing changes beauty, nothing can touch it, nothing
was discordant, nothing was gloomy, nothing had darkened in
the magical, gliding fabric of notes; nothing, nothing had been

done to it at all. Even the old doubts remained: here and there you could hear apprehension, a clumsy, quivering anguish, the exertion of a whirling dancer concealed behind a fixed smile ... Jevíšek recalled the motif of the higher voice that had come to him on the mountain: the thundering cadence of a voice forever giving commands. Jevíšek buried his head in his arms: That's not it. Higher voices don't give orders. Higher voices invoke your pain.

More sorrowful than night is the break of day. Darkness distances itself; little by little, as if in anticipation of a crisis, the air begins to shudder; the contours of things become more refined, colder and more stark. The whiteness of walls gives off a dead luminosity, matter turns pale, and each thing can begin to be seen, vague yet fixed in place; you see more and everything looks so much more unreal. – Dawn is breaking, the world is waking to the distant, unfamiliar dawn; you see everything with an odd clarity, and yet it isn't the light. – People awaken in the stale warmth of their beds, looking toward a day that is worse, more brutal, than the day before.

Just as it was beginning to grow light, someone knocked on Jevíšek's door. Wrenched from drowsiness, the small violinist gave a start and ran to open the door. On the porch stood Slavík, the examiner, and Pilbauer.

"Where did you go last night?" Slavík exclaimed. "We were so worried about you!"

"Did he escape?" Jevíšek whispered.

"He escaped," Slavík said noncommitally. "He fell off a cliff and – "

"Is he dead?"

Slavík nodded. "Dead. He's lying there face down ... covered with brushwood. End of story."

Jevíšek went to light the fire and make coffee for his guests. End of story, he repeated, looking into the flames; dead, covered with brushwood. The flames made his eyes smart, he took off his glasses and wiped his tears. End of story.

Slavík was doing everything in his power to prove to the examiner the clear case he had come up with. Jevíšek didn't grasp a word of it and didn't understand why he was speaking so vigorously. Gesturing with his hand, he brushed against the strings of his violin. The strings plinked, and Jevíšek jerked back his hand as if it had been burned. Slavík stopped in mid-sentence, the examiner shivered, and Pilbauer raised a heavy eyelid.

"Excuse me," Jevíšek whispered.

"It sounded like moaning," Slavík said pensively and uneasily. "Altogether, a sad story. If I'd had any idea that – "

No one in the room moved.

Slavík bit his lips. "There was something great about him," he began again. "Everyone felt it; it was as if he grew to be superhuman. I wanted to meet him, and that's why, that's exactly why I pursued him. We would much rather hold on to a secret than... than..." Slavík frowned. "He's dead, spent."

All of a sudden Pilbauer spoke up. "At any rate – he's finished."

An oppressive silence set in. Jevíšek, blue-eyed, short-sighted, scrutinized his guests: he saw Pilbauer, motionless, brooding with half-closed eyes, as if recalling something; he saw Slavík, chafing under the sorrow of self-reproach and self-torment; he saw how tired, how worn the examiner was, collapsing with sadness, weak as a sick child. But you could have come to an understanding with him, he felt, all of you! He was so unhappy, all he wanted was a way out – how well you could have understood him!

"I talked with him," he said hesitantly. "He wasn't really enigmatic at all."

Slavík looked up, astonished. "You say he wasn't...?"

"He wasn't," Jevíšek repeated, "I mean, he was grieving; he was grieving terribly about everything."

"Weren't you afraid of him?" asked the examiner, suddenly reviving.

"I wasn't afraid. If only you too could have heard. – Oh, how well you would understand him!"

Temptation

For a long time now Růžíka had been going around in a fog. He had fought against it mightily, coming up with reasons pro and con, providing evidence for both sides, growing angry with himself. He had struggled hard to focus his thoughts, and at the same time he yearned: to be endlessly adrift, without thought or direction – much like a piece of driftwood bobbing on a pond in a fog, he mused; above the water a gull cries out and swoops down to clutch the surface in its talons; the water shivers and the gull speeds off like a mischievous boy, sending a shriek of mocking laughter from wherever it has gone...

Růžíka broke off: do I go or do I stay? – All the reasons had gone numb and he could no longer cope with them; they had all gone numb, had petrified, and he could no longer rid himself of them. Reasons that no longer pleased him. They shriveled in this confining room. In this room that no longer pleased him. Reasons to stay and not to go and not to idly toss opportunities aside. Quiet, work, habits, the lamp, the bed, the easy chair – What more do I need, he thought; I will stay and I will fulfill the entire truth of my life. My space is confining, but I can expand it. Yes, stay forever!

Or go, he thought anxiously, try once again to fling yourself into the world like a stone into water ... If only it weren't necessary to make a decision! If only I could, without knowing how, find myself out in the world somewhere and have nothing before me but the day, oh God! what a day that would be! Let it happen to me like fate or coincidence – I would accept all of it, but wanting it is terrible...

Do I go or do I stay?

I will go out, he finally decided (to do at least something! anything!), just a little way out, he hung back at the doorway to sample the evening, he forced himself forward; but "stay," says the lamp, the bed, the easy chair, the ennui, "why go? Going is so effortful, staying so easy; going is so desperate, staying is so desperate, so stay!" No, not today, he forced himself to decide, and he went. "Stay," say the glowing streets, "we aren't troubling you, you've navigated us so often that you no longer see us." Nor do you see me, he objected, and your windows don't flash at me suspiciously like a glance, invitingly like a glance, openly like the glance of coincidence. I walk this way daily: we have become strangers to one another. "Yes, after so many years!"

Preoccupied, Růžíka took shelter in a café, revived, happy to lose himself in the scatter of lights and voices, to disappear into the crowd, happy that the mirrors sparkled and the glasses clinked. He traced a question mark on the table with his finger and was amused by the progress of the veins in the marble tabletop, a network of coincidence, countless aimless paths. "Do I go or do I stay? Eyes! – who is looking at me?"

Young lady, his gaze conveys a smile, what do you want of me? The flawless gray eyes slip away, escape behind the darkness of their lids and sweetly, somberly glance nowhere. Nothing, pale cheeks beneath black hat, an ivory toy, youthful hands holding nothing fidget on her knees. And those other eyes, large, black, are her mama's, they scrutinize the fashions in the room. The gray eyes surreptitiously land, take flight again, are never in repose; beguiling are the eyelids, lowered eyes, beguiling sorrow, love and music, evening, question and nothing, lovely is her glance, her joy, her dress, music and question, lovely flirtation, lovely springtime, violets on the streets, rosy blossoms, rosy smile, lovely glance turned towards him! directly at him, forceful and direct, brief and questioning is that lovely glance! Smooth face suffused with rosy hue.

Beautiful are white and blushing faces, beautiful and sorrowful hair, sorrowful and slender hands on knees, on black mourning skirt.

"Enough," the gray eyes implore, "so much praise, my God – what am I to do now with my eyes, my eyelids, my hands? Don't look at me, put down your glass, I am not looking at you at all."

Slender hands, I imagine them to be full of feeling, like the hands of a violinist: yes, a tremolo, illogical weeping, a song that ends and ends not; haven't I heard that pretty, timorous song? The hoarse, pretty voice of a child?

"God, not that!" the gray eyes exclaim. "What would I say to you? I'm hopeless with words and numbers. Who are you? Why are you looking that way? Why aren't you looking?"

As I look, I think about the people around you, about your breath, about love, about all that I would say to you – I don't know what I think about when I'm looking; but when I don't look, I think about you, about all that I don't see, about myself, about this happy coincidence, and most of all about you.

"Stop! Stop!"

– New people have sat down across from me, and in their midst...

"Oh, look!" the gray eyes blurt out. "How beautiful she is!"

– yes, beautiful, truly beautiful, oh, young lady, how grand and beautiful! Why did she come, for whom is she searching with those dark eyes? Ah, who can bear the crushing glance of beauty? How could a man not tremble with fear and confusion, how could he not cast down his eyes? Woe is he at whom she looks!

Slowly, without doubts or questions, the large, dark eyes of the new arrival came to rest on his face. His heart stopped in wonderment.

"I am beautiful. Many, so many kneel before me. Look at me."

I am going, he answers dispiritedly.

"Stay. I am beautiful. You will see me on the streets, in shops, at festivals. Look for me in my box at the theater. You will meet me, if you wish. We can introduce ourselves and – whom do you know?"

I am going, he repeats, stubborn.

"Stay. I have so few pleasures, so few. I am so beautiful. You will see me often, daily if you like, and so near by! Stay."

No, he says with a sense of urgency, I am going; I am going and I will return with a mouth embittered by foreign seas and lands; I will return with a different soul. A soul with no more wonderment or trembling, a rough, daring, ardent, brazen soul, a cruel and restless soul, a soul for you. And more! a soul that will bring tears to those most beautiful eyes! that will make that beauty tremble! that will make me worse than you! So that you will love me. So that our fate will be fulfilled. So that I will not fear God. So that I will be a match for you. Nothing is more terrible than beauty and courage.

The dark pupils turn away and softly cast their spell into infinity.

So be it, I feel, let it happen to me like fate. I will go so that I might take a risk, be courageous.

"Stay," say the gray eyes, hopelessly, "oh, stay! I could come here again next Saturday. I could meet you somewhere. I won't run off, even if you speak to me. Why don't you want to stay?"

Ah, young lady, his heart wept with sensual affection, I would stay, how could I not want to stay? But you have reminded me of a day in a foreign land, an unhappy man in a foreign land, I don't know why so unhappy and so hopeless; you have reminded me of a happy coincidence, a smile, loving words in a foreign tongue and a lovely glance that is no longer returned: the joy that you would know, and that exquisite day in a foreign land! Nothing is more beautiful than love and happy coincidence, nothing can match a fine, chance meeting that never recurs. I would stay: but you have awakened in me an eternal yearning for coincidence, for chance.

Reflections

CAREFUL," LHOTA CALLED to a fisherman he didn't know from Adam, "you've got a bite!"

"Aha, thank you," the man replied affably, "would you like to land it?"

Lhota promptly slid down the embankment and took the rod. There was nothing on the line, and when Lhota pulled it in, he discovered that the hook had a red string attached to it.

"Isn't this where the worm goes?" he asked, annoyed.

"Yes," the fisherman said with a sheepish smile.

"Have you caught anything yet?"

"Never."

Lhota returned to the embankment, not knowing whether or not to laugh. How is it possible, he thought, how could it ever be possible to fish this way?

"You see, I'm not fishing," the fisherman remarked, "I'm only sitting here with a rod so that people won't laugh when they see me."

"Are you from around here?"

"I live in that cottage behind us. I've been walking over to this place for many years, because I love it here. But I don't fish."

Lhota looked into the fisherman's large, shining eyes. "You're not well, are you?"

"I can't walk well. Not for ages now. I haven't been past this point for years – But it's beautiful here."

"Indeed," Lhota said doubtfully. The bare embankments stretched as far as the eye can see, and between them flowed the wide, gray river.

"You ought to be here at sunset," the sick man said, "or in the morning. I sit here from morning on, and it's never tiresome. Later, when I go home, I sleep without dreaming; night after night I sleep beautifully and dreamlessly. It's only in winter – "

"What happens in winter?"

"Nothing, just dreams. In the winter I can't come here, and I sleep night and day, without pause, until I'm too tired to sleep any longer. In summer I'm here every day."

Deep in thought, Lhota looked at the water: it flowed by, broad and formless, chafing against the rocks in never-ending streams; he watched it rippling, undulating, churning, until his eyes failed him. And then it was a rushing river no more, only a purling sound which did not linger but kept flowing away and disappearing without bounds, without limits, an escape from everything –

"And in winter I dream only of water," the sick man continued. "The same dream appears to me all day and night, for months on end, interrupted only when I wake up frightened. It only ceases in the summer, when I see actual water."

Lhota, his mind slightly reeling, narrowed his eyes. "I wouldn't want to dream about flowing water."

"No, it's not really flowing," the invalid said. "I don't dream about real water. There is this great river which stands without moving, and all along it flow reflections. They drift away much as those leaves are being carried away in the current."

"What kind of reflections?"

"Things mirrored. Riverbanks reflected on the surface. They float by on the water as rapidly as those waves and never cause a ripple. Perhaps they come all the way from the mountains. There are giant trees which slip along quietly with their crowns facing down, as if they were descending into the bottomless sky. Even the sky flows along this motionless river, as do the sun and the clouds and the stars. I've seen reflections of hills and riverside villages go drifting by, and reflections of people, too. Sometimes a white house, standing all by itself, or a lighted window."

"It's an absurd dream," said Lhota.

"Frightening. Sometimes a mirrored city floats by, and the lights burning along its waterfront. The leaves of the trees shiver on the water's surface, as if a wind were blowing, but they too never make the water ripple. A young girl wrings her white hands and is carried farther on. And it seems to me in the reflection that someone standing on the opposite bank wants to look at me or signal me, but the image in the water flows on by, even with my hand placed to my eyes."

The sick man was silent for a moment. "And sometimes," he began again, "it is only the light from a lamppost on some forlorn dock along the riverbank; it sways as if in a November wind and floats on by. Nothing can stop, nothing lingers. Nothing disturbs the water, and nothing is above or outside of it. Eternity is horrifying."

Lhota stared into the water; wave after wave returned without end to the stones beneath his feet and retreated again in persistent play, which both annoyed and comforted him.

"Often," the sick man said, "I wake up covered with sweat and scared to death, and I say to myself: Eternity is horrifying. Wave after wave arrives and breaks against the rocks, rock after rock rolls down into the waves, and the waves scatter them. But I've seen the surface, and the surface doesn't dash or break against anything. The light and shadows of everything on the surface simply pass away. Hills roll away and trees rush past; towns and bluffs flow by, the young girl wrings her hands in vain, and the beginning and the end of the world rush by, mirrored. But the surface is never rippled and cannot be. It touches nothing and can never touch anything, ever. And who-

ever looks upon it sees only the mere reflections of things vanishing, stripped of reality."

On the opposite embankment a man stopped and watched for a moment. "How about it," he finally called over, "are they biting?"

"They aren't," the invalid replied merrily. – "I love to sit here." He was speaking to Lhota again. "When a leaf falls into the water, the water trembles and I tremble, too, but not from any anxiety. Sometimes, at sunset, I think about God. Eternity is horrifying."

Lhota looked at him quizzically.

"At times," the invalid continued, "I've seen such curious ripples on the water that it's impossible to comprehend from whence they've come. Sometimes a breaking wave flashes more beautifully than the others and in the sky there are natural phenomena. – This happens very seldom. But then I think: why couldn't this be God? Perhaps He is precisely that which is most fleeting, perhaps His reality is the sudden breaking and flashing of a wave; it is singular, incomprehensible, but it happens and passes on. – I've often pondered this, but then, I have such a limited horizon, it's been years since I've been farther than here. It's possible that in people, too, just such a ripple or flash occurs, and then it breaks. It must break. True reality must be paid for with destruction. Ah, the sun's already going down."

A young, barefoot girl was now standing behind the sick man. "Yes, we're going," he said. "Good night, sir. Look, now – now," he pointed to the river. "It's never the same twice. Good night."

Slowly and impassively the girl led him home. The river was nacreous, endlessly varied, and Lhota, his mind steadily reeling, went on staring at the unrelenting play of waves.

The Waiting Room

I SUPPOSE I'LL SPEND THE NIGHT in the restaurant, Záruba thought, since the train has already left, or I'll stretch out somewhere in the waiting room; I'll grab three or four hours' sleep and then take the first train out in the morning. God, let the time pass quickly! there's still a little hope left, and it's possible everything can still be saved. So many hours!

But the restaurant was closed, and a detachment of troops filled the waiting room. They were sleeping on the benches and the table tops, they were lying all about the floor, their heads resting on the crossbars of the tables, against the spittoons, on scrunched-up paper, their faces to the floor, piled up like a heap of corpses. Záruba escaped into the corridor; it was cold and damp out there, reeking with the smell of tar and urine from the lavatories, and there were just two gas lamps weakly quavering. There were people yawning and shivering on the benches, impatient with the long wait. But at least there was a bit of space here, a bit of space for a man; at least a bit of space for a weary, unobtrusive sleeper.

Záruba found himself a bench and planted himself down on it, settling in as warm and firm as possible; he fashioned a nook to serve as his sleeping quarters, as bed, headboard, footboard, refuge. – Oh, the discomfort – he wrenched himself out of his half-sleep – how to position my limbs? He thought about it long and hard; in the end he chose to lie like a child in a crib, and he stretched out lengthwise on the bench. But the bench was too short. In despair, Záruba struggled with his dimensions, saddened by such inconsiderate resistance; finally, he lay there as if shackled, motionless, boyishly small, and watched the great illuminated circles that wheeled in the darkness on revolving disks. – Why, I'm already asleep, flashed through his mind, and at that moment he opened his eyes, saw two sides of a triangle drift by, and was terribly confused: where am I? What's wrong? Panicky, he looked around for some sort of orientation, but was unable to figure out the directions; he gathered up all his strength and rose to his feet. Once again he saw the long, cold corridor, but he saw it with greater sadness than before; he knew from the bitter taste of misery in his mouth that he was completely awake.

Resting his head on his knees, he pondered his situation. To hold out, to try and see it through until salvation came, yes; but still so many hours to go! Absently glancing down at the corridor's dirty tiles, he found himself looking at trampled bits of paper, disgusting phlegm, debris from innumerable feet. – That one there has the shape of a face, eyes of mud and lips of spittle, a grotesque attempt at a smile...

Repelled, he looked up. There lay a soldier on a bench, sleeping with his head tilted backwards, groaning as if on his death bed. A nondescript woman sat sleeping, the head of a little girl on her lap; her face grim and pitiful, the woman slept on, but the little girl was looking about with pale eyes, whispering something to herself; she had a long, jutting chin and a wide mouth between thin cheeks, an old woman of a child, with sad, wide eyes that flitted everywhere. And look at that corpulent man, the way he's sleeping, his swollen drowsiness, sagging limply over the bench, doltish and dumbfounded, a flaccid mass rolling off its primary support. Under the brim of a small green hat the lively black eyes of a young man are winking. "Come here," he hisses at the pale-eyed girl through the gaps between corroded teeth: "Come here," he whispers, and smiles. Confused, the little girl fidgets and smiles back with an appalling, old-womanish smile: she has no teeth. "Come here," the young man sibilates, but then he sits down next to her. "What's your name?" And he fondles her knee with the palm of his hand. The little girl gives him a nervous, unpleasant smile. The sleeping soldier lets out a gurgling sound as if at the hour of death. Záruba trembles with cold and disgust.

An hour after midnight. Time scraped forward with agonizing slowness, and Záruba felt it dragging, gratuitously dislocated by a growing, directionless tension. All right, he told himself, I'll close my eyes and hold out, without thinking, without moving, for as long as possible, for a whole hour, while time ticks away. – And so he sat there frozen, forcing himself to hold out for as long as possible; the duration of each minute was endlessly suspended, counting without numbers, delay upon delay. – Finally, after an unsurvivable amount of time had passed, he opened his eyes. Five minutes after one. The corridor, the papers, the child, the same bewildered, old-womanish smile ... Nothing had changed. Everything was frozen in the fixed proximity of a present that did not move forward.

All at once Záruba spied a man sitting stock-still in a corner, awake and alone, like Záruba. He's like me, Záruba thought, he can't sleep either. What is he thinking about? About this endless wait, just like me? The man trembled, as if he found the question disagreeable. Záruba involuntarily gazed at the man's amorphous face, its features twitching as when someone drives away a determined fly. Suddenly the man got up, worked his way down the corridor on tiptoe, and sat down right next to him.

"That was rude, my staring at you," Záruba said in a subdued voice.

"Yes." Both were silent for quite some time. "Look," the man finally whispered, pointing his finger at the ground, "that looks like a human face."

"I already noticed it."

"You already noticed it," the man repeated gloomily. "Then you, too, have felt very – "

"Felt what?"

"Nothing's harder than waiting," the man remarked.

"How do I feel?"

"It's hard. It's hard to wait. No matter what happens eventually, it's a form of deliverance. Waiting is hard."

"Why are you talking about it?"

"Because it's hard to wait. You too have read what's written in the dust and spit. And it troubled you, as well. Nothing is more agonizing than the present."

"Why?"

"Because waiting is hard." The man stared at the ground.

"Where are you traveling to?" Záruba asked after a while.

"I travel only for pleasure," the man replied absently. "That is to say, beautiful places can often be found. You go so far that you're no longer thinking about anything, and then suddenly you're in such a place, a creek or a well in a grove, or children, something unexpected and beautiful. – And then, caught unawares, you understand what luck is."

"What about luck?"

"Nothing. You simply encounter it. In short, it's a wonder. Do you ever think about the pagan gods?"

"No, I don't."

"It's like this: no one expected to see them, people came across them unexpectedly. Somewhere in the water or in a thicket or in flames. That's why they were so beautiful. Oh, if only I could put it into words! if only I could put it into words!"

"Why are you thinking about gods?"

"It's like this: luck has to be encountered quickly and unexpectedly. It's a chance encounter, an event so unexpected that you say: oh, what an adventure! Have you had such an encounter before?"

"Yes, I have."

"It's as if you were dreaming. Adventure is the most beautiful thing of all. Whenever love stops being an adventure, it becomes a torment."

"Why, why is that so?"

"I don't know. It wouldn't endure if it weren't a torment. Look, in the old days people had a single word for luck and chance. But it was the name of a god."

Fortuna, Záruba thought, and he felt sad. If only I were to encounter it on this journey! But it's hard to wait for a chance encounter!

"Waiting is hard," the man said once again, "so hard and painfully awkward that however long you wait, you're waiting for one thing only: for the end of waiting, for deliverance from waiting. So hard that once you've waited until you see it, it can no longer be beautiful or lucky, but somehow, oddly enough, sad and painful from all the waiting. – I don't know how to say it. Every redemption is like that: it's never true luck."

Why is he saying this? Záruba thought; how would I not be lucky to wait until I saw it?

"They waited for God Himself," the man continued. "What manner of man came to redeem them from their waiting? He did not look beautiful, the least of men, a man of sorrows; he bore our grief and endured our pain, as if he weren't a god."

"Why are you talking about this?"

"Look, waiting is hard, it even breaks and humbles a god. You wait all year for some kind of luck, some great and beautiful event; finally it comes, rather trifling and gloomy, the way pain can be; but you say: yes, God, that's it, what I've waited so many years for, in order to be redeemed!"

"What do you mean?"

"I mean this: the only reward for waiting is the end of waiting; and yet it's worth the wait. That's why it's necessary to wait. It makes our belief make sense."

"What sort of belief?"

"Any sort at all," the man said, and he fell silent.

The people in the corridor started to stir and walk back and forth. The toothless little girl had now fallen asleep in her mama's arms, hidden under a shawl. Life began to pour through the corridor, aimless and disorderly, but it moved and kept on moving.

"What did you mean about those gods?" Záruba asked aloud.

"They were beautiful," the man said. "Only luck or chance was needed in order to see them and become oneself a bit of a god. This is what I think: that luck is unusual, so beauty is extremely unusual, and luck, luck can happen only with chance and an astonishing event. But whoever waits is waiting for something that must happen; something must come that completes the waiting. Look, everyone is waiting ... even you; we leave our path with joy, so that we can wait for great things. Oh, waiting is a terrible strain, very much like belief. But the more we wait – *Come what may, we will be redeemed.* Look, it's already morning."

Into the station poured a stream of people with their laughter, coughing, and clamor. The noise whisked through the corridor like a giant broom, sweeping up the silence that had settled and blowing away the stale, dusty voices. The passengers got up off the benches, shook off the cobwebs of sleep, and looked each other over without malice, linked by their shared night, even though out the windows daylight shone.

The man who had spoken with Záruba became lost in the crowd of people. A new crowd, tickets, shouts, bells ringing. – The black and bellowing train pulled into the station, absorbed the crowd, hissed, exhaled, and set off for its destination. God, just go quickly, Záruba thought, all's not yet lost, hope remains.

Help!

H E FOUND HIMSELF on a broad hillside covered with beautiful trees. Why, this is France, it suddenly struck him, I must have boarded the wrong train. It was a most unusual train – full of unfamiliar faces laughing at him as if he were inappropriately dressed; and the train was moving so wildly that the windows rattled.

Brož was wakened from his dream. Someone was rapping on the window.

"What is it?" Brož cried out, his tongue thick with sleep.

"Please," spoke a woman's trembling voice from outside, "please come at once and help us!"

"Go to hell!" Brož replied furiously, and he buried his head deep into his pillows. If only he could recapture the broken thread of his dream! resume sleeping at precisely the place where he had been interrupted! A train, something about a train, Brož forced himself to remember, and suddenly he realized with agonizing clarity: I should have asked her what had happened!

He sprang up from the bed and hurriedly opened the window. The cold, black, empty night blew in from outside. "Who's there?" he called, but nothing answered. Then the cold gripped him, and he went back to lie down; once again he found his own dry warmth under the eiderdown and reveled in it greedily, limitlessly; once again his eyelids sank and his limbs eased into unconsciousness. Ah, to sleep!

His eyes wide open, Brož stared into the darkness. Who could it have been? No one here in the village takes any interest in me. Who would have looked to me for help? It was a woman's voice. It was an unfathomably pained voice. Perhaps it was a matter of life and death. Well, I'm not a doctor. But perhaps it was a matter of life and death.

Tormented, Brož turned to face the window. It was a chill blue oblong in the black, incommodious darkness. No fires were lit anywhere. It was silent, except for the sharp, precise ticking of his watch by the headboard. What could have happened? Some kind of accident? Perhaps right next door someone is dying, someone somewhere is at a loss, struggling with a difficult moment. Even so, I'm not a doctor.

Now the bed burned, dryly, monotonously. Brož sat up and from habit put on his glasses. For that matter, he reflected, how could I be of any help at all? Merely lend a helping hand? Do I know anything that might be useful? My God, I can't even offer advice or consolation; I wouldn't know the words to ease even a portion of someone's burden, nor could I give sympathetic support to anyone. All I want is to be left in peace, to be rid of people. What could have happened?

At this point it occurred to him to light the lamp. Perhaps they'll see the glow, he told himself, and come back. It will shine like a beacon. If they do come, I'll ask them what did happened; at least I'll know then that I really couldn't be of help. – Anticipating that satisfaction, Brož piled the pillows behind his back; he waited expectantly for the creak of the gate and for the same woman's voice to plead outside his window. But the ticking of the watch annoyed him. In vain he tried to stop it. Three o'clock. Little by little, the oppressive weight of his anxieties huddled in his chest. No one was coming.

Reluctantly but hurriedly, Brož began to dress. Surely, he told himself, there will be a light on where it happened, and I can tap on the window. At any rate, I can't sleep now. I won't be of any use to them, but... Perhaps they're completely at a loss – In his haste, Brož became confused and quietly cursed his shoelaces; finally he succeeded in tying an unusual knot and he ran out the front door.

It was dark, utterly dark. Brož set off down the narrow street looking for a lighted window; never before had he seen the village so deeply asleep, so foreign to anything stirring, so foreign. – Nowhere was there an informative night light, nowhere a thin strip of light between the shutters. Alarmed, he stopped in front of the chapel: through its windows came the feeble light of a darting, quivering flame. The eternal light, he realized, and continued on his way; but nowhere was there the glow of a lamp, darkness everywhere, only the walls' pale sweating –

Quietly Brož made his way back home, listening carefully in front of the mute houses. Is there no moan from within, no trembling of hushed impotence? No woman weeping? Apprehensively, Brož probed the closed spaces of silence; nothing, not even labored breathing, nothing. – Is there not, from out of the vast night, from somewhere distant, from some far quarter of the world a single tormented cry for help?

How foreign was this sleeping world that did not speak! That did not call out in pain! That did not cry out for salvation! If just the slightest moan were to start up now, would he not embrace the sound ardently, would he not lean against it as if it were a pillar, would he not respond as to a lamp spilling light into the darkness –

You want to help others, said a mocking voice inside him, yet you cannot help yourself! But, Brož thought in pained astonishment, is that really so? Perhaps because, ah, *precisely* because you cannot help yourself. – People who are capable of helping help themselves, but you, who cannot help yourself, you are precisely not the one...

Brož stopped as if struck by a falling brick. You cannot help yourself! But is that really so? Do I really need help ... from myself, or anyone else? Are things going that badly? No, not at all! I live my life as I please and there is nothing else I want. Only that I may live out my days for myself. I have no unfulfilled wishes. Perhaps I have no wishes at all. I cannot help myself ... there's nothing to be helped. That never occurred to me before. Let everything stay just as it is: day after day, as far as the eye can see.

Day after day? Brož sat on the curb and stared into the darkness, as if he were silently finishing an interrupted dream. Or as if he had dreamed it day after day, month after year, as far as the eye can see. – Nothing has changed; what is there to change? Events are fleeting and years slip by, but day returns each day, as if nothing at all had happened. A day has passed: what of it? It was one and the same as the day that will come tomorrow. Let it too pass!

And every day I can tell myself: I have lost nothing but a day. Nothing more than a day! Then why this anxiety? Brož rubbed his forehead hard. Must shake it off. I've not had a good night's sleep. I've come to a standstill, and the days have grown up around me like bricks in a wall; day after day they've piled up, smooth and solid, like walls. Before long I shall wake: but will it be a new, unprecedented day that I find? Or will it be a day composed of thousands from the past – like walls? And again I'll ask myself: is this yet another day among the thousands piling up – like walls? Why has it come? Yesterday there was only one day less! Is it worth it, waking up for this unprecedented day?

In that instant he and his sleepiness parted ways. Why, it's a prison, he suddenly realized with horror; for so many years I've lived as if in prison! His eyes widened; all those years were sadly illuminated now, strangely foreign, even more strangely familiar; everything, nothing, days without number ... Brož broke free from his reverie: Yes, a prison. What if I never wake up to an unprecedented day? Isn't that what I wait for each day? (– yes, a prison!) and perhaps have always waited for, he suddenly realized (– all those years illuminated)? Isn't that why

I've come to a standstill, just so I can wait for that unprecedented day?

All those years illuminated. Lord, Brož whispered, his eyes raised toward heaven, I shall conceal it from you no longer: I was waiting for your help, for miraculous deliverance, for a great event to occur, a sudden light through the cracks, a forceful knock on the door with a strong voice commanding: Lazarus, rise! I've waited so many years for the strong voice of the conqueror; you never came, and I no longer count on it.

But to the extent that I am still waiting, then it is for help and deliverance. For a voice that will summon me from my prison. Perhaps it won't be strong, but so weak that I must back it up with my own voice. Perhaps it won't be a commanding but a beseeching voice: Lazarus, rise, so that you can help us!

– You cannot help yourself: who then will help you? Who will come to free you, who cannot free yourself? Everything sleeps in unknowing, unsuspecting peace; an infant peeps its grief through slumbering lips; a childish dream, something about a train, an elusive dream sketched on a prison wall. But unexpectedly she comes – she taps on the window and calls you from your dream into an unprecedented day. Will you recognize it and leap up to meet it, wide awake?

Perhaps you've been waiting for an earthquake; listen rather for a soft, beseeching cry. Perhaps the day you await will come not as a holiday, but as an ordinary day, one of life's Mondays, a new day.

Dawn rises over the forest.

Lída

HOLUB WAS STILL ASLEEP early that morning when young Martinec came to him and said, "Our Lída has disappeared." He was extremely pale and distraught; he stammered something about how he and his mother relied on Holub's friendship and needed his advice. Lída had gone out yesterday afternoon, purportedly on a visit, and as yet she had not returned.

Holub would have liked to say a few comforting words, but he couldn't think of any. Suddenly the image of the young woman appeared to him as he had seen her last: curled up on a sofa, quiet, charming. She stared fixedly at whoever was speaking but paid little attention to the words; she made no move to leave, as if preferring to stay off to the side, out of everyone's view. She seemed depressed, not at all herself.

I

Lída truly had not been herself of late. Her voice and even her movements had seemed constrained by sadness, as if sadness had coiled around her and made movement very difficult; she had, however, freed herself of this somehow, speaking and looking on as if from some utterly impersonal void; but even this had passed, and only vague traces remained. On that particular day she had lunched with a good appetite, chatted gaily, and contemplated her next change of clothes. Then it occurred to her to visit her girlfriends. She had left in good spirits and with no sign of distress. There had been nothing to suggest what was to happen.

That evening, when she did not return, the hours of waiting and anxiety began. At each clang of the apartment house gate they held their breath; new hope would spring up, become more certain and more tormenting, raise them to new levels of excitement, stretch on in agony as a few more seconds passed, then crash: no one had come. With increasing uneasiness they waited for the next rattle of the gate; at each barren clank the fleeting moment stopped, became horribly prolonged, for a brief interval suffered, and then once again whirled to the ground like a feather. Finally, around ten o'clock, the building fell silent. Now time spread out before them like an abyss, hopeless and boundless; waiting became an ache which, rather than passing, stayed on and grew in all directions at once. The striking of each hour was like the throb of a festering wound.

Disquietude pressed their faces to the window. There is always a handful of passersby on the damp street below. Each woman looks a bit like Lída, each hurries or dawdles, as if she might be bringing a message. Someone stops directly below, and their eyes fasten on her in vast, breathless anticipation; but she is already walking on, and once again expectation presses against their chests like a massive weight. Suddenly a hackney carriage approaches; its harsh clattering sounds like an eager, hasty explanation in advance. They want to rush downstairs, but the carriage rumbles on, for so long that it seems as if the street had no end. Slowly the pedestrians thin out, with each receding step bleak sorrow spreads further and further; the dwindling number of footsteps can be heard only at a distance now, the quiet ticking of despair. The street is empty, to both right and left an endless strip of desolation. Expectation has died. Everything has meshed into the shapeless fabric of anxiety.

It had been there from the beginning: at first it was pliant, fluid, yielding or tense; gradually it became immobilized and, with silent but tangible pressure, became an immense burden in their breasts. But it was the illusory immobility of an enormous

egg, centering on itself and preparing for life. It grew the way
an ulcer grows, a dull, kneading pressure, apparently endless,
constantly expanding, but then suddenly pulling back into the
center, into a single point of acute pain. In just this manner, all
their anxieties pulled back into the sole suspicion that something
dreadful had happened to Lída. For those who waited, brutal
horror rent the night. The shapeless, fundamentally internal
anxiety clawed its way out and became a dreaded phantom; the
suspicion became a specter that acquired a half-external existence. "I beheld our building's yellow door," Martinec wrote
later, "sprinkled only slightly with something that looked like
blood, I knew that on the other side of the door Lída lay dead,
because it was *obvious;* the fantastic, heartless, monstrously
human-like physiognomy of the door filled me with horror and
dismay. (From that night on, I have observed that *every* door
has some kind of expression.) Not even by the most desperate
efforts could I rid myself of the image of that door. But suddenly that image faded, and I saw a crowd of people, an
ambulance, and a streetcar halted in the barbarous, immeasurable instant of a traffic accident. There were other images,
and each was equally compelling, as if real, imposed from
without, and even now I can't understand where all these
strange, stark, external realities came from, these images created
by sheer anxiety."

Anxiety rooted itself ever deeper in reality. With hysterical
speed the lady of the house threw on her clothes to go looking
for Lída, to knock on the doors of all Lída's friends, to run
hither and yon. Young Martinec restrained her; if Lída had met
with some sort of accident at a friend's house, they would have
sent word.

Martinec himself started off to the police station. The
stairwell gaped beneath him like a dark hole; step by step he fell
into a despair which, with each stride, became more and more
an oppressive, inexorably brutal, external fact. The deathly,

desolate procession of streets was saturated with a murky darkness: the entire incident acquired a grim reality and grew as if it had been permeated by even more harsh, raw substances. Even during the day, the corridors of police headquarters are full of sadness; now their cold, deserted sorrow became an actual component in a vision of misfortune, and the yellow, exceedingly cheerless office stood within it like an alien, tormenting fact. Misfortune acquired an alien sound in the unsympathetic voice of the officer. "Nothing has been reported. What's your sister's name?" – Martinec left, his heart constricted; the matter had grown and was growing more barbarous. His hackney tore through the sleeping city, to shelters, from hospital to hospital; everywhere the waiting, the desolation, the agonizing silence, then finally steps in the hallway and a rough, sleepy voice. – No dead or wounded girl had been transported anywhere that day, but everything actual and external, merciless and alien, that he encountered in the course of his distressing search merged with the phantasm of misfortune into a vast, complex world of misery.

Slowly he trudged home, but at the door he was met with questioning maternal eyes, and he realized that now his hope and hers had collapsed. With a flash of insight he grasped that from the beginning everything had been done merely to cover up the horrible anxiety of suspecting that Lída had been the victim of a crime. As if a hideous wound would be exposed – a cold, vivid horror, almost matter-of-fact yet penetrating in the extreme. Suddenly, they became conscious of their most secret suspicion, that an act of violence had been committed against Lída, that she had been abducted and brutally violated, that she lay somewhere, helpless, cruelly ravaged, or dead. It was a moment of utmost crisis that could not last, and yet it never left them; even when the anxiety had long since died down, that moment continued to cast its shadow like an everlasting memento of pain.

In the midst of the crisis, Mrs. Martincová fell to her knees and said a prayer from her missal, rapidly and aloud.

"Jesus, beam of eternal light, have mercy on us! Jesus, king of glory, have mercy on us! Jesus most wondrous, have mercy on us! Jesus, father of future ages, have mercy on us! Jesus, angel of great counsel, have mercy on us! Jesus, gentle and humble of heart, have mercy on us! Jesus, God of peace, have mercy on us! For the mystery of Thy holy incarnation, deliver us, Jesus! For Thy mortal anguish and Thy crucifixion, deliver us, Jesus!"

The words of the prayers fall monotonously, mechanically, like drops of water or seconds of time; they are a plea that never ceases, to the point of besottedness, as if plumbing the depth of sorrow; they are a cry of pain, each repetition flowing smoothly into the limitless, dull uniformity of a sorrow that has become fixed. With each "Jesus," with each recurring plea, the sorrow becomes more quietly, more numbingly fixed. With cry after cry, a vast emptiness and isolation grows around oneself, everything in the vicinity of the moment grows, as depth increases with the well-digger's rhythmic drill. Every presence empties itself or evaporates, withdraws, retreats far from the excruciating nearness of things, and as if through the boundless emptiness of space, through a numbed consciousness without thought, rapidly, incessantly, "Jesus, have mercy on us."

Each word of the prayers is mysterious, rushing into the infinite. She neither bewails nor laments, grasps nor pronounces upon the pain of man, but rushes into the infinite and is carried away in her human agony. What became of you, pain, surrounded by an endless horizon? What are you, present moment, opening up on all sides to eternity? And you, constricted heart, what is vaster than mercy and deliverance?

"God of Mercy, Whose eyes see my anguish and count my sighs, Who hath so often shown me Thy grace, to Thee this day

I cry out of the depths of my soul. Hear my voice and my pleas, for my fate is in Thy hands."

Gradually, almost imperceptibly, the emptiness is filled. It is as if something both amorphous and plentiful flowed from the prayers. Each word spreads to an indeterminate depth, its content is fluid and unutterable, and it expands beyond the boundaries of sense to the indeterminate and unreal. With each unspoken prayer the nearness of things again tumbles down onto the soul, and there is a need for doubled efforts and the heightened urgency of crying out. Once again things are rent, deadened; endlessly flowing forth from great, inexhaustible quantities and fullnesses of words is a strange atmosphere that bathes things, like depth. They are horrible and agonizing things: they are everything that reminds her of Lída and her misfortune. But all these things are immobile, deadened, flooded to an enormous depth; they are merely corpuscles placed inside a transparent glass globe, in a silent, motionless atmosphere, a prison, a mute depth of resignation.

After many long hours of prayer, Mrs. Martincová rose as if awakening. Everything around her had changed; dust and ash, deposited by reality, had quietly settled on a new order. Everything, including even final, dead things, had taken on a new, fixed countenance, a patient "Thy will be done," an expression of resignation and peace.

Meanwhile young Martinec paces the sitting room until sunrise. The more real Lída's disappearance seems, the more mysterious it becomes as well. What torments him are not the conjectures but the questions. The heinous thing that happened to Lída is not mere phantasm, it is a problem that grows with each question and each answer. Given the utter darkness surrounding the disappearance, *nothing* can be ruled out.

God, what to do, what to do! Entrust the case to the police? But they've already begun their inquiries, starting with

Lída's friends and acquaintances. Her woeful misfortune is being spread about, gossiped about. If Lída does return, it will be as if she'd been taken down from a pillory; she will forever carry the mark of something criminal and shameful. Better that all be concealed. – But in the meantime, Lída's girlfriends are rushing over to her apartment, and they'll be asking what's wrong with her. If she were ill, they would come and visit her; if she had something contagious, their fathers would come and, as always, the right to sit by the bedside of this dearest child could not be wrested from them for all the world. We couldn't keep up the pretense that she had simply gone away, without writing to anyone or sending anyone her greetings. They would sense that something underhanded was going on, they would sniff out the atmosphere of secrecy and lies.

Perhaps Lída will return, but she will find that her familiar, welcoming world has been rendered null and void: drop by drop, small cruelties will permeate her days, thousands of things will touch her wound, for a girl's life is delicately, minutely woven and exposed to countless, minute instances of suffering.

God, what to do, what to do! Yes, search for her, dead or alive. If alive, save her from shame and suffering; if dead, save her from the brutality of sensational news. In either case, save Lída! The day dawns gray and cold, today Lída must be found, but hat on head, young Martinec hesitates and does not go out.

Where is Lída? What has happened to her, where to look for her, where to look? He had a definite plan and a detailed hypothesis, but both he now discards. – He hurriedly outlines a new, alternative plan of action. The mystery of Lída's disappearance unfolds with a new plot, a new set of agonizing particulars, and once again new thoughts and an unexpected hypothesis emerge. Indefatigably, Martinec runs through line after line of reasoning; feverishly and with leaps of logic he hurls himself at each new possibility, deploys it, and then abandons it. God, what to do, what to do!

Patiently, like a miserable spider, his mind continues to weave new alternatives. Each new hypothesis is constructed slowly, meticulously, as if with pebbles. Meticulously, he toils over each new fiber of possibility. More and more often his thinking stops and he begins to horribly overexert himself; time and again, in hushed tones, a single word recurs; but nowhere in the wide world is there a word that would provide a link to her. Young Martinec stands with furrowed brow and strives to catch hold of an elusive notion. Nothing remains but overwhelming fatigue. All his hypotheses have dissipated into nothing.

All his fabricated possibilities fell away like dead flakes of skin, all the workings of his mind split off and fell away, all that was visible and imaginable was shed like useless packaging, and all that remained now was the fundamentally internal, exacerbating, helpless, naked kernel of blind will. There was only a voracious hunger to see this business with Lída through, wholly, headlong, without restraint. He made an unqualified decision, certainty at last.

"I'm going to look for Lída," he said to his mother.

"Go," she whispered, "and may God guide your steps."

II

During his period of uncertainty, Martinec turned to Holub for advice. Holub did his best, said everything he could think of, but there was nothing that could in any way shed light on the mystery of Lída's disappearance. He worried over the facts until there was no longer any doubt that nothing would come of them. Each possible step led blindly into the unknown. There was only utter necessity and the utter impossibility of action. Holub wavered; Lída's huddled form appeared insistently before him, like an idée fixe —

"I think," he began, "that Lída ran away with someone; you don't like hearing this, but I cannot come to any other conclusion. Look, I'd love to find the solution. I haven't known Lída long enough to be able to say what is probable or possible with respect to her nature. You are her brother, perhaps you know her better and can with complete certainty say: she did not run away because this was not within her capabilities."

"I cannot say that," said Martinec, sick at heart. "I don't have any idea what's possible. I can only say that there is absolutely no reason for her to run away."

"We're not looking for reasons: those are strictly hers alone. Every Lída can surprise us by doing something no one would expect from *her*. We do not know her motives. We do not have access to her soul.

"As for reasons, Martinec, it's impossible to count them; it's likely there are an infinite number. But there are far fewer facts, and this keeps the logic very simple. Of motives, an infinite number can be inferred from Lída's disappearance, but of facts – about what she could have done or about what could have happened to her – there is a limited selection. However, action brings an end to the unlimited nature of anything. Actions are not as individual as motives, there is a uniformity to them, a repetition and regularity that have nothing to do with motives and that go well beyond our wishes and drives. Facts are fatal.

"Raskolnikov had uncommon motives for the murder he committed. His plan was thought out in great detail and with great originality, but in the end, the actual deed came off as somehow run-of-the-mill, strikingly similar to a hundred other common murders. But the oddest thing is that, in actuality, it happened purely by chance.

"Let's suppose that the motivation for every suicide is entirely individual: but similar suicides almost always follow. Housemaids almost always resort to poison and not to a noose made from bedsheets; poison isn't a requirement, but it's customary. Unconsciously, our own acts imitate those acts most frequently repeated; they follow in the same direction. Perhaps even reality itself tends in that directon. The more ordinary something is, the more likely it is to happen. Facts ordinarily crop up in association with other facts, not from some sort of requisite causality, but as if by chance, from habit, unwittingly, involuntarily. In short, it has little to do with us. It is sheer concomitance. We can presuppose that, even in Lída's case, ordinariness is playing its role."

"Lída's case is not ordinary," Martinec insisted.

"It might very well be out of the ordinary," said Holub, "but there is a paradox in regard to uncommon cases: they recur. Misfortunes repeat themselves, as do suicides, murders, even records. People who play roulette count on this paradox of chance, on the repetition of uncommon events. In short, the singularity of a case does not foreclose fatal similarities and repetition. Even Lída's misfortune has its striking, recent analogues.

"You want to find Lída, you want to solve the mystery, whose circumstances elude you. All hypotheses are possible; the less we know, the more possible they are. There's only one thing left to do: to find among all the imaginable possibilities the most probable and most possible, which is the most ordinary, familiar, and ready at hand. Anything ordinary is probable, not because the motivation might be better understood, but because it occurs more often. An estimate of probability must deal with the ordinariness of events, with the unwitting repetition of acts; it must take into account the fact that individual, *unknown* circumstances result in regular, similar, fatally ordinary, pre-dictable outcomes. The goal is not to find facts, but to show the workings of fate, which apply blindly and with regularity.

"We don't know the facts of Lída's case, but at least we'll try hard to work out its likely plot. But take care that we aren't tempting fate. Here and there we'll come across the probable, and we can be confident that fate controls even the facts of Lída's case and leads her, unwittingly, in the direction she is going.

"Like you, I imagine that this is a question of – that it relates to Lída as a woman. This is highly probable, because Lída is pretty. The question is whether or not force is involved. You of course think— But force is not so easy as you perhaps imagine. Lída could not simply have been attacked. Look, if you want to dream up everything that *could* have happened, we would never be finished. To kidnap and violate a young woman here in the city would be possible only in fairly remarkable circumstances, and uncommon circumstances are things of fantasy, not of probability.

"Unfortunately, I cannot win you over you with subtle reasoning; I'm lacking in that regard. If we eliminate suicide and accident, we're left with either force or flight. But force most often occurs under other circumstances, in the countryside, among other classes of people – In short, I don't recall such a thing ever happening in circumstances such as ours; yet there are dozens, hundreds of runaways. Thus, Lída is far more likely to have run away than to have been violated, because flight is comparatively common."

"Is Lída common?" Martinec asked rather softly.

"No, and the worse for her if she were to become common. Ordinarily, lovers run away because of some sort of obstacle. In view of the fact that none of you imposed restraints on Lída in her contacts with others, then something else must have done so, something indecipherable, moral, that she had to forcibly transgress. That "something" was perhaps someone whom none of you knew. The hindering was apparently on *his* side. You can imagine romantic scenarios if you like, but ordinary cases are more likely to be less star-crossed. True love has too great a capacity for suffering for it to suddenly resort to such a solution. In the majority of cases, the girl is the victim, involuntarily entangled in passion; in this respect, as a rule, things happen *as if* determined by the deepest of motives. You are young; if you find the man, you will consider it your duty – a matter of honor. — Clearly, you must not treat him as your equal," Holub added, suddenly showing sympathy.

Young Martinec stood up. "Are you finished?"

"Not yet. There is one striking fact here: that Lída left the house quietly and that before leaving she had a good appetite. A good appetite is one of those things it is impossible to feign; apparently she wasn't worried about not returning. Presumably, she merely had an engagement with someone she didn't know very well, but then, in the course of the afternoon, something suddenly happened to her and she ended up in some sort of situation we cannot grasp. You suppose it to be infatuation, but that's only a name for wholly unknown motives. What happened to her must have happened suddenly; if she were to come home, I don't think she would even know how to run away. It's all terribly enigmatic. Martinec, perhaps you will find her, but don't question her, don't force a confession out of her, don't *humiliate* her."

"And where would I find her?" Martinec said peevishly.

"Somewhere outside of Prague. There are tens of thousands of places where she could be, and there are countless circumstances which could influence the choice of destination, but we aren't in a position to know any of them. If Lída acted deliberately, in circumstances unknown to us, then we couldn't begin to guess where she is; but in the event that she chose the destination blindly, due to infatuation, *by chance*, we can have a go at it. This is the paradox of chance.

"When someone places a bet in roulette according to some plan we know nothing about, we cannot guess beforehand what his game is, but if he plays according to chance, at random, we can say with some degree of probability which number he will involuntarily choose: his age, his favorite number, an important date, et cetera. It's the same with lotteries and every other game of chance: we can guess where Lída ran away to only if she acted blindly, out of her senses, as if she had a fever.

"Lída didn't play the lottery unless there was a number that had a certain special flavor for her. Any place Lída would haphazardly choose would have to have a similar sort of flavor. Everyone feels partial to some special place, perhaps because he was there in his youth, or because he hasn't been there yet, or its name appeals to him – it doesn't matter why, that place always stands a greater chance for him than anywhere else in the world. Perhaps you recall Lída talking happily that way about such places, some dream she had, somewhere she always wanted to go, or some particular place she had fixed in her mind. Lída liked to talk about her fantasies; try to recall – words that just popped out of her. Surely you can remember something."

Martinec, coated with the sweat of impotence, said nothing.

"Presumably, then, Lída ran off with someone," Holub concluded in a monotone. "Most likely it was a man with whom she had had contact for some inadmissible reason or other. To all appearances she acted suddenly, in a fit of sorts, erratically, hurriedly, and there's a chance that she chose as her refuge a place in which, at some point, she's shown an interest. It's a simple case of probability, yet it's unreliable because it doesn't take into account a thousand factors unknown to us, and it says only what might have happened, not what did. I assume I haven't said anything out of the ordinary, considering that chance increases with ordinariness. But all this cannot persuade either you or me. And even if I were to stumble upon a fact in my guesswork, what Lída experienced in her innermost depths would remain just as incomprehensible — "

Martinec' silence put Holub on the defensive; I built on sand, he thought, on the sand of many cases. My God, is Lída really just some "case x," one of many? Isn't there anything singular and beautiful about it? Isn't there the wonder of a life? And if I *am* right, what use is it to her, what use are her "unknown motives," her suffering and her choices? Are motives and repentance the only things appropriate to her – the "case" itself doesn't follow her intentions, but its own – to her, her motives would simply be *opportunities* – "

Holub was puzzled: Everything I said was terribly unfeeling, heartless; I had to disregard Lída as an individual, Lída as a woman, just so that I could carry out my dubious calculations. In calculating her, I demeaned her.

Holub was flooded with anguish and regret. How is it, he thought, that it is the very "ordinariness" of my speculations that makes me suffer so? God, our entire life is invested in ordinary things, but we don't know about them, and that is why we can live with them and act despite them. But suddenly, when we become aware of what is most ordinary, it surprises, alarms, seems monstrous to us; suddenly we come face to face with something we do that is not individual, suddenly we find that our will is only apparent, a presentiment of acts that are not dependent on us. There is something of chance in everything we do, and chance is an open road through which fate enters our lives. Fate is not iron necessity, it is iron chance. And the most commonplace, the most ordinary thing of all is horrible, inflexible chance.

Martinec shrugged his shoulders. "I don't know what to do. I can't do anything. I can't shake off my dread."

"Nor can I," Holub said softly.

"I will search for Lída," said Martinec, "but in a different way – I need to take a more internal route. I don't know whether, in the end, you'll be proven right, but that has little to do with Lída. Perhaps I will yet travel that route, but in the meantime I will go blindly, anywhere; perhaps I will find a footprint on the sidewalk and recognize Lída's among thousands. I'll rely upon chance, curious chance. Perhaps something out of the ordinary will happen, something improbable, something that will help me. Perhaps you're right, but you don't know what it is to go searching out of love."

Martinec hesitated, he waited to hear what else Holub would say, he hungered for something that would finally persuade him. But Holub was silent.

"Tell me!" Martinec cried out. "Tell me whether you're certain – "

"I am less certain than you," said Holub.

Martinec went out, but first he thanked Holub and promised that he would come back in the afternoon; but he didn't come back, instead a letter from him arrived that evening.

"Your speculations have been confirmed," wrote Martinec, "but only by chance. I ran around the city without any set destination, I was looking at the ground and in every nook and cranny. – I know that it was crazy, but I didn't know what else to do. Finally I ran into a certain friend, and of his own accord (note how curious this is) he told me that yesterday afternoon he had encountered Lída and accompanied her to the building where her seamstress lives, where she was, supposedly, going for a fitting. But I know that Lída did not go to the seamstress, because she had already gone there that morning. Apparently she only wanted to get rid of her companion, so that she could disappear with someone else. In truth, of course, she was hiding something.

"I must impart to you something most strange: suddenly I became aware that for quite some time I had been standing on the street in front of the train station. I had no idea what I was doing there, and for that very reason I began to examine the railway timetable. The name of the place that had come to mind when I was visiting you had been scratched by a fingernail, but also another quite different place, which I had not thought about earlier, had been underlined, a place about which Lída

had definitely spoken. It was as if Lída had been there, trying
to decide which train she would take. Nothing is certain, but it
was such an extraordinary coincidence that I will travel there.

"Something more: If I find her, do I credit your proba-
bilities or my extraordinary luck? Mother would say that it was
divine dispensation. I don't know. I am leaving in a few
moments."

Holub spent all the next day in a state of heightened
tension. Toward evening he received a telegram and opened it
almost feverishly. All it said was: "No use both places.
Martinec."

Holub felt an enormous, deep sense of relief. He smiled and
ran about as if he had unexpectedly won an prize. It isn't so, he
shouted to himself, it isn't so! That's not what Lída did! He was
seized with infinite tenderness and compassion for her, on his
trembling lips a thousand semi-conscious words he would say to
her or about her.

That evening Holub needed to see people, countless
numbers of people in the streets and in cafés. He was
overwhelmed by the need to prolong that day as long as he
could, on through the night and into tomorrow, and not to let
go of it for anything in the world. In his elevated, poetic state,
it seemed to him that Lída had run away; he was in an ecstasy
of sorts, his joy knew no limits, nor was he aware that for the
entire night he had been alone and silent. He felt that the
moment was too important to be released; he bore within
himself something vast and was afraid that in his thoughts it
would crumble. I have been delivered, he felt; God, grant Thy
favor upon my redemption! may I not awaken! may I sustain it!

Perhaps Lída is asleep, was the sweet image that came to
me, lost in a world like a squirrel in a forest, but I know no
more about her dreams than I do about her steps. But it's good
that she sleep, that she live out of our sight and beyond our
understanding; and if she has gone astray, that she at least go

astray in her own fashion and in familiar places. Let it be wherever! it's simply good that it is not a place marked by fate, that it is far away and inviting, and stands on the threshold of countless steps: so now I will find her. God, I was mistaken; misfortune, crime, or fate – anyone who wants to hit the bull's-eye aims at the black, at the blackest black, but the blackest black deceived me, the darkest, blackest black turned out not to be the *darkest* of all.

That whole night was one of repose after the removal of a great weight, but the next day a new pressure descended on Holub. Didn't I already rid myself of it? Why can't I get Lída's misfortune out of my head? Why am I so concerned about fate? Where did this obsession come from? Once again the young woman appeared to him as he had seen her last, seated on a sofa, all curled up, her movements constrained, quiet, seemingly half there; and then suddenly, vehemently, she was shaking. It was as if she were huddled up in the palm of an enormous hand that was slowly clenching shut. This tenacious, unsparing image clutched my heart.

Finally a new letter from Martinec arrived: "Dear Sir, how I need to speak with you; I must at least write. Lída is upstairs in a room, but not asleep; she is crying like one out of her senses. I remain in the second place I traveled to from Prague. I did not find them there, but I couldn't return to Prague at that exact moment and, in the meantime, while I was waiting for my train, the ones I was searching for arrived. They had spent two nights in Karlovy Vary, then traveled on to here, near the German forests. This is an exceptional circumstance that you did not anticipate. The man in question disappeared; I recognized him slightly, but it is with horror that I recall my conversation with him. Lída simply laments her situation with tears, she doesn't say a word except to indicate to me her burning regret. I cannot take her away from here in the state she is in. It was with great difficulty that I forced her to write a postcard to friends in Prague, that 'brother and sister had gone off on a trip together.' There is within her an outright thirst for becoming an object of scandal, for demeaning herself, to the point of self-destruction. I don't understand this, but I trust that she will awaken from it all tomorrow.

"Of course, Lída herself wanted to leave K.V.; the stay there was only en route to elsewhere, for him. It was reckless and rash. I cannot begin to describe the scenes I lived through; it was as though I were on the threshold of hell or insanity. – I told Lída that I had found her through extraordinary luck, as you already know. I realize that it is deceitful, but I cannot tell her that you are the one who found her. On the contrary, I count on you to visit us immediately upon our return, to be the first person she sees, to not let anyone have the least suspicion – I am anxious that she quickly regain her peace of mind."

Holub dropped the letter. Yes, Lída's peace of mind. This wretched business!

Love Song
(Lída II)

AFTER LÍDA'S PUZZLING FLIGHT, when she was back once again with her family, life at the Martinec' began anew – not actually new, anything but new. Everything new has something redemptive about it, and even the worst of it is a stimulus that moves life forward with greater strength. It was not a new life, but somehow, without words, they concurred on everything in a cautious, reticent attempt to live as if nothing had happened. The moment she returned home, Lída replied to her mother's first questions with nothing but heartrending tears, and after an entire night of scenes and reproaches, during which she allowed not a single word of confession to be wrenched from her lips, no one let fall the slightest allusion to what had occurred. Speaking in careful parabolas, they avoided everything that would remind them of that troublesome incident; but in their ceremoniousness they felt it all too much: it was present, even if they did not speak of it. From the first "Good morning" to the last kiss of Mother's hand before turning in, the days passed, veiled and uniform, so silent that under the surface of the silence they could feel with sorrow the depths of what was left unsaid.

Everything was different, completely different. Even when they wished Lída good morning, it sounded a bit diffident, somewhat guarded; when in the evening Lída bent over her mother's hand, her kiss always descended so humbly, so guiltily, that her mother evaded it with a slight motion of her hand that was equally painful to both. Everything lost its former every-dayness, and yet everyone was afraid to acknowledge their most passionate longing: that everything once again be as it was. It seemed to them that any external change would bring to mind the cruel, horrible fact of Lída's flight, even living the old way, and so without a word each of them swallowed the desperate transformation of everything.

Lída buried herself in self-humiliation. Without a word she evaded her former connections and stayed indoors, within sight of her mother. She handed her letters to her mother, and when they were handed back to her unopened, she let them lie unread – and yet two did reach her, and upset her. It seemed that she was silently thanking her mother and even her brother for their silence, for each word they spoke, for every small task they imposed on her; she accepted everything meekly, humbly, one might even say defenselessly, as if they were unceasing kindnesses of which she was unworthy and which tormented her. In reality, brother and mother both could no longer do anything without the hidden thought that perhaps this would intrigue Lída a bit and distract her. They spoke only for her, concealing their watchful glances of love and anxiousness, and when on her pale, charming face they saw only shamed and tortured gratitude, the two of them vied in thinking up new ways to show consideration, which only pained her more.

Thus Holub found them when, recalling his promise to young Martinec, he dropped in for a visit. Martinec and his mother welcomed him with unmistakable relief; for them, he was the only person who knew *everything* and, consequently, could enter into their tacit collusion, their spidery weaving of cautious consideration. He found all three subjecting themselves to an immoderate love, with mother and brother both on their knees, sacrificing everything for a beautiful martyr lying prone before them in the dust of ungratifiable humiliation. A number of different thoughts went through his mind, and so he turned his attention to Lída. She held up well in his presence, in both her speech and her behavior; here at last was someone who knew *nothing*. It's just as well they're not receiving anyone,

Holub thought when he saw the falseness on the faces of young Martinec and his mother; even the blind could see what was going on. He left soon and gladly, the whole business with Lída seemed to him curiously distant.

But after two days he received an urgent invitation from Martinec. They apparently considered it his duty to dedicate himself to Lída's case. He shrugged his shoulders and submitted.

Soon he saw that the wound was deeper than had appeared to him at first. It wasn't easy for him to adapt to the small family. He was not himself capable of humility, and he found suffocating this atmosphere where no breath was drawn but in solicitude for Lída. He felt strident and common in their midst; so much self-sacrifice, such unselfishness lay in everything they said, each trifling thing was so saturated with attention, love, and concern for Lída that his words fell like cold, muddy footprints in an invalid's bedroom, like a loud conversation in a room where people are whispering, like something coarse and unsanctified. He brooded in his corner, ashamed of what he had brought in from outside.

Lída sat curled up on the sofa, mute and motionless, passively attentive regardless of what was taking place. She did poorly at concealing her sorrow, as her downcast eyes and bitten lips attested, and she was glad when she could be silent. Gradually Holub came to understand that this was not merely pain, it was lassitude. Lída is wallowing in humiliation, perhaps she takes some sort of pleasure from it, who knows – who knows what kind of satisfaction she gets from sinking deeper and deeper; the way she buries herself in shame, without the least will to break free of it and finally let herself be. She does not even make an attempt to forgive herself; perhaps she is clinging to her sin.

Lída is blunt, blunt to the point of frankness; she conceals nothing, she makes no pretense of an innocent heart within nor does she close her eyes to what she has done. Through her shame

and her ruin she sees the world too nakedly, almost brutally, almost brazenly; she doesn't affect timidity in order to hide behind excuses. And perhaps even in this she finds pleasure or satisfaction, to see her sins as clearly and painfully as possible.

If some demon were to appear now and induce her to say what she's been thinking, there would be a confession so harsh, so relentless and unredemptive as to verge on the horrific. And if a single word could purge everything, she would swallow it and prefer to take upon herself each and every humiliation, whether merited or not. And if she says nothing, it is due to the ignobility of silence.

But when he saw Lída again, charming and silent, so beautiful that all the joys of the world, it would seem, eagerly awaited her, he could not comprehend this thirst or passion, this willful drive that reaped such hideous, humbling pain within her, such self-torment.

Lída is possessed, he thought, possessed by the demon of passivity. She is not holding on to her pain of her own will, pain and shame are holding on to her by captivating and subjecting her to their will. It takes a great deal of agility to create joy, joy is born of one's own impulses and initiative; suffering, however, requires nothing but your submission. Perhaps she is darkly satisfied with it: to feel uncared for, dominated, ensnared, it suffices only to submit, nothing more, nothing more than that. Surely, at its deepest depth, every defeat is something both terrible and sweet: a paralysis that frees you of your will.

Suddenly he was overcome by a nauseating, astringent suspicion. Perhaps there was nothing different about Lída's transgression; perhaps she sinned with the same feeling with which she now does penance. The image kept returning to him of the man who had led her astray. He envisaged the type that is a bit adventurous, cocky, worldly, enterprising but without fortitude, aggressively cynical, coarse and common in his temptations; he imagined one of those over-sophisticated, impudent, conceited men who is used to acting without ceremony rather than without reason, and who gets everything he wants by one means only: exploiting opportunities. He imagined how Lída, encountering this man, was overwhelmed rather than enchanted by the naked, unwavering will which, devoid of scruple, treated her like some naïve country girl; how, able to resist more refined efforts, she feebly and numbly yielded to his single-minded pressure, his cheerlessly summoning will that was more primitive and overt than her own. So, with pain and difficulty, did he delineate Lída's case for himself. He saw Lída as obedient to a demon, weak in her self-defense, lost, submissive, fashioned into passivity; he saw her aimlessly wandering the streets, pursued by someone whose words urged her on like a forceful hand; finally, he saw her kneeling passively, no longer concealing anything, without passion or desire, just to get everything over with. When he raised his eyes toward Lída, huddled on the sofa, his look was full of horror and repugnance. He sensed in her something darkly, irredeemably material: slothful, impotent stuff in some ultimate internal hiding place unreachable by the breath of God; he even looked with sorrow at her beauty, the beauty which, despite everything, veiled her with a magical, immaculate spirituality.

The weeks passed, and Holub could find scarcely any change in the relations of the little family other than a bit of listlessness and boredom; even pain becomes mechanized and turns into tedium. They could no longer manage without Holub, they became accustomed to seeing him in the late afternoon, just when it was getting dark. He would arrive breathing the chill of the streets, lively but shy, and eventually even happy, for nothing is less demanding than the family hour. Sometimes they did not even turn on the lights, and in the indolence and tepidness of those evenings Holub felt the breath of woman-hood, powerful and close.

On one such evening, the conversation turned to childhood memories. Holub told about his boyhood, about the mill where he was born, about the weir under which he nearly drowned. When he told this, something happened that no one had dared hope for: out of the darkness they heard the quiet and sad, veiled but charming contralto of Lída. She went on and on, telling stories about her earliest memories, about her first confession, about visits to the country, about her frocks, about something she once lost in a forest, about hundreds of very minor incidents from very long ago. She talked as if she had had it all on the tip of her tongue a hundred times and, in her sorrow, had not found the right moment to speak. They listened spellbound to her voice and to the trivial, painfree things about which she spoke. That evening her mother nearly forgot to turn the lights on, and when she finally did, Lída hadn't shifted from her familiar position, with her legs tucked under her; nothing could break her spell.

There were still distressful evenings when Lída was animated only for moments at a time; Holub noticed that these moments occurred at those times when the conversation came around to childhood, to dreams and premonitions, to superstitions, to people's relations with animals: to things completely instinctive, involuntary and inward. When it came to such topics, Lída loved to talk, she was exhilarated, painted vivid pictures with her words. How wondrously secret, tender, and insubstantial, thought Holub, are the most thirsting roots of life.

Like many disillusioned people, Holub was suspicious of life. Rarely did he trust people or their motives, and far less frequently than that was he convinced by life's more pathetic aspects; he saw through subterfuge and the hysteria of grand gestures. And – as many do – he poured out his love onto those human things that are impossible to place a value on. Always ready to argue with the pretentious and captious, he lost his nerve before people in whom he found a blind, trembling, and imprudent internal life, half weakness, half mania. He litigated every truth and inclined toward anything that spoke to him with the unaffected voice of the soul. So it was under a very special spell that he now listened to Lída; although initially she spoke more to herself, perhaps, she was opening her heart, and Holub was the first to surmise in her the signs of release: the need to talk about herself.

She was reviving: frail as in convalescence, bewildered and subdued, but once again desirous, full of sorrow and wishes. Now the searching glance of an invalid who would like to be liked again, now the narrow-eyed glance of a cat who wants to be stroked, or the eyes of a sick child pleading for something unknown, eyes riveted or fleeting, sweet, sleepy, provocative; hands that play together on her lap, crush something, lie idle; all of it, the restlessness, the sensuousness, the languor, all touched a stimulated and sympathetic Holub. Lída revived by means of countless bits and pieces of life, through the lives of a variety of personas, as if she were without a soul. She had lived through a lot and with little coherence. She found within herself an odd taste for self-revelation, and she monopolized Holub so that he would break it down into syllables for her. She never tired of hearing him read her horoscope aloud; perhaps she was looking for her soul and wanted to know something about herself, something perceptive and special, immediately accepting each acknowledgement as understanding. She plunged into novels and found herself in them everywhere; she argued with him about every heroine, she saw each of them as justified, and she never stopped insisting on some sort of justice in life. Holub was afraid that she would suddenly confess to her trespasses; however Lída never touched on them, as if they had never been. Above all, curiously, it mattered to her that he *understand* her, in an uncommon, romantic sense.

Holub could not hide from himself the fact that Lída asked him about his own life in an oddly intimate way: when they were alone together, she would lean toward him, her bewitchingly flashing eyes riveted on his, and when she rested her head on his shoulder, he would drink in her breath. Weak and spellbound, trembling from a sense of immorality, he was unable to protect himself against the passion they found in this stimulating relationship.

But when he once again found Lída so near and emotional, her eyes full of questions – what should I become? – he forgot the immorality and everything else, and surrendered to the moment, happy and tormented, inwardly sated only if he could take away with him the feel of her hair or the moist touch of her breath on his face. No one paid it any mind, they could see how friendly it all was; why did they change their positions when her mother walked in?

Holub caught the suspicious uneasiness in the old lady's eyes, a look that was sage and admonishing: How can you, you of all people, who *knows*... Suddenly he was ashamed and reminded himself: I too am immoral, I have abused her trust in me, I have even abused what Lída, that bowed flower who is once again raising herself upright before one and all, aimlessly, unwittingly, blindly... Pricked by his shame, Holub walked slowly and heavily home, determined never to return.

For three weeks he did not visit them; finally young Martinec ran to get him and by means of all sorts of fervent nonsense he managed to drag Holub home, like bagged game. The old lady herself welcomed him with a look of conciliation. Lída was now silent and sad. No, she wasn't sad, but lovely as never before, and she looked at him surreptitiously; oh, so sad and hesitant, and yet somehow never more beautiful or intriguing. Even Holub was sad beyond measure and did not know what to talk about, and when the others spoke, their words seemed alien and worthless. He barely kept himself from addressing Lída and he left without shaking her hand.

Young Martinec came to Holub a second time, apparently they missed him very much. On that occasion Holub had a moment alone with Lída but did not sit next to her; it felt like self-denial to him. Lída seemed quiet and resolute, devoid of all the stimulating flaws of days past, so unwittingly harmonious, unselfconscious, and chaste that he suffered from admiration for her.

Now he went there regularly again; nothing, absolutely nothing happened, and yet the old lady was still beset with concern and Lída hardly dared raise her eyes. She radiated with deep life, powerful and pure, contemplative, looking up suddenly during moments alone with him as if she wanted to say something; and Holub himself...

One day, when he was leaving, Lída accompanied him down to the lobby, and at the threshold she said to him quickly and softly, "Come back tomorrow."

That night, Holub arrived home secretly happy and went right to sleep; but after a little while he woke up and began thinking. The entire case of Lída went through his head, right from the beginning, in chronological order. Once again he weighed his calculus of searching, which now seemed to him stupid and yet irrefutable; once again he forced himself to go through Lída's fall, her passive misery and shame; once again he recalled her humiliation and her revival. It made him feel more and more nauseous – not Lída, not Lída at all, but the facts, reality itself. It is not about passing judgment on anyone. It is not about forgiving anything. But without judgment, without condemnation or forgiveness, everything is worse, there is no room for consolation. His distress drove him from his bed. Why, why did I not pass judgment on her? Why did I feel neither anger nor pity? It was as if I had neglected something irretrievable. But then, he challenged himself, why pass judgment at all?

Because with a judgment you might clear her, he suddenly heard himself thinking, because condemnation and forgiveness redeem an act. If there was no sin in her fall, there is no sense in it; nothing can come of it, no reparation, no atonement. It is worse than blame; nothing, nothing, nothing washes away facts.

It became increasingly difficult for him. He paced his room and forced himself back into the secret happiness he had known when he fell asleep. He thought of Lída, her fixed gaze and lovely hands. He could hear the voice of Lída, veiled and dark: "Only you can help me. Oh, what I did! I ran away from home and lived for three days with a bad man. Help me!" Her tears were so sweet. "I can no longer live a life of deceit!"

Holub stopped as if struck, and turned toward the sofa as if she were sitting there. "No, Lída," he thought with sudden fervor, "no, no, you are not to blame; what do you blame yourself for? Don't talk about it again, it has no significance. Apparently, it had to happen – but don't ask why, there is no point in knowing. Don't wrestle with it anymore, don't torture yourself, nothing can come of it, nothing can be accomplished by it. You are beautiful, Lída, and more deserving of love than anyone."

However, Lída falls to her knees – is she then mad? – and sobs: "Judge whether I am bad!"

He too throws himself onto his knees: "How can I pass judgment on you, Lída? I love you, Lída, imagine that! Isn't that more than passing judgment, even were I gracious, like God, or lenient, like the devil? Never will I pass judgment on you!"

Holub began to pace the room yet again. What is this I'm imagining? He was cross with himself. It will never happen, she will never confess, she is not so ... so moral. Better she keep silent and forget – at the very least, let her forget! Even more troubled than when he woke, Holub lay down, with weariness but without sleep.

The next day, standing in front of the apartment house he had entered so often, he found little courage in himself. Lída gave me such a special invitation, what will happen? How should I behave? Full of uncertainty, he pulled out a cigarette and started to pace the sidewalk. At that moment Mrs. Martincová came out of the building, accompanied by her son. His heart thumping, Holub hid inside the entryway next door. Lída is alone in her apartment. This was not something he was prepared for.

Holub stole up the stairs, feeling nothing but a chill and the beating of his heart and an unusual silence in the building. He stood with his hand on the bell, imagining, oddly enough, the sweet, drawn-out sound it makes. Will the door be opened by the maid or by Lída herself? Shaking, he pressed his ear to the door: nothing, silence, perfect silence, no clattering in the kitchen, no footsteps on the tiles. No one is there. Lída is alone. To be so very alone with Lída. So horribly silent. Gripped by panic, Holub leaned against the banister.

The thought suddenly struck him that perhaps Lída had not suspected that she would be alone. She would not have invited him if she had known! But if she did know, what did she want? What will happen? What will I do? What will I say to her when the door opens? Nothing must happen, I have self-control. — What will happen will happen at last! If only it weren't for that old lady!

Why so hesitant? He felt cruel. Yes, if I were first ... Holub was horrified. What if someone sees me leaving? What would happen to Lída? Lída's flashing eyes appeared to him, and her strong, peaceful scent; she was so near, he felt overcome with weariness. Ah, to be able to kiss the door and run off like a boy in love!

Why is it so quiet in there? He listened anxiously. What will she say? His lips dry, he tried not to think about it; his heart beat with fear and confusion. Too quiet. Perhaps Lída isn't even home – the thought grabbed hold of him, carrying both a sting and a sense of relief. He was conscious of only one thing: I must make sure that she is home. He was reaching for the bell when suddenly he heard the slamming of a door upstairs and someone coming down the stairway. He'll see me! Terrified as a burglar, Holub fled.

Outside again, it seemed as if everything had collapsed. With the boundless grief of utter loss he took himself home. This is for the better, he argued to himself; how could I, who knows everything, act like that! How could I ... exploit an opportunity! I would have to be either infatuated or immoral. – This is for the better, he thought, forcing himself toward a good conscience. But shortly after arriving back home, he fell into piteous despair. Perhaps Lída is still waiting for him, disappointed, humiliated. – Perhaps there's nothing to it! Perhaps he should return? And would that really be bad at all – she is so unhappy! Would it really be so bad if she had everything ... behind her ... She is so beautiful, who could pass judgment on her? Holub stood by a window, his throat constricted. There is still time. I can return. But time passes minute by minute, happiness fades, and the greatest happiness of his life is disappearing. Now, surely now it is too late. The end of hope.

At this moment the bell gave a short, hurried ring. Holub, startled, ran to open it. There was Lída.

"You ... Lída," he said. "I didn't know ... I truly meant to come visit you."

"Yes," said Lída. "I must speak with you. I waited for you, and when you didn't – – Don't leave me out here in the hallway!"

Holub stepped back out of the doorway and Lída entered; coolly, sweetly she scented the room with her fresh breath and fragrance. She is standing in the middle of the room now, and he is of two minds; she has a veil over her face (never has he seen her with a veil) and dewy droplets of rain on her fur; she struggles in vain to pull off her gloves, which are split at the seams.

How this place must look, Holub thought anxiously. My God, what can I cover, what can I quickly straighten up? Too many familiar things here, all these books and pens, paper, ashes ... Disconcerted, his eyes wandered over the room. Where do I find space for it all?

"Are you drenched through?" he said abruptly. It hurt to speak.

Lída left on her gloves and raised her dark, glowing eyes. Her face, behind the veil, was pale and tormented. "I must speak with you. I cannot, listen to me, I cannot live like this anymore."

(God in heaven, Holub thought with alarm, here it is!) "What's wrong? Lída, what's happened to you?"

Lída, looking frail, sat down on the sofa. "I cannot," she repeated. "Don't be angry that I came here." She burst into tears. "This is so difficult. What must you think of me? Why didn't I know you before...?"

"Don't talk like that, Lída!"

"I wanted to explain everything, but how could I, God, how could I – I don't know myself, I simply don't know – I've thought so much about how to tell you! You have to know all about me, you have to!" She was raving. "No, don't take away my courage; I should get down on my knees to tell you! I don't want to be bad any longer and keep from you what I want to say."

"Calm down, Lída." Holub desperately wanted to restrain her.

Lída pulled herself together somehow, fixing her eyes on the floor. Suddenly she lifted eyes that were forthright and serene. "It was – before you started visiting us," she said slowly. "I ran away with ... a certain man. After three days my brother came for me." Holub was stunned, it wounded him to hear this. "Why, God, why," he whispered, not as a question.

Tears began to flow from Lída's eyes. "I don't know. I could tell you his name. I don't know how it happened. It wasn't love, no, not love. – It came upon me like an illness. I was enticed to run away and to do I don't know what. I didn't want it, but it was all I thought about. He saw me in the street and started following me, and then suddenly he asked me out. – I don't know why he was so audacious, but for me it was frightening, I'd never known anything like it. He wanted me so simply and directly, so forthrightly. Then he lay in wait for me everywhere, day after day, on and on and on, and he clasped me around the waist and stared into my eyes; he followed me everywhere I went and kept menacing me. Once he got really angry with me and didn't come anymore; and then I wrote him. I don't know anymore, I don't know why I did that."

Holub clenched his teeth, bitter and afflicted.

"Then he wanted me to go to his place," Lída continued in a soft, almost mournful voice. "But it's impossible, surely it's impossible, you understand this. And when it happens, it's forever and ever, like the waters closing over your head. No one knew yet, not Mother, not anyone. 'Run away with me,' I said to him, 'and then kill me.' Then he came to me and said, 'We'll go away. Tell me where you want to go.' I gave him directions and had him bring a knapsack and a revolver, and we left. Already ... the first night, when he was asleep, I woke him and said, 'Shoot me now.' But he kept laughing, laughing at me. – So once again I pleaded with him: 'Shoot me, please shoot me.' So he took the bullets and threw them out the window into the garden. 'Sleep!' was all he said, and I thought that this was the end, forever. But two days later, my brother found me and took me home ... Can someone completely change?"

"What do you mean by 'change'?"

"God, what do I mean? Have a new life. Can anyone truly have the strength to change?"

"D-d-don't worry, Lída," said Holub, trembling.

"What should I do?" Lída was weeping. "I simply can't live like this anymore. When you visited us, it was so – so horrible for me. Either everything would be the same way it was with him – it could have happened; or another way, a new way – I know I can be better." In her anguish, Lída crushed her fingers against the table. "Believe me, believe me, it's true. If I hadn't met you, perhaps I wouldn't know this, but now, now –"

"Lída," Holub said in a raspy voice.

"No, no, let me." Lída wept. "I know you've rejected me, I know this for certain, for certain. – But after what I did, I must make a sacrifice; even were I to never see you again. I know, I knew, that we would go through a horrible and complete reversal of everything; I was terribly afraid of this moment, and only on my way here did the strength come to me – only when I was crossing the bridge..." Suddenly, with a look of terror on her face, Lída fell to her knees: "Judge whether I am bad!"

"Lída," Holub repeated, nearly beside himself.

Lída reached toward him. "No, no – "

"I knew it all long ago!" Holub shouted.

Lída jumped to her feet as if she'd been slapped in the face: "You knew – "

"I knew it all from the beginning. When your family thought you were dead, I knew that you had run away. That you had run away with someone bad, all of it. – I was even the one who found you."

"How, how," she whispered.

"Don't ask me. It was not difficult to figure out. I knew it all, and yet that didn't prevent me from coming to your apartment – coming to see you, Lída. I just want to reassure you," he added, his hands clasped together. "Oh, how could I have rejected you!"

Lída's face seemed ashen under her pall-like veil. "You shouldn't have come," she blurted out, her voice full of pain.

"No, Lída, it's better that I knew everything. I learned to feel for you."

"Not better, no, no, no," Lída said with anguish. "If I had known! If I had only suspected – "

"What then?"

"Nothing, none of what there is now. I couldn't still have wished – Oh God, what you must have thought of me all this time!"

All this time – Holub himself was frightened. Good God, how it must all seem to her now! "All this time, Lída," he said hesitantly, "I have thought of you with love."

"No," Lída shouted, "that's impossible, impossible! How could you have!"

Holub took hold of her arm. "Lída, since you came here, you must have known it!"

Lída did not pull away. "Impossible," she whispered, her voice full of desperation.

Numb, she slipped her arm out of his grasp.

Oh, Lída. Holub felt a boundless sorrow. Then why did you come? Is this what you pulled yourself together for? What sort of repentance did you imagine? A moment of redemption? Atonement via sacrifice? Why did you take everything to extremes, to the very edge? Look how that sharp edge stabs us now! What sort of grand, outlandish act did you want to accomplish? What great and glorious deed are you expecting from me? Humiliated, you stand before a man without glory; every act is in vain, and there is neither victory nor victor.

In despair, Lída shrank back, attempting to delay; first she looked with wonder all around this room where deliverance had taken place, everything she saw was odd, unfamiliar, worn –

"Lída," said Holub, sick at heart, "perhaps you know that your mother – that I can no longer visit you."

Lída nodded.

"If you want to come here again," he said softly.

Into Lída's eyes rushed tears of self-pity for her solitude.

"There is no other choice," Holub added.

With a motion both sad and charming, Lída bowed her head.

PAINFUL TALES

Two Fathers

SINCE MORNING the square has blazed like a hot stove top beneath the cloudless sky. White gables above arcades, cacti and geraniums blooming in the windows, a small rust-colored dog shaking himself on the pavement. The severe facades of luxurious houses breathe a coolness into the burning day; the affluent gloom within is revealed through the large dark panes of latched windows. In front of the pharmacist's house a Saint Bernard lies sleeping like a sphinx. There is silence in the square, there is always silence in this square; the silence of the rain, the silence of the midday heat, the silence of Sundays, the silence of weekdays. The church, like a massive, steep-sided ship, juts into the middle of the square. That is where the little girl used to walk when she was alive.

She died, and never had the small town seen a greater grief than the grief of her father. During those last days he had never left her bedside; only when she slept would he stand at the window and look out into the square. That is where he used to walk with her when she was alive, leading her by the hand and chatting; the pharmacist's Saint Bernard was always sweeping the ground with his heavy tail and standing up for her to stroke him. The old pharmacist would reach into a glass jar and give her a handful of gray throat lozenges. Later the little girl would spit them out in disgust, and her tiny, pitiful fingers would remain smeared and sticky long afterwards.

That was where he used to walk with her, down the hill to the river. She was afraid of certain houses, but never said why; she was afraid of people and bad dogs, of wells with buckets, of bridges, beggars, and horses; she was afraid of the river and afraid of machines. At every tremor of fear she would clutch her father's hand, and he would respond with a firm squeeze of protection: I'm here, don't be frightened. That was where he used to walk with her, on strolls through the woods, rolling fir cones down a hill and forcing himself to joke; the child never asked any questions. Everyone knew them: he, the earnest father, portly, stooped, and solicitous; she, the inappropriately dressed six-year-old with light-colored hair and bony cheeks. Children would shout "sicky-icky" behind her back; he flushed at this, it pained him, and later he would go complain to their parents. This is how their walks would go.

The Saint Bernard stands up and looks around. The little girl was ill for three weeks and then she died. Some beggar-women are already standing in front of the house of mourning; funeral guests gather, bake for a moment in the square, and then go inside. The musicians are already waiting, as are acolytes with lanterns and crosses, four workmen from the father's factory, in new black suits, carrying the bier draped in a long pall, and little girls in white, half bewildered, half pleased. Members of the choir arrive with sheet music under their arms, tall, smiling young women with light-colored dresses and bunches of flowers. Slowly the town notables assemble in their long black coats and silken skirts, heavy top hats, solemn and dignified faces; the entire town comes, because the father is a man of property and position here. Lastly come the dean and two other priests in white vestments signifying celestial joy. The little girl is laid out upstairs in the large drawing-room, a wreath on her fair hair and a broken candle in her small waxen hands.

Silence in the square, and the Saint Bernard lies down again, his head lifted towards the now silent house. Then through an open window comes the powerful voice of a priest: "Sit nomen Domini." The beggarwomen fall to their knees.

"Laudate, pueri, Dominum: laudate nomen Domini." The male choir joins in: "Sit nomen Domini benedictum." The beggar-women start up a mumbled, disorderly prayer that slowly forms itself into the words of the Our Father. "Hic accipiet," intones the powerful voice of the dean. "Kyrie eleison." "Christe eleison." "Kyrie eleison. Et ne nos inducas in tentationem." "Sed libera nos a malo." The Saint Bernard, his tail drooping, slinks home. "Oremus." There is silence in the house, and even the beggarwomen are still. Now the only murmuring comes from the fountain in the middle of the square.

The little girl died, she was frail and not at all pretty; she was afraid of the vast square, she was afraid of the big dog and afraid of the fountain, which seemed bottomless to her; she went through life guided by her father's hand, she lay ill in his arms and now, praise be to God's name, she has died after six pitiful years, so she can be an angel.

Through the burning square a black procession advances: the acolytes with crosses and lanterns, the wailing music, the little girls each with a wreath of rosemary and a broken candle on a cushion, the priests with lighted tapers, and now the small coffin itself, slight amidst all the splendor, with its stiff, broad ribbons, the wax-coated garlands and bands of black crape, the father, head bowed, his features nearly effaced by grief, the wan, diminutive mother behind her black veil, then the people, dark and somber, with bald pates under the glare of the sun, with white handkerchiefs, a slow-moving, whispering throng and, at the rear, like a muttering island, the beggarwomen with their unending prayer.

Along a scorched, rutted path the procession rises to the Calvary of human pain. Behind a bare wall lies the new cemetery, white and dry, the brittle soil of the dead, where nothing grows but white crosses, lilies made of tin, and the gaunt tower of the cemetery chapel. Everything naked and bleached as bone. A white, dead noon. A white, burning path.

The child's coffin moves up the hill, drawing the black crowd behind it; a small child's coffin, a small corpse with white clothing and a broken candle; this is where she used to walk hand in hand with her father –

– Poor soul, he'd loved her so! He married late in life and looked forward to his first child; and then, well, you know, a new choirmaster came to town and swept his wife off her feet. The whole town knows about it. That's why a blonde girl was born to dark-haired parents; she looked exactly like the town organist, his spitting image. Just like she was pointing out her real father.

The small, slight coffin seems to have turned into lead; the bearers come to a halt and place the bier on the ground. Yes, she used to walk to this very place with her father; this is where they used to sit and look down at the road, at the caravans of traveling players, the farm carts, the carriages; from here they used to look down at the street and guess who was walking there –

The whole town knew who his wife was running around with, only he was blind. He had his child, the fair-haired, pale-eyed girl whom he pampered while his wife was running around and indulging in jealous outbursts at every young lady her musician was teaching to bang away at a keyboard. Finally the man had to break with her, for fear of losing all his pupils on her account; later, he let anyone who asked read her letters, and everybody asked –

Once again the musicians wail out a doleful march, and amidst the pealing of bells the slow procession winds heavily uphill. The diminutive woman behind her veil, lips tightly pressed together, stumbles over the hem of her skirt; she regains her footing and holds herself erect to brave all those glances before she shuts herself up in the house again, sitting by the window with her endless embroidery, fading away out of loneliness and rancor.

Yes, he had abandoned her after that, and so she stayed with the child, who was aloof and disobedient, and with her husband, who had no purpose in life other than the lifeless little girl who was not his. He clung to her with all his melancholy affection, and when he would escort her out, absurdly decked out, pale and dazed, from the cool rooms of the house on the square, the town did not know whether to laugh at him or to pity him. After a short peal, the bells fall silent.

The small coffin is banging at the gate of eternity. It rests on planks above the open grave in the midst of the large, hushed throng; in the dead silence there is only the choir rustling its sheet music and the dean leafing slowly through his small, black-bound book. In the crowd a child bursts out crying. The bony shadow of the tower cuts across the burning fallow ground of the dead. This is the first year for burying people here, and perhaps this cemetery is too big, perhaps we will never fill it, perhaps we will never outgrow it, perhaps it will have to remain empty and bare for all eternity. The crowd breathes heavily in its uneasiness. What is happening? Why don't they begin? The drawing out of the silence is hard, agonizing, oppressive –

"Laudate Dominum de coelis, laudate eum in excelsis!" "Laudate eum omnes angeli eius," the choir responds, "laudate eum omnes virtutes eius." The crowd exhales. "Laudate eum sol et luna; laudate eum stellae et lumen." "Laudate eum coeli coelorum–" A faint breeze, as if stirred by the chorus of men's voices, wafts relief over the pale faces; a puff of incense rises, ribbons and wreaths rustle, and from the grave comes the chilly exhalation of earth. The father stares at the coffin, leaning over as if he were about to fall; people stand on tiptoe to see him better: now, now comes the moment of parting.

"Kyrie eleison." "Christe eleison." "Kyrie eleison." A young priest swings the censer, the slender chains rattle weakly, the smoke ascends and quivers – "Oremus." The vast, blazing heavens stretch stiffly over the white cemetery, a moment of agonizing eternity, just the heart beating with the tension of a terrible, sublime, and painfully awkward moment. "Per omnia saecula saeculorum." "Amen." Drops of holy water fall onto the small coffin; the father, moaning loudly, sinks to his knees; little by little the coffin slides into the grave, and the choir breaks sweetly, mournfully, softly into the hymn "God Has Beckoned."

The diminutive woman behind her veil listens, nailed to the spot. Too well she knows that voice: deep, resplendent, self-satisfied. When she heard it other times, other places, she melted under its palpable touch. The whole of the town listens with bowed heads; the choirmaster is singing with the leader of the female chorus, Marie, the town Venus, a tall, blossoming young woman. Of the entire choir, only those two voices can be heard. They say she's keeping company with him, that Marie. The two voices mingle lovingly, embrace under the hot sun. The deacon himself listens with eyes closed, the diminutive woman breaks into convulsive weeping, the blue puff of incense soars heaven-ward, and softly, ever more softly, the finale spreads over the cemetery. The deacon rouses himself as if from a dream and bends down to the ground. One, two, three clods of earth.

One, two, three; everyone presses forward to the open grave, where the father is kneeling on the mound of earth and sobbing as if he could never stop. All have flung their three clods into the grave and would like to leave. They are waiting only for the father to stand up, so they can shake his hand. The priests shift impatiently from one foot to the other, they still have to go to the chapel; the gravedigger blows his nose loudly and begins to shovel the dry, burning earth into the grave. The entire crowd waits, bewildered, in the silence.

Then a ripple of suggestive laughter passes through the choir. The choirmaster's eyes sparkle, he is pleased that his joke has succeeded. Pale Anežka has blushed, Matylda is biting her handkerchief, and Marie is doubled over from suppressing an outburst of hilarity. The choirmaster smoothes his moustache and hair with great satisfaction, leans over to Marie, and whispers something. Marie lets loose a shout of laughter and runs off. The entire crowd turns to watch, half amused, half scandalized.

Suddenly the father rises to his feet, trembles, and starts speaking. "You – all of you – who have paid your respects – my only – beloved little daughter –" But he cannot go on, he bursts out sobbing and, unable to shake anyone's hand, walks off as if in a dream. There is general confusion. While the priests walk to the chapel, the crowd disperses. A few hastily make the sign of the cross three times over the graves of their own departed, others pause for a moment before one tombstone or the other, and almost no one waits for the end of the service; only the choirmaster, with Marie and the other members of the women's choir, laughing openly, pass into the chancel of the cemetery chapel.

A few women in black are saying prayers at the graves, wiping their eyes and straightening the poor withered flowers.

Out from the chapel floats the voice of the deacon: "Benedicite omnia opera Domini Domino."

"Benedicite angeli Domini Domino," the choirmaster intones.

"Benedicite coeli Domino."

With great shovelfuls of earth, the gravedigger buries the child of two fathers.

Three

THE SUN, which since early morning had been beating down on the yellow walls across the courtyard, slowly, in stubborn silence, transferred to the other side. The walls opposite were already in shadow, and this seemed to make it somewhat cooler inside. Now a narrow streak of sunlight gained a foothold on the window sill, soon it would spread, and when it fell into the room her husband would waken, yawn noisily, and come to her, just as he did every Sunday. Marie's shoulders trembled in disgust, and she let her sewing fall onto her lap.

She stared vacantly out the window. The chestnut tree in the yard had blossomed not long before, but now, with only the calyxes remaining, it looked as if something had eaten away at the blossoms. Why was it that even the tree filled her with disgust, when it was hardly to blame? An uneasy, growing, grievous weight had lodged in Marie's breast. If she were to talk about herself, she would say that perhaps it consisted of memories, but she never did talk about herself, neither to her husband nor to the other one. But of course it wasn't a matter of memories at all. It was as if everything in the past had rolled up into a cumbersome ball of thread; she had only to take hold of the end and one incident after another would unwind, those she would be delighted to resurrect for herself as well as those she would prefer to forget for all time. Marie was not thinking about anything, she refused to think about anything, but she was conscious of all that she might be remembering. It was all there, so near that she was afraid to think lest she be touched by memories.

The narrow streak of sunlight had leaped across the window sill.

Above all, there was this impotent awareness that everyone knew about it, that everyone knew even the particulars of her marital infidelity. At first she'd been defiant when so many people had made it clear to her that they knew. Some of them did it crudely, others with prurient familiarity, others reproachfully, and others, still others – there was hardly anyone who didn't feel she had the right to say something appalling to her. One neighbor, whenever they met, muttered audibly about whores, another shook her head and declared that a young man ought to practice whatever chastity he's supposed to possess; another, all hints and insinuations, expressed earnest concern about her husband; another spat, another refused to acknowledge her greetings, another overflowed with shrill sympathy and then proceeded to borrow all kinds of things from her. – Oh God, must she bear all this?

Yes, at first Marie had forced herself to be defiant, but it is not easy to be defiant when you have a bad conscience. Later, she shed furious, resentful, unconsoling tears. She could not even lament her misfortunes to her lover, for she never spoke to him, she was a tongue-tied captive to the silent, oppressive, subjugating love of a passionate but cloddish man. Ultimately, she pretended that she couldn't understand the insinuations, as if they had nothing to do with her; one grows accustomed to everything, though this "everything" does not thereby become purged, changed, or remade...

The narrow streak of sunlight slid across the cords of the window blind.

And then there was her husband. At first he had not perhaps believed what people were saying about his wife, but in time, harrowed with despair and incapable of saying anything to her, he had begun to drink. He drank appallingly, that ever so orderly man, and it was lamentable how he deteriorated. Finally, when his livelihood at the office was threatened, he made an abrupt turnaround, stopped drinking and took up his old way of life again, becoming even more frugal and stay-at-home than before. For a long time he didn't speak to Marie, although eventually it became necessary to talk about expenses, the laundry, meals. ... After his "reformation," he became somewhat fastidious and penny-pinching about his food, he required much attention and managed to content himself with that. Once he came home and found Baudys, Marie's lover, there. He slammed the door and, taking no notice of either one, withdrew into the next room; but no sooner had the visitor gone than he allowed himself to be called for supper. At first he said nothing, but after the meal he began to talk with the painfully awkward hesitance of a man who knows he should remain silent. So Marie chose to go to Baudys' apartment, and several times her husband raised a fuss because she'd been out too long. Yes, he'd had to wait for his dinner. People spoke of him as a good-natured soul. Marie was disgusted by him, partly because she was deceiving him, partly because he no longer took care of himself at all.

The sunbeam glided along the wall. Marie tracked its progress as if it were the fateful hand of a clock. She could still hear her husband's regular snoring, but any minute now the sofa in the next room would creak, her husband would yawn, heave himself up laboriously and, scratching the back of his neck, his vest unbuttoned and nothing but socks on his feet, come to her as he did every Sunday. What he would then do is wander through the room, finger the furniture, inspect damaged spots which had been there for years, mutter about expenses, and cautiously, circuitously, begin his odd weekly conversation ... Marie shuddered. He launched into the topic he'd begun with for quite a while now. A thousand times he had talked about how a wife costs her husband an arm and a leg, how marriage doesn't come cheap. They say the ones who have it best of all are bachelors who take up with married women. Some other man feeds her, some other man clothes her, so it comes cheap to them. A bunch of violets at most, he said, looking straight at Marie. They have it cheap, he repeated at length, as if he'd stumbled on something new. For an entire month he had carried on in this vein, and Marie took it that he was jealous.

One day she was stitching some trimming onto a dress. Fresh from sleep he came to her and asked how much the lace had cost, and how much other things cost as well ... For the most part, however, he seldom opposed her in such matters; perhaps he understood her need to be pretty. All the same, he talked about it and complained about the expense. These days, he began, *one* man isn't enough to keep his wife in clothes; no, as things are today, *one* man by himself can't earn enough. Some men, of course, have it cheap, they get a wife for free, since she isn't theirs ... Marie began to understand what he was getting at, and she felt her heart suddenly freeze, but she said nothing, as if it had nothing to do with her. Her husband looked straight at her, took a hard look, and suddenly asked: "And Baudys?" It was the first time he had uttered the man's name.

"What about Baudys?" Marie was frightened now.

"Nothing," he said evasively, and then after a pause: "I wonder how much he earns."

That's how it began, Marie remembered. And from that time on, it was the same every Sunday. He would come in and scratch his back. "Have you talked to Baudys this week? How often? How much does he make?" Then he would start in about himself. There was no money and he needed a new hat – his old one was truly a disgrace – but what was the use "when household expenses eat everything up?" He would go on talking. A lump of disgust would rise in Marie's throat, and she'd wish she could disgorge it. Her husband would shake his head and end by saying, in an oddly sad voice, "You, of course, don't have a thing to worry about."

Marie stared at the advancing ray of sun and dug her fingernails into her palms. If only she could be spared that memory! It had happened at her lover's apartment one day – after just such a Sunday as this. Baudys had placed her on the sofa, but she had resisted him and begun to cry; she considered it necessary to cry, and for quite a while she let him beg for the explanation: that her husband was stingy, that he didn't want to give her money for clothes or anything else ... Her lover listened, frowning and somewhat cool; he was so ... cloddish, perhaps, that he mentally calculated how much it would cost. Finally he had said, reluctantly, "Let me worry about that, Marie." Marie felt that now she could cry without pretense, but first she had to let herself be kissed, no, more than that, more than before!

The next time, he was waiting for her with a gift: material for a dress, and she didn't like it; she returned home racked with shame. Prior to that day, her relationship with her lover had been like that of a wife with her husband; her caresses had been sincere and affectionate. Now, however, she had to close her eyes to what she was doing, so as not to shudder. While she was cutting some material, her husband came in. "Is that from Baudys?" he asked, and the thought excited him.

Marie sighed and began to sew, taking long stitches. She was working on a silk blouse, now, with other fabric her lover had bought for her. It was odd how much it pleased him to shower her with costly, extravagant, and attractive presents. Sometimes it delighted her to think about how fond he was of her. Sometimes, however, she felt otherwise, appallingly ill at ease. Her passive, temperate love was a thing of the past; his gifts exhaled the breath of something feverish and profligate, and Marie forced herself to assume an unnatural, lighthearted vivaciousness that was entirely alien to her firm, placid being. It was a sudden change of course which her lover embraced like a thirsty drunkard, but Marie found its persistence abhorrent.

It seemed unspeakably sinful to her because it was against her nature; she could not oppose him, however, and endured it all, striving desperately, but in vain, not to think about it. The week before, when he himself was intoxicated, he had urged her to drink some wine. She refused, but when she felt his drunken, burning, impassioned breath, she could have screamed in horror.

The streak of sunlight gently shifted onto the photograph of her mother. She had the round, serene, cheerful face of a country woman who had borne children and given back in abundance all that life had given her. Marie's hands dropped to her lap, her husband's breathing grew quiet, the heat was sweltering and the silence utterly oppressive. Then she heard her husband, in the next room, grunt, the sofa creak, the floor rattle under unsteady footsteps. Marie began to sew rapidly. Her husband opened the door, yawned loudly and, all unbuttoned, torpid from his sleep, sweaty, scratching at his neck, approached her. Marie did not raise her eyes, she went on sewing even more rapidly.

Her husband wandered through the room in his stocking feet, and then he stood unsteadily over her, yawned, and asked:

"What's that you're sewing?"

Marie did not reply, she merely spread out her work so that he could see it.

"You got this from Baudys?" her husband asked indifferently.

She stuck the needle in her mouth and again did not reply. Her husband sighed and fingered the silk, as if he knew something about it. "You got this from Baudys," he answered his own question.

"Ages ago," Marie said out of the corner of her mouth.

Her husband yawned and once again started wandering through the room.

"You might at least put your shoes on," Marie remarked.

Her husband said nothing and continued to walk around. "Rags," he said, "always more rags! Why do you ... it's such nonsense. Money doesn't mean a thing to you. No, Marie, money doesn't mean a thing to you!"

"You're not paying for it," Marie said, her voice hard. She knew this was the beginning of the same conversation they'd had so many Sundays.

"I'm not paying for it," her husband repeated. "Of course I'm not paying for it. Where would I get the money? I ... have other things I have to pay for. For one thing, I have to pay the insurance ... We don't have any money for useless things. You don't keep track of what's spent. A hundred and fifty for rent. Plus insurance. It's all the same to you. Did you talk with Baudys?"

"I did."

"To be sure." Her husband yawned and contemplated Marie's work. "No, Marie, money doesn't mean a thing to you. How much does it cost, material like that, do you know?"

"No."

"How many times did you talk with him this week?"

"Twice,"

"Twice," he repeated absentmindedly. "What a waste of money. You've got plenty of rags like this already! Now listen, Marie."

The young woman bowed her head: now it was coming.

"It's been two years since we set aside any savings. That's how it is, Marie. And if one of us got sick or something... But all you care about is fancy clothes, right?"

Marie remained stubbornly silent.

"We ought to set something aside ... and then there's coal for winter. I'd be glad if, for old age ... if you could have ... At least you could provide for your own old age!"

There was an agonizing silence; Marie drew her needle through the fabric, hardly aware of what she was doing. Her husband gazed out the window, past her pale hair, and tried to say something, and his chin, woefully unshaven and preserving a few crumbs from supper, suddenly began to tremble ...

"Stop it!" Marie cried out.

His chin fell, he gulped and said: "Look, I need clothes myself, but I know we don't have the money for them. That's how it is, Marie."

He sat down, hunched over, and gazed at the floor.

Marie dug her needle into the silk. Yes, a week ago today he'd said the very same thing. She could have wept over his shabby clothes. She went over them every day, was familiar with each frayed thread; she was ashamed when he wore them to the office.

Yesterday she had been with her lover; she had gone to see him with a plan in mind, but it had not turned out as she had hoped. She sat in his lap (thinking this necessary, given the circumstances) and worked herself up to a wanton gaiety; he was immediately on his guard and asked what it was she wanted. She laughed and asked him not to buy her any more presents, she would rather buy them herself, buy what she wished, if only she had the money. He looked at her and then let go of her. "Get up," he said, and then he rose; he wandered through the room, counted out two hundred crowns, and placed them beside her purse. She had purposely left it on the table, she had thought it all out in advance. Why did he not understand, why did he leave it to her to gather up the banknotes as she said goodbye, and hastily, awkwardly, cram them into her purse? Why did he not at least turn aside while she did it, why did he stare at her, why did he pay such close attention? Marie contemplated the tip of her needle with dry, unseeing eyes, and without realizing it she began to tug at the silk, tearing a jagged hole in it.

"That's how it is, Marie," her husband said, his voice grave. "We don't have enough money."

"My purse," said Marie, irritated.

"What?"

"Get ... my ... purse!"

He opened the purse and in it he found the crumpled handful of banknotes, just as she had stuffed them in the day before. "These are yours?" he gasped.

"Ours," said Marie.

Her husband stared with astonishment at his wife's bowed neck; he didn't know what to say. "Should I set this aside?" he asked softly.

"Do as you wish."

He shifted from one stockinged foot to the other, trying to find a word of outrage or tenderness; finally, without a word, he took the money into the next room. He was there for a long time; when he returned, he found Marie, her head still bent, tearing at the silk with her needle.

"Marie," he said softly, "wouldn't you like to come for a walk with me?"

Marie shook her head.

Her husband lingered, completely perplexed. It seemed impossible to have their conversation *now*... "Look, Marie," he said, relieved to have finally broken the silence, "maybe I'll go to a café today! It's been years now since I..."

"Go," Marie whispered.

He dressed, not knowing what to say. Her round, comely face bent over the multicolored silk, Marie was silent.

He dressed hurriedly, as if about to take flight, yet at the door he hesitated and said, uncertainly, "You know, Marie, if you'd like to go out ... well ... you may. I could eat dinner out."

Marie lay her head on the lacerated silk. She was not, that day, granted the gift of tears.

Helena

H E MET HER AT A SPA TOWN, that tall, curious girl with
her long legs and bony frame. She had beautiful gray
eyes, and the flesh of her cheeks beneath them clung
tightly to her skull. She was manly in her smart grooming,
forthright yet uncertain in her movements, half tomboy, half
virginal nymph, full of timidity and a most complicated shame;
she was, in short, the type of character that fascinated him,
especially in the setting – summer forest, sunny languor, and
mental repose – in which he was indulging himself. She was
studying something, philosophy perhaps; she had a touch of
pedantry and her own "ideas," according to which she thought
and observed, and she was uncommonly well-educated. She
wore clothes with large pockets for tucking away her books. In
combination with a certain boyish naïveté, her store of learning
embellished her chaste, cloistered maturity, the maturity of a
remarkably strong and introspective woman. In speaking of the
learned Pallas, do not forget her virginity.

They became friends easily, amused, perhaps, by each
other's peculiarities. He felt that this wise girl was making an
effort to read him as if he were a new, rather surprising book,
and this delighted him. There are women, may the good lord
help them, who have a mania for regarding people as if they
were psychological novels: they expect people to be either types
or characters, endeavor to read their souls, make profound
judgments about them with singular self-assurance, and consequently arrive at conclusions that are either plain and simple
injustices or enormously complicated mistakes. Helena was, in
her mistakes, forthrightly but mysteriously complicated; this
man with whom she went on strolls in the surrounding forest,
who loved to talk, contemptuous of many things and amused by

all the rest, smart, shrewd, skeptical about everything, was for her something on the order of Hamsun's Falk. Back in her room she analyzed him, broke him up into ingenious but not very elucidating bits and pieces of information; he, meanwhile, was either bored or asleep, finding nothing in himself to be of any more interest than a pinch of snuff.

On their walks together, though, Helena had no time to think about him; she was too busy listening, her pretty eyes looking ahead, amused by his restless animation. At times she herself spoke up, softly and hesitantly. She didn't know that, to him, her voice rang with melodious clarity among the myriad accompanying sounds of nature; she didn't know that, to him, with her serious voice and boyish face, with her severely cut and coarsely textured clothes, to him she was a clear, roughly graceful, high-spirited note filled with purity and harmony, Pallas Athena's note amidst the woods, the sunlight, and the elements. She was not aware of all this, but she had a new, unprecedented feeling that she was pretty; never had this feeling repeated itself before her mirror at home, but here, on these forest paths, she sensed it with blushing pleasure. The pleasure was the greater when he, the sceptic, told her that between man and woman there was a finer sentiment than love, that there are sources of harmony which are infinitely more capacious and more natural. For these words Helena wanted to give him her hand in gratitude, but she felt self-conscious about her hands, she fancied them too big and was forever hiding them in gloves. She walked by his side, scarcely saying a word; she was surprised to discover that it so suited her to be wholly female, and that she harbored within her not the slightest rebellion against this natural male dominance. It was a fine and memorable day. Relieved of the burden of artificially maintained pride, Helena experienced a sense of camaraderie that brimmed with admiration for this man who had given her back the pleasure of being a girl.

Before long, Helena was put to a fairly demanding test. There came to the spa town a young woman, a plump, blonde, dissolute beauty. On the very first evening, she singled out Helena's friend and gave him to understand that his attentions would not be in vain. This did not escape Helena; God forbid that she should ever be jealous, but it was a shock, and she found her face disgusting and her body foolishly clumsy. When he talked with her, she responded to him in a disagreeable manner, as if she were angry. She hated herself for feeling such intense pain and tried valiantly to control it. That night she cried, but then it struck her that, if truth be told, the man was a show-off, a vacuous pleasure-seeker, and a commonplace egotist; with these consoling thoughts, she happily fell asleep.

The next morning she went out early, so as not to encounter him, and climbed the high wooded hillside to the summit where they had once "discovered" a seat formed by boulders which provided a more or less beautiful view of the spa town. She sat there filled with the spirit of sacred solitude; fully experiencing the peace of renunciation and exaltation, she pardoned the entire world. But there, look, wasn't that yesterday's show-off climbing up the sunny hillside amidst the flowering mullein and the blackberries? She wanted to flee, but only offended Pallas ran away; Helena stayed and had to put up with the fact that her eyes had filled with tears. She turned so that he couldn't see, so that he couldn't look into her eyes, but mostly, mostly because she was not at all pretty today. He sat down and talked – not a word about anything having happened, about looking for her, about having anything to explain; he spoke seriously and gave her nothing to feel cheerful about. And so blazing midday found them together on the stone seat, in friendly conversation, which meant simply that everything was deeply, infinitely back to normal. Down below, across the spa town square, floated a white speck with a red parasol; perhaps it was the blonde beauty. Yes, it was midday, and the man knew very well that they should have started back down the path a long, long time ago; must he sit there with her till evening? Helena continued to sit with her large hands pressed between her knees, smiling not with her lips, nor even with her eyes, but only with her soul. "How late is it?" she finally asked. "Two o'clock," replied the man, brutally practicing self-control so as not to sound discontented. But what was time to Helena? There really is "a higher feeling than love," and Helena felt herself infinitely above all love, above all passion; never, never would she know weakness. At last she rose, and on the way back she picked a few flowers and placed them in her belt, fully intending to preserve them as relics. The man sighed: it's not easy to perform an act of charity. They arrived down below at four o'clock, which in the life of the spa town was a noteworthy scandal.

There followed undisturbed days of wandering together in unclouded joy. God scattered discoveries and adventures along their path: they found nesting birds and they startled a hare; one burning afternoon, beside a country ninepins alley, they sat in solemn silence amidst hens and chicks; another day they were overtaken in a field by a heavy shower that drove them, happy twosome, to seek shelter inside a deserted farm hut, and then a rainbow erected before them a magic triumphal arch; one morning they came upon a clearing where a family of deer were grazing, and they found a place in the undergrowth, a place unknown to anyone else, where a mushroom of record size was growing. They buried a dead goldfinch, found gentians and sweet cyclamens, encountered an old woman who sold them milk and who delighted Helena by calling her "young madam." They were mutually grateful for the countless adventures and incidents they experienced together. Helena accepted all his boyish fascinations as her own, revitalized by a double joy, a joy in new things and a joy in sharing. They were in perfect agreement about everything that pleased him. She said "our cyclamens," though it was he who found them; everything was his doing, everything passed through his eyes first and flowed from his abundance; poor Helena, where was your contribution to this mutual world? Helena didn't know, she just smiled with downcast eyes; her doing was this concord and her value was great, her heart was pure and humble; although knowing that he discovered everything, she made of it a mutual joy and a fullness of harmony. "Goodbye for today, Helena, tomorrow we'll go somewhere else; thank you for such a beautiful day."

He left the spa town, and Helena started writing him. At first he was alarmed by her rough, disorderly, overly large hand; he perceived in her a violence that had not hitherto been apparent. Her rhetoric seemed artificial, her cheerfulness forced, and he couldn't see why he should have to read about the gentians, now withered, or about finding the bones of a dog in "our quarry." He didn't know how to respond. It's strange how little of the most beautiful concord survives when people are no longer together.

Helena came back to Prague in the autumn and lost much, so much, on the city soil. He liked to walk with her on the outskirts of Prague, where small, pick-and-shovel struggles were taking place between country and city. These were unforgettable moments, full of gloom and desolation, when it feels as if you're standing on a now-silent battlefield where the country is wounded and the city almost done for, expiring on piles of debris. Then, too, there were places of great simplicity, such as White Mountain; the woods, the gently sloping, unpeopled hillsides, and most of all the Vltava River, beautiful and mysterious beyond all the rivers in the world. There were the morning hours, most precious of all, unknown to city-dwellers. Set out early on the morning in a small steamer, against the current, and you will hear voices so intimate, you've never envisioned human habitations so near at hand.

One morning they were walking together along the Braník towpath. It was a silvery autumn day. The Vltava appeared to be a stream of light filled with a soft, metallic murmuring. This unusual softness rubbed off on everything, and there was so much pacified sorrow that involuntarily he began talking about himself. He talked about what he had wished to be and what he had not become, what he had wanted to do and what had eluded him; he opened up his heart and, abandoning all reserve, poured out all his discontent in one unbroken stream. He felt that by his confession he was ridding himself of all his pettiness and weakness. It seemed as if he were looking at the stony towpath from afar, or perhaps from the opposite bank: two small pedestrians utterly insignificant in the presence of the river, the valley, and the sky, as if illustrating the loneliness and desolation of it all. There was infinitely more solitude than in the depths of the summer woods.

"Helena," he said, "this isn't life. It's growing old, tedium, killing time or what have you, but it isn't life. I'm good for nothing, I can't do a thing, and if I do start in at something, I'm already thinking: what's the use? I don't get anything out of it myself. Myself! I myself! My whole life long I've thought only of myself, and look, never have I actually done anything for myself. This isn't life. Help yourself! But how can an egoist help himself? Helena, I've experienced many different things, but the saddest thing of all is to feel your own weakness. I'm tired of so many things. You're listening to me, and all I say is worthless. Your patience amazes me. Look at the huge fish that man has caught."

He pointed with his finger. Helena raised her downcast eyes, but not to follow his finger; rather, she looked at him with shining eyes. He was confused by how wholeheartedly she looked at him, and he didn't know how to go on; he qualified

what he had said before, broke free of the topic, and started to joke. Helena was so dumbfounded, she neither spoke nor listened. By the end of the walk, they were both out of sorts. Going back on the steamer they didn't talk; this made him feel bored and he was glad to say goodbye. The remainder of the day was of no importance to him, but the next morning brought a letter from Helena. His heart filled with uneasiness, he opened the envelope.

"While it is still today," began the letter, in agitated hand, "I must thank you, my dear, my dearest..."

He put down the letter as if struck by a blow; this sudden use of the familiar form of address and this "dearest" – was the girl out of her mind? He paced the room, the better to digest it; he felt ashamed and humbled and wished he could sink straight through the floor. What more is there?

> While it is still today, I must thank you, my dear, my dearest for the most beautiful day of my life. You have given me everything, you have given me love. Yesterday I lived in a bad dream that was not life. Today I stand at the window with arms outspread, is it you is it you for whom I spread them wide, dearest is it you? I know I'm mad and maybe in a short short time I will regret what I have written you. I am hurrying as fast as I can to say everything before that time of regret comes, because I would rather regret it than not say it. I kiss you, I kiss you, my dear, don't ask me why because I don't know what is happening to me! No it was not life but a terrible dream darling Thank you thank you   I am yours and I don't want anything that isn't yours   Jesus keep me from saying everything! I wish I could embrace your feet, humble myself with my whole body because I am so much yours I can't be any other way. Bear me up my darling I have no control, I will put my head on your shoulder and you will kiss me don't you know cruel one that nobody ever kissed me before? Ah if only I were with you!

> Helena

> Dear dearest, I am afraid of evening give me your hand
> think of me, it is my first night!

Astonished, painfully embarrassed, he read it through again, relentlessly noting each error of punctuation, every instance of desperate incoherence in the wild, confused letter. And all the time he felt ashamed. What did I do, how did I bring this about? God in heaven, did I make some confession of love to her? What happened to her? A fit of hysteria? Perhaps this was mailed to some other address, it occurred to him, and he quickly scanned the crazy letter again. Alas, no doubt about it: the "darling" is me. But when did I speak to her about love, when did I lie to her about anything? She was dear to me, certainly, but only because, yes, precisely because there was no question whatsoever of love … My God, what happened?

He read her letter once more, sensing in it her sobbing, feverish breathing; how savage, how frantic must have been the struggle of that manly maiden before she lost her head. Maliciously dubious, he paused: but is that altogether how it was? Perhaps she was only waiting for my first sign of weakness, so that she could assault me with her hysterical embrace. All right, I did complain, I was suffering: an opportune moment indeed for her to unload her burdensome virginity on my bed. Oh, Helena, forgive me, you didn't do that. He was trembling now. You wanted to help me in my disappointment, you wanted to sacrifice yourself, do something grand. You foolish girl, how on earth could you have imagined such a thing?

Once again he carefully went over her letter, but it sickened him as much as before. The handwriting was deranged, written in a dark room, the hand wet with perspiration, the letter evidence of a crisis. There was no hint of calculation here, but neither was there the least hint of either magnanimous or foolish sacrifice. She wanted kisses, more than kisses. She's twenty-five years old. The body's rebellion is powerful, formidable. He recalled her Pallas-like harmony, the sexless purity of her unblossoming womanhood. Something, some taint had descended on her. Poor Helena, if only you were beautiful, at least then no one would be surprised at your passion and no one would disparage you. But you are not beautiful, and there is nothing left but to be unjust to you. Go, Helena! If anything is certain in this world, it is that I am not in love with you.

Again he thought of her, thought kindly of her and saw in his mind her lovely eyes. No, Helena, wise Helena, I don't believe it was the monthly female disturbance, nor a carnal insurrection, but rather some peculiar mistake. Your heart is deranged, but tomorrow it will be serene again, at peace again; but sadly, you will remember what you've done and it will be horribly shameful and humiliating for you. You will despise yourself, harrow yourself with burning reproaches, and never, never will you want to set eyes on me again. Oh, Helena, how can I say this? Don't give it another thought. I knew at once that's not the way things are and I've burnt your letter and scattered the ashes, and I no longer know what was written there. I only recall that it was something about your loving me in the most noble fashion.

He rushed to the table and wrote:

Helena,

Thank you for the words of love. I feel unworthy of them. You give me more than my poor heart can ever repay. I am a tired, worn-out man, my dear, and the world has not made me as good as you deserve.

And now, dear Helena, we can be wise once more. You have spoken words that had to be said, you are brave and admirable. It was indeed necessary that we sincerely...

He put down the pen. It's quite clear that I am not in love with her; how is it possible that I can't simply say it? He was scribbling on the writing pad the word "never" when the bell rang. He heard the servant open the outer door; someone spoke softly and knocked on his door. He called "Come in," but no one entered. He went to open the door himself, and there was Helena leaning against the doorframe, pressing both large hands to her breast.

"Come in, please," he said through clenched teeth, and he shut the door behind her, wringing his hands. "How could you, Helena, how could you?"

Helena looked aside, her lips trembling in anguish. "I came to tell you..." she began.

"I know what you want to say," he interrupted her. "Sit down, Helena."

Her eyes downcast, she sat on the edge of the sofa and crushed her purse between her fingers. "I came to ask – – to ask you to return my letter."

"I had just begun a letter in response," he said softly. "What a scare you gave me!"

She raised her eyes and looked at him with despair.

"So, Helena," he said, "how did you sleep?"

She stood up, threw her purse on the sofa, took off her hat, and started to remove her coat. It was horrible that he hadn't asked her to do this when she entered the room. The coat was caught on a button, and with her trembling fingers she could not unfasten it, but he still didn't move to help her. She yanked violently and blindly, until something ripped. She let the coat fall to the floor, and when he leaned down to pick it up, she clutched his head in both her hands.

He rose violently, his eyes dark with hatred, and though she held him tenaciously, his rising caused her to stagger and she would have fallen had he not caught her with both his arms. Her hands loosed their grip, and he felt her quivering fingers on his face, a loving, ardent trembling as she fell with all her weight into his embrace. Her head thrown back, her eyes closed, her dry lips upturned as if for a final, fatal kiss, her teeth exposed and chattering, the point of her tongue trembling between them, her face pale gray yet impassioned: thus did she lift her face to him in the wonderment of fervent expectation. She was unequivocally plain; when her eyes were closed, everything in her face was extinguished. Hissing with repugnance, he kissed her lightly on the cheek; tenderly, as tenderly as could be, he removed her hands from his face and said slowly and severely, "Sit down, Helena."

She sat down as if intoxicated, and covered her face with her hands.

Walking across the room, with pauses between his words, he said, "Helena, I don't want this meeting to upset you. I beg of you, be reasonable. I don't recognize you, and God knows I don't know what has happened, but I'm afraid that tomorrow you will think of me reproachfully."

Helena sat as if turned to stone.

"Forgive me," he went on, resentment in his voice, "for thinking today about tomorrow. It would be better if there weren't one. Tell me, can you be certain that tomorrow won't revenge itself on you?"

Helena, her face covered, shook her head.

"You came to place yourself in my hands. Here I am, do as you will with me! But is it possible? Am I to hold you for a while, grasp you firmly, set you down somewhere else, what? How can I know in what way I would hurt you most? Oh, Helena, spare me this; please don't ask me to decide what to do with you. My will is gone, but I am fond of you. Get hold of yourself, Helena!"

She sat there motionless, rigid, mute; he was incredibly sorry for her and anxiously sought to find the tenderest words with which to explain matters to her. So as to be nearer to her, he sat on the back of the sofa and looked down on her coarse hair.

"Get hold of yourself," he repeated gently. "You're pure and proud; don't throw everything away. I hardly know you at all; I have a feeling that today was sent to us by fate, so that I can think infinitely more highly of you than before. Helena, I delighted in your company as an innocent girl; now I will respect you as a woman who has surmounted herself. You will be self-assured, an accomplished woman."

Then Helena did something unexpected yet very simple. She uncovered her face and placed her chin on his knee, a movement that was at one and the same time childlike and amorous. She held that position and closed her eyes, as if she were saying: now say whatever you wish.

He was confused by the sudden realization that all he was saying was false, and when he spoke again, it was with sadness. "Helena, is it a great fault on my part that I'm no longer young enough to – believe in love? Is it a great fault on my part that when I hear the word 'love,' I think immediately of pain and disappointment, crude sensuality, the most vulgar sorts of relationships, lies and break-ups? Is this a great fault?"

Helena, her eyes still closed, shook her head. He could feel the violent beating of the artery in her throat; pale and as if asleep, she breathed rapidly through parted lips. Now, her fawning expression seemed to say, at this moment all is one to me, let me stay thus. She became almost beautiful, looking up at him like that, her face set like an ivory mask. He bent over her and said in a whisper:

"Helena, it's not love that you should desire; love is hard and always humbling; it's not for you. If I ever saw you go down that road with someone else, whoever he might be, I would call to you with dread: 'Helena, Helena, don't go that way, it's not for you, you cannot travel where others go, what others endure would crush you.' I don't know whether it's because you're wiser or more unhappy. I don't know what happened to you, but I'm afraid for you. What more can I say to you?"

Helena's cheeks turned pink, suddenly she looked oddly attractive, her features softened, her eyes looking out mysteriously, in no particular direction, through narrowed lids. He stroked her hair and said softly, "Helena, you must never come see me again."

Not the slightest tremor showed on her face; she could have endured any blow, it seemed, sitting in that position. He sighed and touched her face.

"Goodbye, Helena."

Obediently she stood and allowed him to put on her coat. He helped fasten her hatpin in her hair; she smiled at him.

As she was leaving, she turned suddenly, almost violently, and shook his hand with all her strength. "You are ... so ... noble," she said, blushing, with eyes downcast, as though thanking him for having done nothing to her. In spite of everything, he had to bite his lips.

From that day on, they no longer walked together; of course, it was hardly possible. Years later he heard about Helena. He learned that she spoke of him with unconcealed animosity, as one who had hurt her badly.

He was sorry for that – even years later.

At the Castle

D, MARY, D," Olga repeated with mechanistic patience. Little Mary reluctantly hammered out a very easy piano étude they'd already been at for fourteen days, but the more time they spent on it, the worse the result. That detested childish melody haunted Olga even in her dreams.

"D, Mary, look: C D G D," Olga hummed the notes and played them on the piano. "Try to pay better attention: C D G D – D, Mary, D! Why do you persist in playing E?"

Mary didn't know why she was playing badly, she only knew that she was being forced to play. Her eyes flashed with hatred, she kicked her legs against the piano bench, and at the earliest possible moment she would run off to her papa; meanwhile, she willfully played E and then E again. Olga abandoned her efforts and gazed out the window with the eyes of a martyr. The sun shone, the great trees on the park-like grounds bowed before the hot wind, but there was no freedom, no lack of constraint out on those grounds, not even in the rye fields beyond – ah, when would the hour end? E again, once again E!

"D, Mary, D" Olga repeated, filled with despair, and suddenly she burst out: "You'll never know how to play!"

The young girl rose to her feet, scorched Olga with a glare of ancestral pride, and replied: "Miss Olga, why don't you say that in front of Papa?"

Olga bit her lip. "Play!" she shouted with undue sharpness. She caught sight of the child's hateful glance and emphatically, impatiently, she began to count: "One, two, three, four. One, two, three, four. One, two, three, four. C D G D. Wrong. One, two, three, four..."

The door to the drawing room swayed. No doubt the old count was standing behind it, eavesdropping once again. Olga lowered her voice. "One, two, three, four. C D G D. Much better, Mary!" Much better it certainly was not, but the old count was listening. "One, two, three, four. Much better now. That wasn't so difficult, was it? One, two..."

The door flew open and the lame count entered, his cane clattering. "Mary, Mary, wie gehts? How beautifully you play! Eh, Miss?"

"Oh, yes, my lord," Olga fervently agreed as she rose from the piano bench.

"Mary, du hast Talent," the lame old man cried out, and suddenly – it was terrible to see – he fell to his knees with a loud thump, and with what sounded like a sobbing wail he nuzzled his child's neck, planting wild, noisy kisses. "Du hast Talent," he murmured, "du bist so gescheit, Mary, so brilliant! Tell me, what sort of present should Papa give you?"

"Danke, nichts," replied Mary, her small, ticklish shoulders wriggling beneath his kisses. "I'd just like..."

"What, what would you like?" asked the count enthusiastically.

"I'd just like to have not so many lessons."

"Ha, ha, natürlich," the count laughed, enchanted, "wie gescheit bist du! Eh, miss?"

"Yes," Olga said in a whisper.

"Wie gescheit," repeated the old man, and he started to stand up. Olga sprang to help him. "Let me be," the count fiercely shouted, and on hands and knees like an animal he tried to rise to his feet. Olga turned away. Then five convulsive fingers gripped her arm, and thus supporting his entire weight, the old count stood up. By some miracle, Olga did not collapse under the weight of this huge, frightful, apoplectically palsied body; it was an act above and beyond courage. Little Mary laughed.

The count straightened himself, affixed his pince-nez, and gazed at Olga with some surprise, as if he'd never seen her before.

"Miss Olga," he said, now addressing her in English.
"Please?"

"Miss Olga," he continued in English, "you speak too much during the lessons; you confound the child with your eternal admonishings. You will make me the pleasure to be a little kinder."

"Yes, sir," Olga whispered, blushing to her hairline. Mary understood that her papa was scolding Olga, and haughtily pretended that it did not concern her.

"My respects to you, miss," the count said in his odd, old-fashioned Czech.

Olga curtsied and left. But on her way out, she was struck by a need for revenge, and she returned, her eyes flashing, to say, "Mary, you might acknowledge it when I take my leave."

"Ja, mein Kind, das kannst du," the old count benignly agreed. Mary smirked and tossed off a quick little curtsey.

Scarcely had Olga gone beyond the door when she pressed her hand to her forehead. Oh, heavens, I can't bear this, I can't! Oh, heavens, for five months not a day, not even an hour has passed when they haven't tormented me ... But in fact they don't torment me, she said to herself as she proceeded along the chilly hall with her fingers pressed to her temples. I'm a stranger here, a servant, and no one gives me a thought. This is simply the way they are, God knows, and no one is ever so alone as when among strangers. But Mary is wicked, something within her fiercely shouted, and she hates me, she wants to bedevil me and she knows how to do it. Osvald is a rascal, but Mary is wicked. The countess is a proud woman and she insults me, but Mary is wicked. The child I so wanted to love! The child with whom I spend the entire day, the entire day! My God, how many more years will I be here?

Two chambermaids came giggling along the corridor. As soon as they noticed Olga, they fell silent and greeted her with sidelong glances. From pure envy of their laughter, Olga nearly snapped at them; she would have liked to order them about in a lofty way, but she didn't know how. If at least she could be in the servants' hall with those girls, it occurred to her, squealing well into the night, gossiping and chasing each other, and Franz the footman with them, every moment one or another of them screaming with laughter – oh, heavens, it was disgusting! A frightful memory forced its way into her head: yesterday she had surprised Franz with the scullery maid in an empty guest room next to Olga's bedroom. Olga could have struck him in the face with a small, raging fist for the idiotic way he grinned while buttoning himself up. She buried her fingers in her face. No, no, I can't bear this! C D G D, C D G D ... But at least the servant girls enjoy themselves. At least they're not so lonely, they don't take their meals with the gentlefolk, they jabber all day long, and in the evening they sing softly in the courtyard ... If at least they would let me join them in the evening! Sweetly, melodiously she could hear the duet they'd been singing last night under the old linden:

> Oh, how my heart is aching,
> Oh, how I could weep.

She had listened at her window, her eyes filled with tears, and sung along with them under her breath; she forgave them everything and extended her hand to them in ardent friendship. Girls, I am truly just like you! I too am only a servant girl, the unhappiest of us all!

The unhappiest of all, Olga repeated to herself as she proceeded along the hall. What was it the count said? "Miss Olga, you speak too much during the lesssons. You only confuse the child with your – everlasting – reprimands. You will do me the pleasure of being – a little – kinder." She repeated it word by word, so as not to lose a drop of bitterness. She clenched her fist, burning with anger and pain. Yes, this was her weakness: she took her work as governess too seriously. She had arrived at the castle glowing with enthusiasm, already in love with the little girl to be entrusted to her care. She had hurled herself passionately into instruction. Zealous, meticulous, brimming with knowledge, she had believed wholeheartedly in the importance of education. But now she merely drudged wearily through her bits of grammar and arithmetic, letting herself become upset over and over again, banging her knuckles on the table and then fleeing the schoolroom in tears, while little Mary stayed there, victorious in her defiance and her mistakes. At first she had played with Mary exuberantly, passionately, always in high spirits, as engrossed as a child with Mary's toys, but eventually she found that she was being toyed with under Mary's cold, bored, mocking glance, and the game was over. Olga trailed along behind her little charge like a shadow, not knowing what to say to her or how to amuse her. Accepting the task as a sacred trust, filled with resolutions of love, gentleness, and patience, but now look at her blazing eyes, hear how violently and erratically her heart beats, that heart which now feels only pain, not love. "A – little – kinder," Olga repeated to herself, horrified: God in heaven, can I ever be kind again?

All upset, her cheeks blazing, she ran between the two rows of metal-plated figures, knights in armor, which used to make her laugh. A thousand replies to the count's admonishments occurred to her, words of great dignity, replies both decisive and proud, which would ensure her importance forever in that house. My lord, she might say with head held high, I know what I want: I want Mary to gain a thorough understanding of all things and to learn self-discipline; I want to make of her someone who will not permit herself to take the wrong path in anything. My lord, it is not a matter of false notes on the piano, but of false upbringing. I cannot love Mary and not be concerned about her faults; it is because I love her that I will be as strict with her as I am with myself. – Upon saying all this to herself, her eyes shining and her heart lifted from its recent pain, Olga became almost cheerful; she felt relieved, and she firmly resolved that soon, tomorrow, she would have a word with the count. The count himself was not so bad, he had his generous moments, and after all, he suffered so much! If only there weren't those frightful, pale, domineering eyes staring out from behind his pince-nez!

She went out in front of the castle, dazzled by the sunlight; damp air rose from the glistening pavement, which had been sprinkled with water not long before. "Watch out, Miss Olga," Osvald shouted in his breaking voice, and then a wet soccer ball bounded up into Olga's white skirt. Osvald howled with laughter but stopped when he saw the poor girl standing there stunned. The skirt was splattered with mud; Olga gathered it up and without a word of reproach began to sob. Osvald turned red and stammered, "I didn't see you, miss."

"Beg your pardon, miss." These words, in English, came from Osvald's tutor, Mister Kennedy, who in white shirt and trousers was lolling about on the lawn; with a single movement he leaped up, gave Osvald a cuff on the head, and lay down again. All Olga could see was her skirt; she had been especially fond of this white outfit. Without a word she turned and went back inside, controlling herself with all her might to keep from bursting out in tears.

By the time she opened the door to her room, her throat was shaking with the need to weep. She stood there in complete amazement, unable to understand what was happening: in the middle of the room, seated in an armchair, was the countess, and a chambermaid was rummaging through her, Olga's, wardrobe ...

"Ah, c'est vous," the countess greeted her without turning around.

"Oui, madame la comtesse," Olga forced out, scarcely breathing, her eyes staring in alarm.

The chambermaid pulled out an entire armful of clothing. "My lady, it's not here, I'm sure of it."

"Very vell then," replied the countess, rising heavily to go. Olga, stunned, did not even think to step away from the door. The countess halted three steps in front of her. "Mademoiselle?"

"Oui, madame."

"Vous n'attendez pas, peut-être, que je m'excuse?"

"Non, non, madame!" exclaimed the young woman.

"Alors il n'y pas pourquoi me barrer le passage." The countess's r's rumbled in her throat.

"Ah, pardon, madame la comtesse," whispered Olga, swiftly making way for her. The countess and the chambermaid left, and all that remained were the scattered articles of clothing on the table and the bed.

Olga sat in the armchair as if made of wood; tears passed her by. They had been going through her wardrobe as if she were some thieving maid. "You are not, perhaps, waiting for me to apologize?" No, no, countess, God forbid that you should ever apologize to someone in your service! Here are my pockets, there's my purse, have a good look through everything, to see what I have stolen. I am poor and surely dishonest. Olga stared at the floor, stunned. Now at last she knew why she had so often found her dresses and linens in disarray. And I eat with them at the same table! I answer, smile, provide companionship, force myself to be cheerful ... Olga was overcome with boundless humiliation. Her eyes were staring, tearless, her clenched hands were pressed against her breast; she was incapable of thought, there was only her heart pounding painfully, horribly.

A fly settled on one of her her clasped hands, rubbed its tiny head, attended to its wings, scurried to and fro – but the hands did not move. From time to time a hoof stamped or a chain rattled in the stable. Crockery clinked in the pantry, a hawk shrieked out over the grounds, a train whistled at a distant curve in the track. Eventually, it was too long a time even for a fly, it jerked open its wings and flew through the open window. Absolute silence stretched out over the castle.

One, two, three, four. Four o'clock. Yawning noisily, a kitchen maid came to prepare tea. Rapid steps crossed the courtyard, at the well the winch screaked, and a certain haste was noticeable in the house. Olga rose, passed her hands across her forehead, and set about arranging her dresses neatly on the table. Then she knelt by the bureau, took out her linens, and laid them on the bed. Her books she placed on the chair, and when she was quite ready she stood above it all, as if standing over the ruins of Jerusalem, and rubbed her forehead: What do I really want from them?

Why am I doing this?

I will leave, a clear, distinct voice within her replied. I will give an hour's notice and I will leave tomorrow at five o'clock in the morning. Old Vavrys will take my trunk to the station. But that can't be done, protested Olga, dismayed; where would I go from here? How would I manage without a position? – I'll go home, replied the voice that, so far, had thought everything through for her. Of course Mama will cry, but Papa will approve. It's good this way, my little girl, he'll say, better honor than a good table.

But Papa, Olga objected with quiet joy and pride, what do I do now? – Go to the factory, replied the voice that had thought everything through. You'll work with your hands, you'll bring home a weekly paycheck, and you'll help Mama at home; she's old and frail. You'll do the wash and scrub the floor; you'll go to sleep tired and eat when hungry. My little girl, you will go home!

Olga threw out her hands in joyous rapture. Away from here, away! By tomorrow evening I'll be home! How is it possible that I didn't think of this long ago? How did I bear it? Immediately, right after tea, I'll give notice and go home; this evening I'll put everything in order, bring the countess in here, and show her: here is what I'm taking home; if there is a single thread that belongs to you, tear it off. Only the mud on this dress is yours, my lady, and that I will take with me.

Ruddy with joy, Olga pulled off her mud-spattered clothes. Tomorrow, tomorrow! I'll hide myself in a corner of the carriage where no one can see me; I'll fly like a bird from a cage! A rascally mood came over her, and she whistled and donned a red scarf. Smiling at herself in the mirror, proud, her hair tousled, she whistled as loudly as she could: C D G D, C D G D.

People were rushing around the courtyard; a gong clanged for tea. Olga flew downstairs; she didn't want to miss, for the last time, the spectacle of the ceremonial entry of the count's family. There descending, behold, the old count, half-crippled, leaning on the arm of the spindly Osvald. The countess, with her heavy, bloated, sickly belly, was nagging at Mary, jerking her along by the ribbon in her hair. At the rear lounged the athletic Mr. Kennedy, loftily indifferent to all that was going on around him.

The courtly old man reached the door first, opened it, and said: "Madame?"

The countess, with heavy steps, entered the dining room.

"Mademoiselle?" The count looked around for Olga, who entered with her head held high. After her came the count, Kennedy, Mary, and Osvald. The count seated himself at the head of the table, with the countess on his right and Olga on his left. The countess rang the bell. The maids entered, with downcast eyes and inaudible steps, like puppets who only hear orders and only see what they are told to see, as if those young lips never uttered a sound and those downcast eyes were never raised in a show of interest or understanding. Olga's eyes were fixed on this dumb show, "so that I will never ever forget it..."

"Du beurre, mademoiselle?" asked the count.

"Merci." She drank plain tea with dry bread; in a week, the invigorating thought danced in her head, I will be working at the factory. The count struggled to adjust his false teeth, the countess ate nothing, Osvald spilled his cocoa on the tablecloth, Mary ignored the food and sucked on a sugar plum. Only Mr. Kennedy was preparing to eat, spreading a centimeter of butter on his slice of bread. Triumphant disdain of everyone and everything filled Olga's heart. Wretched people, tomorrow I shall be the only one of you who is free. I shall look back with horror on your dinners, where you have nothing to say to each other, no exchange of laughter or groans.

With every bit of haughtiness within her, Olga looked down on Mr. Kennedy. She had hated him heartily from the first day; she hated the indifferent ease with which he managed to live as he pleased, caring not a whit for what anyone else might think; she hated him because no one dared stand up to him and because he slighted everyone and everything with his indolent superiority. God knows why he was there; he boxed brutally with Osvald, rode with him on horseback, and allowed himself to be idolized by the boy; he went out to shoot whenever he was so inclined, and if he was lolling somewhere on the grounds, nothing could induce him to budge. Sometimes when he was alone he would sit at the piano and improvise; he was a highly accomplished pianist, but he played without feeling, thinking only of himself. Olga used to listen in secret, offended that she could not penetrate that cold, complex, egotistic music. He took no notice of anyone or anything; if he were asked a direct question, he would barely move his lips to answer, in English, "yes" or "no." A young athlete, cruel, vain, and lazy, who did everything as if out of charity. Sometimes the old count ventured to propose a game of chess; without a word, Mr. Kennedy would sit down to the chessboard and in a few undeliberated, frighteningly savage moves checkmate the old gentleman, who, sweating with anxiety and prattling like a child, would give each move a half hour's deliberation, drawing back his piece fully a dozen times before deciding. Olga would watch these uneven contests with unconcealed rage. She herself used to play chess occasionally with the count, and found him a good, deliberate player; a game with him would be endless, filled with much meditation and thoughtful plotting, which required flattering her opponent for his shrewdness and evaluating his play. Olga did not ask if she had any right, but she felt herself far superior to the accomplished Mr. Kennedy, whose accomplishments cost him not the least effort, and who dominated everyone and everything with his self-confidence and sovereign haughtiness. She despised him and made him aware of it; yes, all her girlish pride and conceit, struck down so many times day after day, was restored again and again in this show of scorn.

Meanwhile Mr. Kennedy took his afternoon tea with great composure, completely disregarding Olga's lethal glances. He ignores me here, thought Olga, provoked, and yet every night, on his way to his room, he knocks at my door: "Open, Miss Olga ... "

It was one of the castle's mysteries, and Olga never suspected how greatly this mystery amused the servants. The young English fellow, who, insultingly, paid no attention whatsoever to the chambermaids, had conducted this secret escapade for quite some time. It was his "fancy," as he called it in English, that they prepare a room for him in the castle tower which, as everybody'd said for generations, is haunted. Of course, Olga did not believe in ghosts, and she saw in Kennedy's whim only the affectations of a show-off, but this did not prevent her from being in mortal fear on the staircase and in the passageway at night. Besides, it's God's truth that sounds were heard at night which could be attributed neither to Franz's philandering nor, still worse, to the erotic goings-on in the women's quarters. In a nutshell, one night, after Olga had gone to bed, Mr. Kennedy knocked at her door: "Open, Miss Olga." Olga threw on a dressing-gown, opened the door a crack, and

asked what he wanted. Mr. Kennedy then began to rattle off no
end of foolishness in English, of which she scarcely understood
a quarter, but enough nonetheless to grasp that he was calling
her "sweet Olga" and other interesting things. This sufficed for
her to slam the door on his nose and lock it, and upon
encountering him the next morning, she asked him, with an
extremely severe look in her eyes, what he had been doing at
her door last night. Mr. Kennedy didn't think it at all necessary
to explain, or indeed act as if he remembered it at all, but from
that time on, he knocked every night, said, "Open, Miss Olga,"
turned the door handle and prattled in the most comical
manner, while Olga hauled the covers up to her chin and
screamed tearfully in English, "You're a rascal" or in Czech
"You're mad" – mortified to despair that this rascal, this
madman was laughing. That was the only time he laughed the
whole day long.

Now Olga was gazing at Mr. Kennedy with shining eyes.
As soon as he looks this way I'll ask him, in front of everyone,
"Mr. Kennedy, what do you mean by trying to gain entrance to
my room every night?" There will be a scandal, but before I
leave I'll have still other things to tell. This appetite for revenge
exhilarated her. Then Mr. Kennedy looked her way with calm,
steely-blue eyes; Olga began to move her lips, but suddenly she
blushed. She remembered...

Those beautiful moonlit nights about a week ago were to
blame. Inexpressibly enchanting nights, nights of a clear full
moon in the height of summer, silvery nights, the sort of
moonlit nights sacred to pagans! Olga was wandering about in
front of the castle, she had no intention of going to bed on such
a magical night. She was alone and happy, filled with a soaring
astonishment at the excess of beauty which flooded the sleeping
world. Slowly, with an awe full of pleasure and delight, she
ventured out into the grounds. She saw handsome birch trees
and deep black oaks in silvery meadows, mysterious shadows

and wondrous light; it was more than can be endured. She set off across a large meadow to the pond with a fountain, and as she came around a thicket she spied at the edge of the lake a white statue of a naked man, his face upraised to the full moon, his hands clasped behind his head, his powerful chest arched above his firm abdomen. It was Mr. Kennedy. Olga was not a silly girl, she didn't scream or run away. Her eyes half-closed, she stared at the white figure. With a compact movement of its muscles, the statue came to life. From the calves a wave of taut sinews gradually rolled upward, across the thighs and abdomen to the chest, and flowed into the beautiful, powerful arms; and then a new muscular wave rose from the slender calves, once more to swell the biceps sculpted as if from boulders. This is how Mr. Kennedy exercised, without moving from his place. Then suddenly he arched his back, raised his hands, and dived backwards into the pond. The water spurted, glittered, and purled. Olga silently disappeared and, thinking no more about the mysterious, fearsome shadows of the night, she made her way straight home; oddly enough, she saw no more the beauteous birches or ancient oaks on silvery lawns. This is why she blushed.

Truth be told, she really didn't know why she blushed; there was nothing whatsoever to be ashamed of and so much marvelous beauty to that adventure. But something worse happened, and it happened the very next day. It was a clear, charming night, and once again she took a walk in front of the castle, but this time she didn't go out into the grounds. She thought about Mr. Kennedy, who might be swimming this evening as well, about the secret depths of the grounds, and about the white statue of the young man; when the gossipy housekeeper came near she avoided the woman, wishing to be alone. By then it was quite late, eleven o'clock, and Olga was afraid to go home alone up the staircase and along the passageways. Kennedy returned to the castle, his hands in his pockets. When

he saw Olga, he wanted to start in on his bizarre nightly courtship, but Olga cut short his speech and commanded quite imperiously that he light her way home. Somewhat puzzled, Kennedy lit a candle and didn't say another word until they were at her door, when he rather tamely said, "Good night." Olga turned fiercely, shot him an abnormally threatening look and, as if having taken leave of her senses, thrust her hand into his hair. It was damp and softly disheveled, like the coat of a Newfoundland puppy fresh from a bath. Olga released a brief hiss of delight and, unmindful of what she was doing, gave his hair a hard tug. Before he could recover from the shock, she had slammed the door and locked it. Mr. Kennedy left for his own quarters as if in a daze, but in half an hour he returned, barefoot and half-undressed, knocked gently, and whispered, "Olga, oh Olga..." She made no reply, and eventually Mr. Kennedy stole away.

That was the incident which now caused Olga such mortification. It was, of course, shamefully stupid, and Olga wanted to sink through the floor because of what she had done, but at least she had doubly avenged herself on Mr Kennedy, who was somehow to blame. The next night she took the shaggy-haired terrier Fritz to her room, and when Kennedy came to knock on the door, Fritz let out a frightful racket. For the next few days Mr. Kennedy left Olga in peace, but then twice he came back, cutting loose with the most lyrical twaddle, but Olga, fed up with it all and full of fastidious spite toward the brazen man, buried her ears in her pillow so as not to hear.

That was all that passed between Olga and Mr. Kennedy, and that is why Olga was so unutterably and painfully embarrassed that she turned red under his glance, and she could have smacked herself for it. She was immensely troubled in her irritably virginal heart. So much the better that I leave, she told herself, if for no other reason than that man. She felt weary from her nightly struggle and humiliated by her powerlessness;

such a torrent of distaste and defiance rose in her throat that she could have screamed. But she succeeded in lightening her mood: Hallelujah! I'm leaving! And were I to stay one day longer, I'd set off the most appalling scandal.

"Prenez des prunes, mademoiselle."

"Pardon, madame?"

"Prenez des prunes."

"Merci, merci, madame la comtesse."

She broke her thoughts away from Mr. Kennedy and turned her gaze on the handsome face of Osvald. Her heart was a bit consoled by his cheerfulness. It was no secret to her that, in his own way, the boy was in love with her, although he was, naturally, unable to admit it other than by unnecessary rudeness and averted eyes. On the other hand, Olga took special delight in tormenting him; she would place her hand around his nice, slender neck and drag him out to the castle grounds with her, inordinately amused by his grumbling and light-hearted fury. At that very moment, sensing her glance, he swallowed an enormous mouthful and glared fiercely. Poor Osvald! What will become of you here, in this frightful house, child on the verge of young manhood, burdened at one and the same time by an excess of delicacy and an excess of savagery? How will your heart awaken, what examples will you have before you? Olga suddenly felt resentment at the memory of having gone recently into Osvald's room to find him wrestling and boxing with the chambermaid Paulina, the worst of all the girls. Needless to say, it was only the juvenile play of a spirited pup, but there was no need for Osvald to blush, no need for Paulina's eyes and face to be so inflamed, in short, no need for it to have happened at all, no need, no need at all. Highly suspicious, Olga was on the alert from that moment on; never again did she tenderly run her fingers through Osvald's hair, never again did she place her hand around his neck; she kept watch over him with Argus eyes, pervaded by anxiety, stooping even to spying, determined not to surrender Osvald's childhood to premature and shameful experience. Often when she was with Mary she would suddenly run off to keep an eye on Osvald; she was coldly severe with him, but this resulted only in his youthful love becoming riddled with rebellious hatred. But why, Olga now asked herself, why should I be keeping such a watchful eye on him? What have I, a stranger, to do with whatever lessons about life he receives from Paulina or anyone else? Why should I plague myself with anxiety and my own severity, when it hurts me more than him? Goodbye, goodbye, Osvald, I won't tell you that you are my dear child, I won't tell you of my love for your boyish innocence, more loveable than a girl's. I'll no longer keep an eye on you, you'll just open your eyes and arms and seize the first opportunity – I won't be there to weep over you.

And you, my lady countess, all at once Olga switched to a brisk reckoning, you have suspected me. You have spied on me during my lessons with Osvald; you have made it unmistakably clear that "it is better for him to be in the company of Mr. Kennedy." Perhaps it is also better for him to be in the company of Paulina; you trust Paulina. When one night Osvald secretly went out with Kennedy to see an otter, you came into my room, I had to let you in, and you searched for the boy even under the coverlets on my bed. Very well, my lady, he is your child, but you send Paulina to his bedroom to awaken him, Paulina, a woman over thirty and as depraved as the devil himself. You hunt through my wardrobe and sniff around my bureau, then you order me into your carriage and demand that I entertain you. You offer me prunes, oh, thank you, madame, you are so kind! If you consider me frivolous and a thief, then send me from the table to the servants' hall, or still better, to the laundry; I'll swallow a bit of bread with my tears of rage and humiliation, but at least ... at least I'll not be obliged to smile!

— — "Aren't you listening, miss?"

"Pardon." Olga reddened.

"Perhaps you are – a little – unwell?" asked the count, staring fixedly at her. "Are you not perhaps – feverish?"

"No, my lord," Olga hastily objected. "There is nothing whatsoever the matter with me."

"So much the better," said the count slowly. "I don't like people who are – unwell."

Olga's spirits suddenly fell. I didn't grow up among these people, she thought despairingly, I don't know how to stand up to them. God, grant me the strength to give notice today! God, grant me the strength! She anticipated the horrible state of nerves that would accompany her speaking about it to the count. He would most certainly raise his eyebrows and say, "An hour's notice, miss? Such a thing is not done!" What excuses can I dream up now? How can I explain that I must ... I must go home immediately, this very minute? I'll run away if I'm not allowed to go, I'll definitely run away! Olga waited fearfully for the next moment to arrive.

The family rose from the table and settled down in the adjacent drawing room; the count and Kennedy smoked, the countess picked up some embroidery, and then they all waited for the afternoon mail delivery. As soon as the children go out, Olga decided, I will speak about it then. In the meantime, her heart pounding, she forced herself to think of her home. She pictured her mother in a blue apron, the scrubbed, unpainted furniture, her father sitting coatless with his pipe, reading his newspaper with prudent thoroughness. That is my only salvation, she felt with growing anxiety, I cannot bear this another day. God, grant me the strength this very moment!

Paulina, her eyes downcast, brought in the letters on a silver tray. The count scooped the letters into his lap; he wanted to grab the last letter as well, which lay apart from the others, but Paulina respectfully plucked it away. "For mademoiselle," she murmured.

From a distance Olga recognized her mother's handwriting on the pitifully scrawled envelope with its obvious rustic origins and atrocious spelling, a letter like all those others of which she was ashamed and yet which she carried next to her heart. She turned red even today – forgive me, Mama! She picked up the rustic letter with trembling fingers; moved, she looked at the address, written with great thoroughness, as though the world were wicked and would not, without detailed directions, deliver a letter into the right hands so far away, among other sorts of people – but that moment a weight fell from her heart: Mama, what a help you are! I'll read the letter and suddenly cry out that my father is ill, I must go to him, I'll collect my things and be off, and no one will be able to hold me back; in a week I'll write that I must stay at home and have them send my trunk to me. Much the easiest way, she told herself joyfully. Like every woman, she found it easier to help herself by means of excuses than by making a good case for herself. Filled with joy, she tore open the envelope. When she drew out the letter, her heart was pierced; she held her breath and began to read:

Dear little Daughter,

I must write you with sad news, your Papa is sick the doktor says its his hart and he is week and his feet swelled up and he cant walk, Doktor says he cant get upset, Doktor says dont complane when you write as Papa frets about it so dont do it just write that your fine then he wont be upset as you know how he loves you and Thank The Good Lord you have a good job

Pray for Papa and dont come its to far but your money came thank You Many Times, its very bad, Papa must lay down Frantík stole his watch we cant tell him what happened it would kill him so we say its geting fixed. All the time he says when will it be fixed as he cant tell the time and I cant cry in front of him.

Dear little daughter I must write you to Thank God you have a fine job so Pray for the Master and Mistres and serve them faithfully theres no place so good if you eat good there, do it for your Health as your week in the chest and send us something every month daughter dear and we Thank you the Good Lord will reward you for your Family.

Pray for your Master serve them many years they will Take Care of you till you Dy like a goverment office job and dont get yourself talked about Greet the Master and Mistres, its bad with Papa hes like a candel hes almost gone.

Kisses from your Mother in Kostelec no. 37

The count left off reading his letters and stared at Olga.

"Mademoiselle, you don't feel well," he exclaimed, genuinely concerned.

Olga rose, as if completely drained of her spirit, and pressed her fingers to her temples. "It's only – only a headache, my lord," she gasped.

"Go and lie down at once, miss, go and lie down at once," exclaimed the count, disturbed.Olga curtsied mechanistically and slowly left the room.

The count looked quizzically at his wife; she shrugged her shoulders and said sharply in German, "Osvald, sit up straight!" Mr. Kennedy smoked and gazed at the ceiling. There was a disconcerting silence.

The countess went on sewing, her lips tightly clamped together. After a while she rang and Paulina appeared. "Paulina, where has mademoiselle gone?" she asked, scarcely opening her mouth.

"To her room, my lady," replied the maid, "and she's locked herself in there."

"Have the horses harnessed."

The carriage wheels rattled on the sand in the courtyard, and the coachman led out the horses and buckled their straps.

"Papa, may I ride?" ventured Osvald.

"Ja." The count nodded, numbly staring nowhere at all.

The countess turned on him a searching, hostile glance. "Will you be joining us?" she asked.

"Nein," he said, preoccupied.

The groom brought the riding horses and saddled them. Kennedy's horse danced all around the yard before allowing itself to be saddled, while Osvald's half-blooded gelding peacefully and sagely pawed the ground, sadly contemplating his hoof.

The family went out to the courtyard. Osvald, a good horseman, vaulted right onto his horse. He couldn't keep from casting an upward glance at Olga's window, for she often waved her hand to him when he was setting out for his ride. The window was empty.

The countess climbed heavily into the carriage. "Mary," she said peremptorily. Little Mary made a face and reluctantly followed her into the carriage. "Paulina," the countess called to the chambermaid, "go see what Miss Olga is doing. But don't let her catch you at it."

Mr. Kennedy threw away his cigarette, and with one bound was in the saddle, gripping the horse with his knees. The horse broke into a gallop; its thundering hooves pounded across the wooden planks lining the vaulted entry to the courtyard and struck an explosion of sparks from the cobbled pavement beyond. "Halloo, Mr. Kennedy!" Osvald shouted, and he hurried after him.

Paulina came running back, her hands in the pockets of her white apron. "Madame," she reported confidentially, "Miss Olga is hanging up her dresses in her wardrobe and arranging her linens in her bureau." The countess waved her hand. "Go," she called to the coachman.

The carriage rolled out of the courtyard; the old count waved to them and was now alone. He sat down on a bench beneath the arcade, his cane between his knees, and forlornly, in an ill humor, he stared out into the courtyard. For perhaps half an hour he sat there, then he rose and clumped heavily on his palsied legs into the drawing room. He seated himself in the armchair beside the chessboard where the game he had been playing yesterday with Olga lay still unfinished. He scrutinized the board; obviously he was at a disadvantage: Olga had moved her knight and was threatening an attack. Bending over the board in an effort to anticipate her moves, he discovered the neat little scheme by which she intended to defeat him, thoroughly. Then he stood, raised himself upright and, cane clattering, went upstairs to the guests' wing. He stopped before Olga's door. It was quiet, absolutely, frighteningly quiet; nothing stirred. Finally he knocked. "Miss Olga, how are you?"

A moment's silence. "Better now, thank you," replied Olga, her voice full of distress. "Did you wish anything, my lord?"

"No, no, just lie down." And suddenly, as if he had said too much, thereby spoiling things again, he added, "So that you will be able to teach again tomorrow." And conspicuously making noise, he went back down to the drawing room.

If he had remained only a moment longer, he would have heard her softly groaning, and then quietly, ceaselessly weeping.

Hours of solitude are long, very long. At length the carriage returned, the heated horses were led up and down the courtyard, and from the kitchen came the usual hurrying clatter, as happened every day. At half-past seven the gong rang for dinner. All were seated, but Olga was missing. For a while all went on as if no one had noticed this, until the old count raised his eyebrows and asked with surprise, "Was, die Olga kommt nicht?"

The countess shot a look at him and said nothing. Not for a long time did she call to Paulina, "Ask Miss Olga what she would like to eat."

Paulina was back in an instant. "My lady, Miss Olga wishes to thank you, but she's not hungry. However, she'll be up and about tomorrow." The countess gave a brief toss of her head; there was more than dissatisfaction in her gesture.

Osvald barely pecked at his food and cast beseeching glances at Mr. Kennedy, as if imploring the tutor to rescue him by taking him outside as soon as possible after dinner; Mr. Kennedy, as usual, chose not to understand.

By now, twilight had come, bringing merciful night for those who are weary, boundless night for those who are sad. There is light, it dims, and night is here; one cannot tell exactly when it sets in, this darkness that stifles and oppresses one so; darkness, that abysmal hole whose depths are dug by human despair.

You, silent night, you know this, you who hear the breathing of sleepers and the groaning of the sick, for you have listened carefully to the feeble, feverish breath of a girl who has wept long and now weeps no more. You have held your ear to her heart and cruelly constricted the throat that is wound about with tousled hair. You have heard cries smothered in a pillow and then the silence even more terrible to hear.

You know, mute night, how the silence spreads through the entire castle, floor by floor, room by room, you who with burning fingers stifle a woman's shrieks of passion in a corner of the stairwell. You accommodate the echo of a young man's footsteps as, hair still wet from bathing, whistling softly, he makes his way belatedly to bed along the lengthy castle corridor.

Dark night, you see how a young woman, exhausted from weeping, trembles at the sound of those youthful footsteps. You see how she bounds off the bed as if hurled forward by some blind force, throws her hair back from her burning forehead, and dashes to the door, unlocking it and leaving it ajar.

Then she again lies rigid on her feverish bed, waiting in dreadful expectation, as one for whom there is no help.

Money

AGAIN, ONCE AGAIN it had come over him: scarcely had he swallowed a few mouthfuls of food when he felt faint, his head strangely heavy, and a sweat broke out on his forehead. He left his dinner untouched and leaned his head on his hand, firmly rejecting his landlady's excessive solicitude. Finally she left, sighing, and he lay down on the sofa to rest, but actually to listen with both attentiveness and dread to the agonizing sounds of his body. His dizziness persisted, his stomach seemed to have stones lodged inside, his heart beat rapidly and irregularly; he was so exhausted that even lying down he was covered in sweat. If only he could fall asleep!

An hour later the landlady knocked and handed him a telegram. He opened it with apprehension and read: "19/10 7:34 coming tonight Růža." He had absolutely no idea what it meant. His head still reeling, he stood up and once more read the numbers and words, until finally he understood: it was from Růžena, his married sister; she's arriving this evening, and of course I must go and meet her. She was probably coming to do some shopping; the thought of feminine pother and disregard for others, imposing on a man for no reason at all, put him in a bad mood. He paced the room, angry that his evening had been spoiled. He thought about how he would have spent it, lying on his eternal sofa, book in hand, his electric lamp buzzing familiarly away at his side. He had passed tedious, interminable hours there, but now, God knows why, they struck him as particularly attractive, filled with wise musings and tranquillity. Tonight, a wasted evening. The end of peace and quiet. Filled with childish, resentful bitterness, he tore the unfortunate telegram to bits.

But that evening, as he was waiting for the delayed train in the cold, damp, high-ceilinged station, an even greater feeling of distress assailed him: distress at the squalor and misery he saw all around him, the weariness of people who were arriving, the disappointment of those waiting for people who hadn't come. He had trouble finding his slender, diminutive sister in the thick of the hurrying crowd. Her eyes were apprehensive and she was dragging a heavy suitcase behind her, and he grasped at once that something serious had happened. He bundled her into a cab and headed for home. Only when they were on their way did he remember that he'd forgotten to find a room for her; he asked if she wanted to go to a hotel, but this only provoked an outburst of tears. Of course, in that state he couldn't take her anywhere, so he resigned himself, took her slender, nervous hand in his, and was tremendously cheered when at length she looked up at him with a smile.

Once home, he looked at her with scrutiny and was alarmed. Trembling, tormented, in a strange, excited state, her eyes burning and her lips parched, she was seated on his sofa, surrounded by the cushions he had heaped around her, and she spoke. ... He asked her to speak softly, for it was already night. "I've run away from my husband," she blurted out. "If you knew, Jiří, if you knew what I've been through! If you knew how mean he is to me! I've come to you for advice," she said, and then she burst into tears.

Gloomily, Jiří paced the room. One word after another drew a picture for him of her life with an overfed, greedy, and vulgar husband who insulted her in front of their servant, was brutish in bed, and bored her with his never-ending scenes about nothing. The fool had foolishly squandered her dowry, was penny-pinching at home yet extravagantly indulged his idiotic hypochondria ... He heard of food doled out bite by bite, of reproaches, humiliations, and cruelties, of shabby generosity, of frenzied, savage quarrels, demands for love, foolish, overbearing gibes ... Jiří paced the room, choking with disgust and sympathy: he was suffering tremendously, he could not endure this endless torrent of shame and pain. And there sat the diminutive, agitated girl he had never really known, his fierce, proud little sister. She had always been combative, had never listened to reason, had displayed wickedly flashing eyes even when she was small! There she sat, her chin quivering with sobs and her ceaseless flood of words, so haggard, so feverish! Jiří wanted to soothe her but was half afraid. "Stop," he said roughly, "that's enough, I know it all now." But how on earth could he restrain her?

"Let me go on," Růžena said through her tears, "I have no one but you!" And once again, out poured a stream of accusations, more broken now, more slow, more hushed; details were repeated and incidents enlarged upon. Then suddenly she asked: "And you, Jiří, how have you been?"

"As for me," Jiří mumbled, "I can't complain. But tell me, aren't you going to go back to him?"

"Never," Růžena swore. "It's not possible. I'd rather die than... If you only knew what it was like!"

"Then what are you going to do?" asked Jiří.

This was the question Růžena had been waiting for. "I made up my mind about that a long time ago," she replied eagerly. "I'll give lessons or go somewhere as a governess, work in an office or something ... I'll be a good worker, you'll see. I'll make a living all by myself, and how glad I'll be, oh my, how glad I'll be to do whatever it is I'll do! You must advise me ... I'll find a room somewhere, something small ... I'm so looking forward to working! Tell me, something'll turn up, won't it?" She was so worked up, she couldn't sit still, she jumped up and began to pace the room beside her brother, her face glowing with excitement: "I've thought it all out. I'll take the furniture, you know, the old furniture our parents left us; just wait and see how nice it'll look. I want nothing more than

to have a room, even if I'm poor, as long as I don't have to ...
I want nothing, nothing, nothing more from life, the least
morsel will be enough for me, I'll make do with anything, as
long as I can be far away from ... from all that ... I'm so
looking forward to working, I'll do all my own sewing and
sing while I'm doing it ... Why, I haven't sung in years! Oh,
Jiří, if you only knew!"

"Work," Jiří wondered aloud. "I don't know if there's any
to be found ... In any event, you're not accustomed to it, Růža;
it would be hard for you, very hard..."

"No," countered Růžena, her eyes shining, "you don't
know what it's like to be reproached for every mouthful, every
rag, everything ... To be told all the time that you don't work,
all you do is spend ... I want to break free from everything
that's made me so bitter. No, Jiří, you'll see how glad I'll be to
work, how glad I'll be to live! I'll enjoy every mouthful, even if
it's only dry bread; I'll be proud of it ... I'll go to sleep proud,
dress in calico, cook for myself ... Tell me, I can be a working
woman, can't I? If nothing turns up, I'll go work in a factory ...
I'm looking forward to it all so much!"

Jiří gazed at her in joyful astonishment. Good heavens,
what radiance, what courage after such a downtrodden life! He
was ashamed of his own lassitude and fatigue, he suddenly
thought of his own work with affection and joy, infected by the
glowing vitality of this strange, passionate girl. She really had
become a young girl again, blushing, animated, naïve – It will
turn out just fine, how could it not?

"It'll turn out just fine, you'll see," Růžena said. "I don't
want anything from anyone, I'll make a living all by myself, I'll
surely bring in enough, at least enough for food and for flowers
on the table! And if I didn't have enough for flowers, I'd walk
down the street and just look at them ... You can't imagine
how much joy I've gotten from every little thing, ever since the
moment I ... decided to run away. How beautifully, delightfully

different everything is! A new life's beginning for me ... Until now, I had no idea how beautiful everything is. Oh, Jiří," she exclaimed, tears running down her face, "I'm so happy!"

"Foolish girl," Jiří smiled at her, filled with joy. "It won't be ... all that easy. But we'll try. However, now you need to lie down, you mustn't make yourself ill. Please, let me be alone for a while, I need to think things over. In the morning I'll tell you what I think ... Go to sleep now, let me be."

Nothing he could say would induce her to sleep in the bed. She lay down on the sofa, fully dressed, he covered her with everything he had that was warm, and turned down the lamp. It was quiet except for her rapid, childlike breathing, which seemed to appeal to heaven for sympathy. Jiří quietly opened the window to the cool October night.

The peaceful sky was bright with stars. Once in their father's house they had stood before a wide open window, he and little Růžena, and shivering with cold she had pressed close to him as they waited for falling stars. "When a star falls," Růžena had whispered, "my wish will be that I be changed into a boy and do something glorious." Their father was sleeping like a log, they could hear the bed creaking under the heaviness of his exhaustion. For Jiří it was a solemn moment: he thought about grand things, and with the gravity of a man he sheltered little Růžena, who was shivering with cold and excitement.

High above the garden a star flew across the sky.

"Jiří," Růžena's voice called to him softly from the room.

"I'll be right there," Jiří answered, and he shivered with cold and enthusiasm. Yes, to do something great; there is no other deliverance. You're so naïve, what great deed did you want to accomplish? You have your own burden to bear; if you want to do something great, bear more: the greater the load you carry, the greater you will be. Are you a weakling, foundering under your own burdens? Rise up, so that you can lift up someone else who is foundering. You cannot do otherwise, lest you yourself fall!

"Jiří," Růžena called in a hushed voice.

Jiří turned from the window. "Listen," he began hesitantly. "I've been thinking about it ... I think that – that you won't find work to suit you ... There's work enough, but you won't earn enough to have ... Oh, it's foolishness."

"I'll be satisfied with anything," Růžena said quietly.

"No, you don't know what it's like. Look, I'm making good money now, thank God, and I can take on some afternoon work as well. Sometimes I don't even know what to do with... It's quite adequate for me. And there's money I could let you have..."

"What money?" Růžena gasped.

"My share from our parents and the interest on it, which comes to ... comes to about five thousand a year. No, not five thousand, only four ... That's just the interest, you understand. It occurred to me that I could let you have the interest, and that way you'll have something."

Růžena bounded off the sofa. "That's not possible!" she shouted.

"Don't shout," Jiří muttered. "It's only the interest, you know. When you no longer need it, you can stop drawing on it. But for now, at the beginning..."

Růžena stood there in astonishment, just like a little girl. "But that won't do, what would you have?"

"Don't worry about that," he said. "I've wanted to work in the afternoons for a long time now, but ... I was ashamed to take work away from my colleagues. You can see how I live; I'll be glad to have something to do. That's how it is; you understand, don't you? That money was only getting in my way. So then, do you want it or not?"

"I want it," Růžena gasped, and she came over to him on tiptoe, placed her arms around his neck, and pressed her moist cheek to his face. "Jiří," she whispered, "I never expected this, not even in my dreams; I swear I wanted nothing from you, but since you're so good – "

"Let go," he implored, flustered. "That's not it at all. The money doesn't matter to me. Růžena, when a man's fed up with life, he must do something ... But what can he do when he's alone? Whatever you do, in the end you only meet up with yourself again; it's like being surrounded by mirrors: wherever you look, you meet up with your own face, your own tedium, your own loneliness ... If you knew what that's like! No, Růžena, I don't want to talk about myself. But I'm so glad you're here, so glad this has happened! Look how many stars there are; do you remember how once, when we were small, we watched for falling stars?"

"I've forgotten," Růžena said, raising her pale face toward him. In the frosty darkness he saw her eyes shining like stars. "Why are you like this?"

Seized by the cold, shivering, he stroked her hair. "Don't talk about the money. It's so good of you to have come to me! Oh Lord, how glad I am! It's as if a window had opened ... among all those mirrors! Can you imagine? All that time I was concerned only with myself! I was sick of myself, I'd grown tired of myself, I had nothing else ... No, it served no purpose. Do you remember what you wished for that night the stars were falling? What would you wish for today if they were falling again?"

"What would I wish for?" Růžena smiled sweetly. "Something for myself ... Yes, and something for you, for something to come true for you."

"I have nothing to wish for, Růžena. I'm so glad that I've rid myself... Tell me, what arrangements have you made? No, tomorrow I'll find you a nice room with a good view, all right? From here, you can only see into the courtyard; in the daytime, when no stars are shining, it's a bit depressing. You need a more open view, so that you can have a better..." Enlivened by excitement, striding about the room, he began to plan the future, enthusiastic about each new detail, laughing, chattering, promising all sorts of things. An apartment! a job! money! all would be forthcoming. The main thing is that it be a new life! He sensed her eyes shining in the darkness, smiling, following him with their intense brilliance. He could have laughed outright with joy, and he didn't stop until, exhausted, overcome by happiness and too much talking, the two of them enjoyed long respites of silent understanding.

At last he made her lie down; she did not resist his comical, motherly solicitude, which did not allow her to thank him, but when he raised his head from the piles of newspapers in which he was looking through advertisements for rooms and realtors, he found her eyes fixed on him with an enthusiastic, formidable brilliance, and his heart was wrung with happiness. Thus did morning find him.

Yes, it was a new life. He was no longer sick and exhausted, now that he was bolting down his dinner and racing through countless inspections of rooms, coming home sweaty as a hunting dog and happy as a bridegroom, and then devouring piles of extra work at night, until finally he fell asleep, worn out but elated by a rich, full day. Still and all, he'd had to settle for a room without a view, a loathsome room, upholstered in plush and sinfully expensive; he placed Růžena there for the present. Sometimes, admittedly, he was seized in the midst of his work by a fainting fit, his eyelids would tremble, and the dizziness would make sweat break out on his suddenly pallid brow; but he succeeded in mastering it, set his teeth and laid his forehead against the cool desktop, saying resolutely to himself: Bear up! You must bear up! You are no longer living for yourself alone – In truth, he did get better as the days went by. It was a new life.

Until one day he received an unexpected visit. It was his other sister, Tylda, who lived somewhere just outside the city and was married to the owner of a small factory that wasn't doing well. She always called on him when she came into the city – she did all the business traveling, took care of everything herself. She always sat with her eyes cast down and to the side, and used frugal words to talk about her three children and her thousands of troubles, as if there were nothing else in the world. Today, however, she alarmed him; she was breathing heavily, struggling in her web of endless troubles, and her fingers, disfigured by writing and sewing, touched his heart with harsh sympathy. Thank heaven, she said, the children are healthy, they're good children, but the plant is idle, the machines no longer fulfill the customers' requirements. In fact, we're looking for a buyer...

Trying in vain to raise her eyes, she said suddenly, half question, half statement, "And Růžena's here." Oddly enough, wherever her eyes landed there was a hole in the carpet, a frayed slipcover, or something else that was old, shabby, and in disrepair ... Actually, neither he nor Růžena noticed such things. It bothered him that Tylda noticed, and he looked away; he was also ashamed to meet her eyes, busy as needles and relentless as her unceasing troubles.

"She's run away from her husband," she said. "She says that he tormented her. Maybe he did, but ... everything has a reason..."

"And he had a reason, too" she continued when no questions were forthcoming. "You know, Růžena is ... I don't know how to put it." She fell silent, her hard eyes stitching a huge hole in the carpet. "Růžena is no housekeeper," she began again after a moment. "And of course she has no children, doesn't have to work, has nothing to worry about, yet..."

Jiří looked out the window, frowning.

"Růžena is a spendthrift." Tylda forced out the words. "She ran him into debt, as you know ... Haven't you noticed the kind of clothes she wears?"

"No."

Tylda sighed and rubbed her forehead. "You have no idea what it costs ... She buys furs that cost ... thousands, then she sells them again for a few hundred so she can pay for shoes. She used to hide the bills from him, but then the lawsuits started ... You don't know about this?"

"No. He and I don't talk."

Tylda nodded. "He's a bit strange, if I do say so ... But when she never mends a stitch of clothing for him, and he's got loose threads falling off him everywhere, while she goes around like a duchess ... And she lies to him ... And she runs around with other–"

"Stop," Jiří pleaded. This was torturing him.

Tylda's sad eyes mended a torn bedspread. "Maybe..." she began uncertainly, "maybe she's offered to keep house for you? Suggested you find a bigger apartment? Offered to cook for you?"

Jiří's heart missed a beat. None of this had occurred to him. Nor had it to Růžena! Good heavens, how happy he would be! "I wouldn't want her to," he said curtly, trying with all his might to master himself.

Tylda succeeded in raising her eyes. "Maybe she wouldn't want to, either. This is where she has ... her lieutenant. They transferred him to Prague. That's why she ran away ... and he's married. She's not likely to have told you."

"Tylda," he said hoarsely, searing her with his eyes, "you're lying."

Tylda's hands and face were shaking, but she would not give up. "See for yourself." She was stammering. "You're too kind-hearted. I wouldn't have said this to you, if ... if I didn't feel for you. Růžena never liked you. She said you were–"

"Get out," he shouted, beside himself with rage. "For God's sake, leave me in peace!"

Tylda slowly rose. "You should ... you should find a better apartment, Jiří," she said with heroic calm. "Look how filthy it is in here. Would you like me to send you a small box of pears?"

"I don't want anything."

"I have to go ... It's so dark in here ... Oh, Jiří, goodbye then."

The blood hammered in his temples, his throat constricted. He tried to do some work, but he had only just sat down when he broke his pen in rage, leaped up, and hurried off to see Růžena. He ran to her apartment and, out of breath, rang the bell. The landlady opened the door and said that the young lady had been out since morning, did he want to leave a message?

"That's not necessary," Jiří mumbled, and he plodded home as if carrying an immense burden. He sat down to his papers again, leaned his head on his hand, and began to work, but an hour passed and he hadn't turned a page. Dusk was followed by darkness, but he hadn't turned on the lamps. Then the bell rang briskly, cheerfully, there was the rustle of skirts in the entryway, and Růžena flew into the room. "Are you asleep, Jiří?" She was smiling sweetly. "Heavens, how dark it is in here. Where are you?"

"Um, I've been working," he managed to say drily. There was a chill air in the room and a wonderfully delicate scent.

"Listen," she began merrily.

"I wanted to go see you," he interrupted her, "but I thought perhaps you wouldn't be home."

"Where would I have been?" she asked, genuinely surprised. "Oh, how nice it is in here! Jiří, I'm so glad to be here with you!" She exuded youth and joy, she sparkled with happiness. "Come sit by me," she begged, and when he was seated next to her on the sofa, she placed an arm around his neck and repeated: "I'm so glad, Jiří!" He rested his face against her cool fur coat, dewy from the autumn drizzle, allowed himself to be gently rocked, and thought: Let her go wherever she likes – what business is it of mine, after all? At least she's come right back to me again. But his heart stopped and was gripped by a strange mixture of stabbing pain and sweet fragrance.

"What's the matter, Jiří?" she cried out in alarm.

"Nothing," he said, deluding himself. "Tylda was here."

"Tylda!" she repeated, horrified. "Let go of me," she said after a pause. "What did she say?"

"Nothing."

"She talked about me, didn't she? Did she say anything bad?"

"Well – a few things."

Růžena burst into angry tears. "That damn woman! She never, never wants me to have anything! How can I help it if things go bad for them? She must have come only because ... because somehow she found out what you've been doing for me. If things were going better for them, she wouldn't give you a thought. It's so disgusting! She wants everything for herself ... for her children ... for those detestable children!"

"Don't talk about it anymore," Jiří entreated.

But Růžena went on crying. "She wants to spoil everything for me! The minute I start to have a little better life, there she is slandering me and depriving me ... Tell me, do you believe her insinuations?"

"No."

"Well, I don't want anything except to be free! Don't I have a right to be a bit more happy? I want so little, I've been so happy, Jiří, and now she comes along – "

"Don't worry," he said, and he went to light the lamp. Růžena stopped crying. He looked at her, scrutinized her, as if he were seeing her for the first time. She was looking at the floor, her lips were trembling; how pretty and youthful she was! She had on a new dress, new silk stockings, and new gloves stretched almost to the point of splitting ... Her small, nervous fingers picked at the worn upholstery on the sofa.

"Excuse me," he said with a sigh, "I have some work to do."

Obediently, she rose. "Oh, Jiří," she began, but she didn't know how to continue. Her hands clasped to her breast, her lips pale, she gave him an agonized glance and just stood there, the image of fear. "Don't worry," he said, and he sat down at his desk.

The next day he sat over his papers, trying to settle into a smooth, unconscious, mechanistic mode of work and forcing himself to go faster and faster, but all the while he was working, a small fissure of pain had opened and expanded. Růžena came at twilight. "Go on with your work," she whispered, "I won't disturb you." She sat down quietly on the sofa, but he felt as if her vehement, vigilant eyes never left him.

"Why didn't you come see me?" she finally burst out. "I was home all day." He sensed a confession in this, and it touched him. He laid down his pen and turned to her: she was dressed in black, like a penitent, and paler than usual; her hands were folded in her lap and even from a distance they appeared to be cold and pitiable. "It feels almost like winter in here," he muttered apologetically, and he tried to converse as usual, without touching on the previous day's events. She replied like a grateful child, sweet and submissive.

"About Tylda..." The words suddenly escaped her lips. "The reason things are going so badly for them is that her husband's a fool. He co-signed for someone and then he had to pay ... It's his own fault, he should have thought of his children, but it's as if he doesn't understand a thing! He had a salesman who robbed him, yet he goes on trusting everybody ... Did you know they're bringing charges against him for insolvency?"

"I don't know anything." Jiří saw that she had been thinking about this all night long, and he felt somewhat ashamed. Růžena was oblivious to his quiet resistance; her fighting spirit took over, and carried away by her zeal she immediately produced her highest card: "They wanted my husband to help them out, but he got the story and just laughed at them ... They say that giving money to them is like throwing it away: they're three hundred thousand in the red. A man would be crazy to put a single heller into that company; he'd lose it all."

"Why are you telling me this?"

"So you'll know." She forced a lighter tone into her voice. "The thing is, you're so good-natured you'd probably let yourself be swindled out of everything."

"You're very kind," he said, not taking his eyes from her. She was tense as a bowstring, burning with the desire to say still more, but his scrutiny made her uneasy. She was afraid she'd gone too far, so she asked if he had found her any work and said that she did not wish to be a burden to *anyone*, that she had cut her expenses, that she didn't need such an expensive apartment ... Now, he thought, perhaps now she'll offer to keep house for him! He waited with a pounding heart, but she began talking about something else altogether.

The next day he received the following letter from Tylda:

Dear Jiří,

I am sorry that we parted in such a state of misunderstanding. If you only knew everything, I am sure you would read this letter differently. We are in a desperate situation. If only we could pay back fifty thousand now we would be saved, because our plant has a future and in two years it will begin to pay. If you were to lend us this sum, we would give you our guaranty. You would be a partner in the business and have a share of the profits as soon as it starts to pay. Come to our plant and you will see for yourself that it has a future. You will get to know our children too, and see how nice and good they are and how eager to learn, and you will not have the heart to ruin their whole future. At least do it for the children, because we share their blood, and Karel is already big and smart and has a great future. Forgive me for writing you like this, we are extremely upset, but have faith that you will save us and that you will like our children, because you have a kind heart. Be sure and come.

When little Tylda is grown up, she will be glad to be a housekeeper for her uncle, you will see what a dear girl she is. If you don't help us, it will be the death of my husband and the children will be beggars. I hope you are well, dear Jiří, from your unfortunate sister Tylda.

P.S. In regard to Růžena, you said that I told lies. The next time my husband comes to Prague he will bring you evidence. Růžena does not deserve your assistance and magnanimity because she brings shame on us. She had better go back to her husband, he will forgive her, and she shouldn't be eating the bread of innocent children.

Jiří flung the letter aside. He felt bitter and nauseous. From the unfinished work on his desk a forlorn emptiness seemed to blow up into his face, and a heavy lump of disgust rose in his throat. He abandoned it all and went to see Růžena. He was already at the top of the stairs, in front of her door, when he dismissed the idea, went down the stairs, and began trudging aimlessly through the streets. In the distance he saw a young woman in furs clinging to a lieutenant's arm; he ran after them like a jealous lover, but it wasn't Růžena. He saw the woman's bright eyes, heard the laugh on her rosy lips; she was radiating, ringing with happiness, full of trust and joy and beauty. He returned home at last, weary. On his sofa lay Růžena, in tears. Tylda's open letter lay on the floor.

"That miser!" She was fiercely sobbing. "And not the least bit ashamed! She wants to rob you, Jiří, rob you of everything. Don't give her a thing, don't believe a word she says! You have no idea what a crafty, tight-fisted woman she is. Why is she persecuting me? What have I ever done to her? For the sake of your money, to ... to disparage me that way! It's all ... all because of your money. It's absoutely disgraceful!"

"She has children, Růžena," Jiří softly observed.

"Nobody forced her to," she exclaimed harshly, choking with sobs. "She's always robbed us, all she cares about is money! She married for money, and when she was little she bragged about how rich she'd be ... Well, she's disgusting, vulgar, foolish – tell me, Jiří, what is there in her? You know what she was like when things were going better for them – fat, snooty, hostile ... And now she wants to ... to take it out on me ... Jiří, are you going to let her do it? Would you turn me out? I'd rather drown myself than go back!"

Jiří listened with head bowed. The girl is fighting for everything, for her love, for her happiness; she's weeping with rage, her voice is crying out in fierce hatred of everyone else, of Tylda and even of him, who could take everything from her. Money! The word stung Jiří like a whip whenever she said it, it struck him as shameless, filthy, offensive...

"...It was like a miracle to me when you offered me money. It meant freedom to me, and everything! You offered it, Jiří, all by yourself, and you shouldn't have offered it at all if you meant to take it away. – Now, when I rely on it..."

Jiří was no longer listening. From a distance he heard accusations, exclamations, sobbing ... He felt immeasurably demeaned. Money, money – did it have only to do with money? God in heaven, how had it come about? What had coarsened the careworn, motherly Tylda? Why was his other sister wailing? Why had his own heart coarsened and become tired of it all? What had money to do with it all? In an odd way he felt a strange readiness, almost a desire to hurt her by saying something cruel, demeaning, imperious...

He rose, feeling more at ease. "Wait," he said coldly. "It's *my* money. And I," he concluded with a lordly gesture of dismissal, "shall think it over."

Růžena jumped up, her eyes filled with alarm. "You – you..." she stammered. "But of course ... that's understood ... Please, Jiří, perhaps you didn't understand me ... I didn't mean..."

"That's enough," he broke in. "I said I'd think it over."

A flash of hatred blazed in Růžena's eyes, but she bit her lip and went out with her head bowed.

The next day a new visitor was waiting in his room: Tylda's husband, an awkward, red-faced man whose manner displayed indecisiveness and a dog-like submissiveness. Choking with shame and fury, Jiří refrained from sitting down in order to force his visitor to stand.

"What do you want," Jiří stated in the tone of an official.

The awkward man trembled, but managed to say: "I ... I ... that is, Tylda ... has sent some documents ... that you asked for..." and he hunted feverishly in his pockets.

"I certainly did not ask for any papers." And Jiří waved them away. There was a painful pause.

"Tylda wrote to you, brother-in-law..." the unfortunate factory owner started to say, now redder than before, "she wrote that our business ... in short, if you'd like to participate..."

Jiří purposely let him flounder.

"The fact is ... things aren't all that bad, and if you wanted to participate, in short, my line has a future and ... as a partner..."

The door opened softly and there stood Růžena. She froze when she saw Tylda's husband.

"What do you want?" Jiří asked sharply.

"Jiří," Růžena gasped.

"I have a visitor," Jiří remarked, and then he turned back to his guest. "I beg your pardon."

Růžena did not stir.

Tylda's husband began to sweat with fear and shame. "Here are ... please ... The evidence, letters her husband wrote to us and other papers ... intercepted..."

Růžena leaned against the door. "Show me," Jiří said. He took the letters and made a pretense of reading the first one, but then he crumpled them all in his fist and brought them over to Růžena. "Here you are," he said with a malevolent smile, "and now excuse me. And don't go to the bank to draw anything out; you'll have made the trip in vain."

Růžena withdrew without a word, her face ashen.

"Well now, your factory," Jiří continued hoarsely, closing the door.

"Yes, the prospects are ... of the very best, and if there were capital ... that is, of course, without interest..."

"Listen," Jiří brusquely interrupted, "I know that you're to blame, I've been informed that you are not prudent or – or even accommodating – "

"I'd do everything in my power," Tylda's husband stuttered, gazing at him with dog-like eyes, which Jiří evaded.

"How can I have any confidence in you?" he asked.

"I assure you that ... I would highly value ... and do everything possible ... We have children!"

Jiří's heart was racked with frightful, painfully embarrassing compassion. "Come back in a year's time," he finally said, holding on to the last vestige of his shattered will.

"In a year's time ... God..." Tylda's husband gasped, and his pale eyes filled with tears.

"Goodbye," said Jiří, extending his hand.

Tylda's husband did not see the proffered hand. He went to the door, stumbling over an armchair, and groped through the emptiness for the doorknob ... "Goodbye," he said in a broken voice from the doorway, "and ... thank you."

Jiří remained alone, the sweat of tremendous impotence on his forehead. He spread his papers out on his desk and called the landlady; when she came, he was pacing the room with both hands pressed to his heart, he had already forgotten what he had wanted from her.

"Wait," he called as she was leaving. "If my sister Růžena comes here today ... or tomorrow, or at any time, tell her that I'm not well, and that ... I would rather not see anyone."

Then he stretched himself out on his old sofa and fixed his eyes on some new cobwebs, which had been added to those in the corner above his head.

The Bully

THE BOOKKEEPING DEPARTMENT, lit up like an operating room by its score of electrical fixtures, rumbled and shook with the roar of the factory, but since it was drawing near to six o'clock, the clerks were already getting up and washing their hands. Suddenly the in-house telephone jangled; a bookkeeper lifted the receiver and heard a single word: Bliss. He put down the receiver and winked at a young man who, leaning against the office safe, gold fillings agleam, was chatting with a couple of typists. The young man displayed all his teeth, tossed his cigarette aside, and left.

Taking three steps at a time, he bounded up to the second floor. In the anteroom, no one. Bliss shifted from one foot to the other, coughed, and then made his way through the double doors into Pelikan's private office. He saw the factory's general manager standing at Pelikan's desk the way a soldier stands when reporting for orders. "'Scuse me," Bliss muttered, and he started to withdraw. "Stay!" the command flew after him. The general manager was suffering from a tic that caused one whole side of his face to twitch, so distraught was he from full-bore attentiveness. Pelikan, who was writing, spoke brusquely out of one corner of his mouth while simultaneously biting on his cigar with the other. Suddenly he threw down his pen and said: "Tomorrow you'll announce a lock-out."

"That means a strike," the general manager observed with a frown.

Pelikan shrugged his shoulders.

The general manager's face twitched again; evidently he had much on his mind. Bliss, meanwhile, was discreetly looking out the window, to give the impression that he wasn't really there. He knew exactly what was going on; for a year now he had observed the great Pelikan fighting for his life. Day by day, German competition was killing this huge, roaring factory, and tomorrow it might well fall silent for good. Do what you do, the Germans were still thirty percent cheaper. A year earlier, Pelikan had expanded the factory and invested an insane amount of money in new machinery in order to reduce production costs; he had bought new patents which, he calculated, would increase production by one-half. It had not increased at all; worker resistance had made itself felt. Then Pelikan had pounced upon these new enemies, brutally attacked the shop stewards and ousted them from the work force. This provoked two unavailing strikes. Eventually, he raised wages and saw to it that bonuses were provided. Outlays rose preposterously, yet the amount of work done continued to decline; the silent enmity between workers and owner broke out in open combat. The week before, Pelikan had called the shop stewards together and offered the workers a share in the profits; he was choking with hatred the entire time, but he said some very beautiful things nonetheless: increase production, show a little good will, and the factory will be half yours. The shop stewards rejected the offer. Very well then, a lock-out. Bliss knew that Pelikan only wanted some breathing space, that he did not feel beaten yet.

"That means a strike," the general manager tried again.

"Bliss!" Pelikan shouted, as if he were calling an amiable dog, and he went back to his writing.

The general manager took his leave, hesitating as if he still expected to be called back, but Pelikan paid him no attention.

Bliss leaned against a cabinet and waited; he smiled at his glossy boots, his fingernails, the pattern of the carpet ... His soft Jewish eyes blinked like those of a contented cat, lulled half to sleep by the warmth and the whisper of pen on paper.

"You're going to Germany," Pelikan announced, without looking up from his writing.

"Where to?" Bliss smiled.

"To our competitors. To have a look at... You know what to look for."

Bliss was flattered. He was an industrial spy, born to gather intelligence. Had a statesman appeared and made use of his easy elegance, his breathtaking audacity, and his feminine eyes, Bliss could have served any political or traitorous cause; as it was, he prowled all over the continent, drinking in through his smiling, half-shuttered eyes the secrets of industrial establishments, products, patents, and markets, in order to sell them to their rivals. He was curiously, gratefully devoted to Pelikan, who had discovered something special in the wretched, poverty-stricken Polish refugee he had once been, and set him on his feet. It was just a matter of playing a trick or two on the German competition; it was the first time Pelikan had required such a service from him.

"To Germany," Bliss repeated, giving his gold-filled smile. "No further?"

"If you have the opportunity, why not?" Pelikan seemed to chew the words. "But be back soon."

With inaudible footsteps Bliss walked to the window and looked out. Its great windows lit up, the now silent factory looked like a glass palace.

Pelikan went right on writing.

"I saw your wife this morning," came a strained, unsmiling voice from the direction of the window.

"Is that so," Pelikan remarked. The whisper of his pen suddenly stopped, as if in anticipation.

"She went to Stromovka Park," Bliss said without turning around. "She got out there and took the ferry to Troja. Waiting for her at the palace was..."

"Who?" Pelikan asked after a moment's silence.

"Professor Ježek. They walked along the towpath ... Your wife was crying. They parted at the ferry."

"What were they talking about," Pelikan said as if not asking a question.

"I don't know. He said: 'You must decide, it's become impossible, impossible like this – – ' She cried."

"And his manner – "

"Suggested intimacy. Then he said: 'Until tomorrow.' This was at eleven o'clock this morning."

"Thank you."

The pen once again whispered across the paper. Bliss turned around; he was smiling with his eyes half-closed, as before. "I'll go have a look at Sweden," he said with his golden grin, "they have something new at the steelworks there."

"Pleasant journey," Pelikan replied, and he handed him a check. Because it was obvious that Pelikan wanted to go on working, Bliss quietly slipped out.

But now it is silent in the office, as if Pelikan has turned to stone; waiting down below, beneath the window, his chauffeur is stamping his feet, numb with cold; the voices from the courtyard are coated with frost. An agreeable bell strikes the metallic hour of eleven. Pelikan locks his desk, grabs the telephone, and calls the number of his apartment.

"Is Madam at home?"

"Yes," the telephone replies. "Shall I call her?"

"No," and hanging up the receiver he sits down.

This morning, he repeated to himself, the words fixed in his mind. That's why Lucy had been so distracted, so ... God knows what ... When he came home at noon, she had been playing the piano; he listened from the next room, and it had never occurred to him that there could be anything in the world so terrible, so harrowing, so captivating, as the jubilation and sobbing in her music. She came to lunch pale, her eyes burning feverishly, and ate practically nothing; they said very little, as he had little to say to her of late, being too preoccupied with the strife at the factory, about which she knew nothing. After lunch she played again; she did not hear him come, nor did she hear him go. What dreadful strength, what desperate yet lofty resolve, what hidden intimations was she trying to find in this rolling torrent of notes; or with what was she intoxicated, with whom was she communicating in such fiery exaltation? Humbled, he bowed his head, thick as wood for, deafened by habit, his brain had learned to labor calmly amid the clanging of steam hammers and the piercing whine of lathes shaping iron. But this outcry of tenderness and pain that flowed out of the open piano was like a foreign tongue to him, one which he strove in vain to decipher. He waited for her to finish playing and rise from the piano; he would have called her to sit beside him on the sofa and he would have told her that he was exhausted, that what he was doing now was beyond a man's strength; he even refrained from lighting a cigar, lest the smoke trouble her. She had taken no notice of him, however, immersed as she was in another world, and eventually he looked at his watch and on tiptoe left to return to the factory.

Pelikan tensed his jaw, as though he were biting through something with all his strength. So Ježek then, the friend of his youth ... He remembered when he had introduced Ježek to his wife in their drawing room: a shaggy-haired, bushy-bearded, stoop-shouldered, bewildered and somewhat ridiculous scholar with a child-like look of wonderment behind his spectacles. He had nearly had to force the introduction on Ježek, and he did it with good-natured superiority, as if Ježek were some kind of new, comical toy. Ježek seldom came; he was shy, and in addition he was soon desperately in love with his young hostess. Pelikan had noted this with the pleasure of ownership, for he was proud of this thrilling, radiant woman with her intense, incomparable spirit. He had urged his friend to come more often, but Ježek, startled, had been evasive, had reddened with embarrassment and distress, preferred never to show his face again. Nevertheless, after a while he did return, more tormented, more reticent, more flustered than ever, happy and harrowed beyond measure when his hostess fished him out from amongst the other guests and pulled him over to the piano where, her white hands improvising on the keys, she talked, talked, talked, her radiant, slightly mocking eyes fastened upon the bushy head of the unhappy professor. Then, yes, even then Pelikan had not felt the least sympathy for this tormented man; he had amused himself royally at the expense of his friend. His sense of his own vitality was too powerful for him to have ever imagined...

His strong, ruminating jaw trembled. For the first time, Pelikan recalled that, indeed, it was not only at the house that these things happened. On rare occasions he accompanied his wife to concerts; he would sit there, happy to be next to her, thinking about his own affairs. And yes, there too, without exception, was Professor Ježek, his head bowed, leaning against a wall. God knows what the music was all about, but before long Lucy would tremble, grow pale and agitated, and then Ježek would raise his head and fix upon her, across the distance, a fiery, formidable gaze, as if all that music were pouring from his heart.

And Lucy would raise her eyes to look for him or close them in mute complicity; somehow they understood each other from a distance; they conversed in the transcendent notes that were overflowing the space. Then, on the way home, Lucy would not speak to him or answer him, she would cover her face with her fur collar, as if she were trying with all her might to hold on to a great moment created by the music and by ... God knows what else.

Pelikan put his head in his hands and groaned in anguish. To be sure, it was probably his own fault that matters had gone so far! Over the past few months he had indeed neglected Lucy, had indeed built a wall of silence around himself, but there was so much work, it was such a brutal struggle! He had to be at his office, at the bank, at a dozen board meetings; he needed money and the plant wasn't giving him enough; he needed money ... above all for Lucy. Lucy spent far too much; he had never told her so, but dammit, it took every second of his time to provide the wherewithal for her to live like that. Every second, every day. These last few months there had been moments he felt that something was going on, that something had already happened: why was Lucy sad and evasive, why had she grown pale, thin, and pensive, why had she shut herself off from him? He had seen this clearly and with deep concern, but he had shoved it all aside, almost violently. He had had other, more urgent matters to attend to ...

Suddenly he recalled Ježek's last visit with agonizing clarity. Ježek had arrived late, disheveled and jittery; he had sat apart and spoken to no one. The young hostess, blanching slightly, had approached him with a tremulous smile, then Ježek rose and, as if compelling her with his eyes, directed Lucy's steps to a window alcove. In hushed tones he said a few words to her there, Lucy bowed her head in a sorrowful "yes" and turned back to the other guests. It was then that Pelikan, under the thrall of a hunch, had determined to be on his guard. But there had been so much work, so many pressing concerns!

That delightful bell struck eight.

On the embankment at Troja, two people are standing. A beautiful woman is weeping, a handkerchief pressed to her lips, and bending over her is the bearded face of a man whose teeth are bared in grief and passion. He is speaking ... "You must, you must decide, it's become impossible like this..." This image tortured Pelikan with its brutal clarity. That's how far things have gone with them, he told himself, crushed, but good God, what should I do about it? Should I speak to Lucy or to him? And what am I to do if they say, Yes, we love each other? And why would I choose to hear that, when it's already ... so obvious ... His heavy hands were clenched tightly together on his desk. He expected to be seized by a paroxysm of rage, but instead all he felt was infinitely feeble, and this suffocated him. From this very desk he had resolved so many conflicts, from here he had commanded men and events, here he had parried and dealt so many blows with the formidable, instantaneous speed of a skillful boxer. And now, with horror and dark rage against himself, he felt incapable in every way of responding to this assault. In his weakness he measured the magnitude of his defeat. Something must happen, I will do something, he stubbornly repeated, but then he once again saw Lucy at the piano, her eyes blazing yet sullen, Lucy pale, recoiling, the beautiful woman on the Vltava embankment, and once again he was filled with the overflowing, unbearable torment of impotence.

At length he managed to stand up and go down to his car. The automobile was gliding quietly toward the center of Prague when all at once Pelikan's eyes reddened and he began shouting at the driver, "Faster! Faster!" He was breathing heavily, in the grip of a sudden rage; he needed to fly into people like a projectile, crush them, crash into some obstacle with a horrifying din. "Faster! Faster! You idiot driver, why are you swerving?" The astonished chauffeur unleashed the car at full speed; although the horn blared nonstop, shrieks could be heard: the car had almost run over a man.

He walked into his house, seemingly calm. Dinner passed in silent evasiveness. Lucy did not speak, she merely answered despondently, and after eating no more than a few bites she asked to leave. "Wait," said Pelikan, and with a lighted cigar he came over to look into her eyes.

Lucy's eyes, which she raised to meet his, suddenly filled with horror and resistance. "Let me go," she implored him, and she pretended to cough, as if she were choking on the smoke.

"You're coughing, Lucy," he said, not taking his eyes from her. "You must go away from here."

"Go where?" she whispered, alarmed.

"To Italy, to the sea, anywhere. You must go to a health spa. When can you go?"

"I won't go," she said vehemently. "I don't want to go anywhere! There is nothing the matter with me!"

"You're pale," he continued, with an probing, unswerving gaze. "It doesn't suit you here. You need two or three years of treatment."

"I will go nowhere, nowhere, nowhere," she burst out, terrified. "Please ... No, I won't go," she shouted in a voice filled with tears, and she ran from the room to keep from bursting out in a fit of weeping.

His shoulders slumped, Pelikan went to his study.

That night, in the antechamber to the master's bedroom, an old servant was waiting to prepare the evening bath. It was midnight and his master had not come. On tiptoe the servant approached the door to the study and listened: he heard heavy, regular footsteps from wall to wall, back and forth, endless. He went back to his servant's armchair and fell into a fitful sleep, waking now and then from the cold. At about half-past three he was startled out of a deep slumber and saw his master getting into a fur coat; he jumped up and began stammering a thousand apologies for having fallen asleep.

"I must go away," Pelikan interrupted him. "I'll be back this evening."

"Shall I call your car, sir?" the servant asked.

"That isn't necessary." Pelikan went on foot to the nearest railway station. There was a thin layer of ice on the sidewalks, and the streets were deserted, as those in a dream, desolate with the solitude of death. At the station a few people were lying asleep on the benches; others, freezing patiently in silence, sat huddled together like animals. At the "Departures" board Pelikan chose the first train leaving for anywhere and then went off to pace up and down the long corridor. Meanwhile, he forgot all about his train, chose another, and at last rode off in an empty carriage, having no idea of its destination. It was still night, so he turned off the light and settled himself in a corner. Everything dissolved in his immense fatigue. Wave after wave of weakness seemed to roll over him with every lurch of the train; he was mortally melancholic and yet somehow, at the same time, incredibly comfortable, as if for the first time in years he were profoundly passive, at rest. He did not resist, for the first time in his life he took a blow, and he felt with a peculiar sort of satisfaction how deeply, how mortally, the wound had penetrated. He had escaped from home in order to be alone for an entire day, to clearly and ruthlessly think through what was to be done about Lucy, how to resolve this horrible entanglement. But now he couldn't, and perhaps didn't even want anything other than to be adrift in his own suffering. Look, there is the first glimmer of the new day, people are waking up, regretfully abandoning their warm oblivion. And Lucy, Lucy is still asleep. He can see her wide pillow and beneath her cheek her tousled, strawberry-blonde ringlets; perhaps her cheeks are still damp with the tears that had streamed down them, the tears of a tired child. She is pale and beautiful – oh, Lucy! truly this weakness is nothing other than love! What manner of resolution did I expect to find? Truly, the only resolution is that I love you!

Do something! do something! do something! chanted each powerful stroke of the wheels. No, no, no, what can be done? Once again, love is the only thing to do! But if Lucy is unhappy, then something must be done to stop this. Do something! do something! Wait, Lucy, wait and I'll show you what love is; you must be happy, even if I... What manner of resolution? If I love her, then I must show it. What sacrifice is great enough to make for her?

Daylight began to spread over the countryside.

Quietly yet vigorously beats the heart of a man taken with great suffering. Lucy, Lucy, I will give you back your freedom;

follow your love and be happy. I will make this sacrifice; you are frail and beautiful – go, Lucy, and be happy. A constantly changing landscape slipped by outside the window; the hard, tenacious brow leaned against the frozen pane, the better to conquer the intoxication of suffering, but the heart, like a wide, gaping wound, had already accepted the peace that comes with resolution.

I will tell her this evening, Pelikan thought. I'll tell her that we will get a divorce. After a brief moment of alarm, Lucy will accept. Within six months she'll be happy; Ježek will take her on his arm, he will understand her better than I; and Lucy will...

Pelikan jumped up as if he'd been struck. How on earth could Lucy be happy being poor? Lucy, who is luxury itself, the definition of expensive whims. Lucy, who had been introduced to his wealth direct from the luxuries of her great mercantile family just prior to its downfall. Lucy, who from some instinct, passion, or inner need, out of naïveté or who knows why, must, must throw ridiculous sums of money about. In fact, all that Ježek earned would not be enough for a single gown! – But what of it, he argued to himself; after we divorce, I'll be paying alimony, and it will be a substantial sum...

Alimony? He suddenly recalled that she would be marrying Ježek, and then, of course, he would no longer be able to pay her alimony ... She can't possibly marry Ježek! She must remain single in order to receive money from me – But what would become of her? Her relationship with Ježek will necessarily take its course, and if they don't marry, it will become a more or less public ... a public concubinage. The circles in which she travels will make her only too aware of her situation: they will single her out and humiliate her. And she herself, proud, vehement Lucy, will make herself suffer most horribly. She was brought up with a definite outlook ... This must not happen! If we divorce, let her marry Ježek and learn to live in poverty, if she can, and I, thought Pelikan, I will offer Ježek money from time to time. – Then he felt ashamed of himself: this is something Ježek would never accept!

Fully confused, he jumped off at the next station. He had no idea where he was. He simply could no longer remain seated, he wanted to seek refuge across the black fields with their bands of hardened snow, to pull himself together. Daybreak was gray and damp. Scarcely had Pelikan left the station than he sat down on a stone by the high road and was lost in contemplation.

Perhaps I could say to her: I will go away, but I will leave you a dowry of sorts. So that you can live on the interest, you understand? And then let her marry! He quickly calculated how much he might be able to settle on her; it was next to nothing. In truth, he lived from day to day. No use, Lucy, you must economize; you will sew your own clothing, you will stand over a stove, night after night you will anxiously calculate how much you've spent that day...

He began shivering from the cold, and so he stood and walked aimlessly along the high road. Lucy, Lucy, what am I to do about you? I simply cannot abandon you to a life of poverty! No, that's not for you; oh, child, you don't know how ordinary and exhausting poverty is! Be sensible, Lucy, just think of all you're accustomed to having – – – Deep in thought, he grew warmer as his pace increased. He himself did not know how it came about, but he began to map out new plans, on a grand scale, a mammoth industrial venture that would throw millions of crowns his way. In a flash he saw the necessary actions, even the details; he calculated, broke all those who resisted, and through it all he shuddered from the thrill of the wild idea that perhaps Lucy would see everything in a different light if he lavished her with new and even greater riches. He stopped, breathless, at the top of a hill he had stormed in a single charge.

Neither the high road nor the train tracks could be seen now; all around were the undulating, russet-colored southern Bohemian hills rising above dark forests. He set out across the fields, frozen and immensely weary. At last he reached a village and tumbled into the nearest inn.

He was alone in the low-ceilinged taproom, served by a scruffy youth who brought him red tea with rum, which smelled like snuff. He drank the scalding abomination eagerly, in one gulp, and then slowly thawed back to life. No, Lucy will not suffer hardship; I exist, Lucy, to prevent that. Perhaps at this very moment she is awakening, she is getting out of bed, looking like a small child, and she is remembering yesterday's pain. He was so tired, he felt old, as if he were her father. You will not live in poverty, Lucy; nothing, nothing at all must happen, neither my words nor my eyes will indicate that I know anything. Live your luxurious dream, my love, do as you wish: in any event, I am away from home all day, and I can give you nothing but wealth. Have all that you wish, Lucy, and be happy; your proud heart will keep you from falling too hard...

Now and then, the youth would come in from the passageway, sullenly watchful. What was he doing here, this big gentleman in a fur coat, sitting there in the corner, twirling his empty glass in his fingers and smiling to himself like that? Why didn't he pay up and go about his business?

But it's impossible, Pelikan suddenly realized with a shock. Lucy already suffers from her relations with Ježek, suffers now, when there is barely anything more between them than idle talk! She already flees from me in guilty fear, weeping bitter tears. What might she do tomorrow or the day after, when things have gone further? Lucy, proud and ardent Lucy, could she even bear – infidelity? Her humiliation would suffocate her, and terror and disgrace would dig into the depths of her heart! Can I let that happen? Pelikan asked himself in anguish. Surely I can prevent it somehow...

"Aren't you going to pay?" the youth asked, scowling.

Pelikan pulled out his watch. It was eleven o'clock. "When is the next train to Prague?"

"Eleven-thirty."

"How far is the station?"

"An hour's walk."

"Can I get a car?"

"No."

Eleven o'clock. Now, precisely this moment is when they are to meet on the towpath at Troja. He saw the long stone terrace, Lucy turning toward the gray water and crying into her handkerchief. Perhaps at precisely this moment they are making their decision, frantically, senselessly, perhaps foolish Lucy is selecting her fate now, while I am here...

He sprang to his feet, bereft of reason: "You must find me a car!"

The youth left, grumbling. Watch in hand, Pelikan went out in front of the inn, his heart beating. God, was no one going to come? He was raging with impatience, and ten minutes passed without result. Finally, rattling toward him was a small, rustic wicker cart drawn by a white pony. Pelikan threw himself into it, shouting: "Hurry! I'll give you anything you want if you catch the train!" "Ya don't say," the aged driver replied, and he gently urged the pony forward.

Up hill and down jounced the cart. "Faster!" Pelikan would shout, and each time the old man would affably pull on the reins, and the little white mare would move her legs a little faster. Suddenly a powerful form rose up behind the old man, snatched the rains and whip, and lashed, lashed, lashed the pony's head, and legs, and back. Whipped until the blood ran, the poor beast dashed down the road. There was the railroad track already, but at a bend in the road one of the rear wheels collided with a milestone, the stone was pried from the ground, and the cart turned over on its side, its rear wheel breaking like

a toy's. Pelikan shouted with rage, punched the pony on the
jaw, and in his fur coat he galloped over to the station. The
train was just pulling in.

"Do something, do something, do something," chanted
each stroke of the wheels. In the overcrowded carriage, streaming with sweat, Pelikan stamped his feet and clenched his fists
in a raging fit of impatience. How slow, slow, slow it is, opposed to human will! Stations moved slowly from ahead to
behind; tree-lined avenues unwound, a small bridge, a forest –
one thing after another, telegraph poles – – – Pelikan yanked
open the window and looked directly down under the wheels of
the train; here, at least, the endless strip of gravel and crossties
rushed along drunkenly, furiously, with blind speed, as in a
feverish dream.

Prague! Pelikan ran from the station and took a cab
straight to Ježek's building. Breathlessly he rang at the door.
"The professor's not at home," the landlady announced, "but
he'll be coming back soon from lunch, around two-thirty
perhaps..."

"I'll wait," Pelikan muttered, and he sat down in Ježek's
room.

Three o'clock had long since struck and four o'clock drew
near, but Ježek had not returned. It began to grow dark in the
room. Pelikan was panting as if someone were chasing him.
Perhaps he had come too late. Finally, long past four, the door
flew open and Ježek stood on the threshold; he saw Pelikan and
froze.

"You ... waiting here," he said in what could hardly be
called a voice. "But you went away!"

Pelikan suddenly regained his poise. "How do you know
that I went away?" he asked coolly.

Ježek realized that he had tripped over his tongue; he
flushed crimson and his forehead grew damp with anxiety, but
he said nothing.

"I'm back now," Pelikan began after a moment, "and I want to set some things straight. Allow me to smoke."

Ježek's heart was pounding so hard, he felt it must be audible, and he drummed his trembling fingers against the table. The tiny flame of the match lit the hard mask of Pelikan's face, with its half-closed eyelids and bully's jaw.

"To be brief," Pelikan stated, "this must come to an end, do you understand? You will ask to be transferred."

Ježek still said nothing.

"My wife must be left in peace," Pelikan continued. "I trust that you will not have the audacity to write to her ... from the next place you are employed."

"I won't go away," Ježek proclaimed, his voice quivering. "Do as you please, but I'm not going. Oh, I know you look on it as... You don't know what has happened! You don't understand at all..."

"I understand nothing," said Pelikan, "except that it must come to an end. Nothing, nothing ... can come of this. You must go away."

Ježek leaped to his feet. "Give her back her freedom," he said passionately, "release her, release her from your golden cage! I don't ask you for myself, but take pity on her! For once in your life, have a heart! Don't you realize that she cannot endure you, that she is desperate in your presence? Why must you keep her bound to you? You two haven't a single thought in common, not a single interest! Tell me, have you anything to talk with her about, anything at all to give her other than ... money?"

"... No," came the reply from out of the darkness.

"Give her back her freedom! I know ... she knows that you may be fond of her, in your way, but... and then these past few months ... You've been so distant! If only you'd give her a divorce!"

"Let her ask for that herself."

"Why can't you understand? She doesn't have the courage, she can't ask you for it herself ... You're so generous to her! But you don't understand her, you don't know how sensitive she is; she would rather die than tell you ... She's so very delicate and ... dependent! She couldn't bring herself to... But suppose you were to say to her yourself that you were setting her free! It's a question of her happiness ... Pelikan, I know you're not accustomed to talking about love; for you, it's probably just so many words ... you can't understand a woman like that! And you're not even happy yourself! Tell me, what do you get from her? What use is she to you? You merely torture her with your gifts ... Don't you realize how horrible it is?"

"You would marry her, then?" Pelikan remarked.

"I don't know – God, how willingly," Ježek burst out with the immense relief of hope. "If only she'd consent! I would think of nothing but her happiness ... If you knew how we understand each other! If that's what she decided," he said, nearly weeping with joy, "I would do anything for her ... It's as if I've lost my senses, I breathe for her ... You don't know ... I had no idea that it was possible to love someone so much!"

"How much do you make?"

"What?" Ježek asked.

"What's your income?"

"As to that," Ježek stammered in bewilderment, "you know it isn't much ... But she would economize, we've already talked it over ... If you knew how unimportant money is to us! You don't understand, Pelikan, that there are other, greater things ... Money makes no difference to her! You see, she doesn't even want to talk about how it will be ... later. In fact, she's absolutely contemptuous of money!"

"But how do you feel about it?"

"Me? Yes, you're a different breed, you can think only of material things – – Lucy is so much above you! She wouldn't take a pin of yours with her, if you let her go. In fact, I would-

n't want her to, do you understand? It would be an absolutely new life for her..."

The glowing red tip inched farther along the cigar. "What a pity," Pelikan said. "I would gladly listen to you longer, but I must be off to the factory. So listen, Ježek!"

"The truth is, your wealth keeps her bound."

"Yes. Consequently, you will ask for that transfer. Cheers, Ježek. And if you come to our apartment again, I'll have you thrown off the premises. As long as you're still in Prague, don't be surprised if you find yourself being followed. And don't walk on the towpath, if you don't want to be thrown in the river. You will not speak to my wife again."

Ježek was breathing with difficulty. "I'm not leaving Prague!"

"Then she will. If you want to take matters that far ... But you will not see my wife again. Cheers."

When the landlady came down from the top floor a few minutes later, she found the gentleman in the fur coat seated on the stairs.

"Don't you feel well?" she asked with concern.

"Yes ... no..." the gentleman said, as if he were only just waking up. "Would you be so kind as to call me a cab."

She ran for a cab, and as he clambered into it, it occurred to her that he was drunk probably. Pelikan gave the driver his address, but after a few minutes he tapped the man on the shoulder: "Turn around. I'm going to the factory."

The Shirts

THOUGH HE WANTED TO THINK about other, infinitely
more important matters, an unpleasant thought kept
coming back: that his housekeeper was robbing him. She
had been with him so many years, and by now he was entirely
out of the habit of concerning himself with his personal
belongings. There stood his wardrobe; each morning he opened
it and took a clean shirt from the top of the pile. From time to
time, Johanka would come and spread a tattered shirt before
him, declaring that they were all that way, and that Sir needed
to buy new ones. Very well, Sir would then go out and buy half
a dozen shirts at the first store he came to, with the dim
recollection that he had bought something or other there not too
long before. It's odd, he thought, that goods are so badly made
these days. It was the same with collars and ties, boots and soap
and the thousand and one things a man needs even when he's
a widower. Everything must be renewed in the course of time,
but on an old man everything somehow grows aged and shabby
right away, or else goodness knows what was happening with
them: he was constantly buying new things, yet it sufficed
merely to open the wardrobe to see that swinging from the
hangers were numerous items of clothing so worn and faded
that you couldn't tell when they had been made. But after all,
there was no need to be concerned: Johanka saw to everything.

Now, for the first time after all these years, it entered his
head that he was being systematically robbed. It happened like
this: that morning he had received an invitation to a banquet
given by some society or other. Good heavens, for years he
hadn't been anywhere at all, and his circle of friends was so
small that the unexpected invitation utterly bewildered him; he
was immensely pleased, but also a bit panicky. The first thing

he did was begin searching to see which of his shirts would be sufficiently splendid; he pulled them all out of the wardrobe, but there was not one which wasn't frayed at the cuffs or around the buttons. He called Johanka and asked whether he didn't have some more presentable shirts somewhere.

Johanka gulped, and then after a pause declared sharply that Sir needed to buy new ones anyway, that there was no point in mending them, they were no better than cobwebs ... Although he had the vague impression that he had bought some not too long ago, he wasn't sure and therefore said nothing, and at once began putting on his coat to go shopping. But having already started on "tidying things up," he pulled some old papers out of his pockets to see if he should save them or toss them out. Among them was the last bill for shirts: paid on such and such a date. Seven weeks ago. Seven weeks, half a dozen shirts. That was his moment of revelation.

He did not go out to the store, but stayed in the room thinking back on his many, so many years of solitude. Johanka had kept house for him since his wife's death, and never, not even for a moment, had there been the least suspicion or mistrust, but now the uneasy feeling came over him that he had been robbed the entire time. He glanced about him. He couldn't say what was missing, but he suddenly noticed that the room was empty, downright desolate, and he tried to remember whether there hadn't been more things here, more familiar things in the room, more of everything ... Uneasy, he opened the wardrobe, in which dresses and linens belonging to his late wife had been kept in her memory ... A few worn, threadbare items were there, but all breath of the past was gone from them. Heavens, the number of things his wife had left behind when she died! What had become of them all?

He closed the wardrobe and forced himself to think about other things, the banquet that evening, for instance. But the past few years returned with persistence. They seemed to him now more dreary, bitter, and miserable than when he was living through them; it was as if all at once they had been despoiled, as if they now exuded a more desolate anguish. To be sure, he had been content at times, lulled as if in sleep, but now, appalled, he understood it as the slumber of an isolated man whom strange hands had robbed of even the pillow beneath his head, and in his heart there opened up a more intense pain than any he had known since the day ... the day he had come home from the funeral. He suddenly felt old and weary, like one to whom life has been too cruel.

One thing, however, he couldn't fathom: why would she steal my things? What would she do with them? Aha, he suddenly remembered with a certain malicious satisfaction, that's it! She has a nephew somewhere whom she loves with the foolishness of a doting aunt. Haven't I had to listen to non-stop twaddle about that prize blossom in the flowering of the human race? She's even showed me his photograph – curly hair, upturned nose, and an exceptionally impertinent moustachio – but she was wiping her eyes with pride and emotion. So that's where all my things have strayed, he said to himself! – He was seized by a horrible rage. Running to the kitchen, he shouted at Johanka something on the order of "you damned old witch!" and then bolted off, leaving her appalled, tears streaming from her eyes, which were round as the eyes of an old sheep.

He did not speak to her again the rest of that day. She sighed as if mortally offended and banged around every household item that came to hand; she didn't have the least idea what had happened. In the afternoon he embarked on a complete overhaul of his wardrobes and drawers. It was terrible: he remembered first one thing and then another which he had at once time possessed, various family heirlooms which now seemed to him especially precious. Today there was nothing, nothing, none of them were left. Like the aftermath of a fire. He could have broken down and wept with anger and loneliness.

He was sitting in the midst of pulled-out drawers, out of breath, covered with dust, holding in his hand the one solitary relic that remained: his father's beaded coin purse, now with holes at both ends. How many years must she have been looting if nothing at all was left? He was nearly beside himself with fury; if he had come across her at that moment he would have slapped her face. What shall I do with her? he asked himself, shaking with emotion. Chuck her out on an hour's notice? Turn her over to the police? But who would cook for me tomorrow? I could go to a restaurant, he decided, but who will heat the water and light the fire for me? With a supreme effort he dismissed these concerns: I'll think it over tomorrow, he assured himself, something will turn up, it's not as if I were dependent upon her! Nevertheless, the problem weighed on him more heavily than he cared to admit, but a sense of injustice and the necessity of punishment buoyed him up the way courage does.

When twilight came, he pulled himself together enough to find Johanka and say to her, indifferently: "There are a few places you need to go." He then enumerated some complicated and lengthy errands of a somewhat questionable nature which, he said, had to be taken care of at once and which he had very painstakingly concocted. Johanka said nothing, but set off with the air of a martyr. At last the door slammed behind her and he was left alone. Heart thumping, he stole to the kitchen on tiptoe and then hesitated: he was overcome with fear and shame, and felt that he could never bring himself to the point of opening her cupboard; he felt like a thief. But just as he thought about giving up the whole idea, it simply happened: he opened the door and went in.

The kitchen literally shone with cleanliness. There stood Johanka's cupboard, but it was locked, and there was no sign of a key. This discovery only hardened him in his resolve; he tried to force the cupboard with a kitchen knife, hacking away at it, but the cupboard wouldn't open. He pulled out every drawer in search of a key, and he tried each of his own keys, until at last, after half an hour of raging, he found that the cupboard wasn't locked at all, that it could be opened with a button-hook.

Carefully folded and beautifully ironed, clothing lay in separate compartments. And right there on top lay his six new shirts, still tied with the blue ribbon from the shop. In a cardboard box was his wife's brooch with the dark amethyst, his father's pearl cufflinks, his mother's portrait on ivory – great heaven, what good is that to her? He pulled everything out of the cupboard: he found his socks and collars, a box of soap, toothbrushes, an old silk waistcoat, pillowcases, an old officer's pistol, any number of things, even a smoke-stained and truly useless amber cigarette holder. But these were mere leftovers, the greater portion had evidently been transferred long ago to the curly-haired nephew. The flush of anger passed, nothing remained but melancholy reproaches: So this is how it is ... Johanka, Johanka, how have I deserved this from you?

Item by item he carried his things back to his room and spread them out on the table; it was a thorough exhibit of every imaginable article. Whatever belonged to Johanka he threw back into Johanka's cupboard; he had even wanted to arrange them neatly and in order, but after a few attempts he retreated helplessly, leaving the cupboard wide open, as if it had been burgled. And then he began to fear that Johanka would return and that he would be obliged to have a serious talk with her ... The thought of it sickened him so, he began at once to dress. Tomorrow I'll give her a severe talking-to, he told himself; today it's enough for her to know that I've found her out. He picked up one of his new shirts; it was stiff, as if made of cardboard, and for the life of him he couldn't manage to fasten the collar. And Johanka would be coming back any moment...

He quickly slipped into one of his old shirts instead, despite the fact that it was frayed, and then the moment he was dressed, he slunk out of the house like a thief. For an hour he hung about the streets in the rain, until it was time to go to the banquet. He felt lonely at the gathering; he tried to enter into conversation with some old acquaintances, but lord knows how it happens, the years had come between him and other people; who would have guessed that we can barely understand each other now? But he held no grudges against anyone, he merely stood to one side and smiled, dazzled by the glare of lights and the hum of activity ... until, from some unknown source, new panic welled up inside him: what on earth must I look like? Look here, threads dangling from my shirt, and there's a spot on my dress coat, and as for my shoes, my God! He wished he could sink into the ground, and he looked around for somewhere to hide, but on all sides there shone the glare of brilliant shirtfronts – where could he possibly, inconspicuously, lose himself in the crowd? He was afraid to take a step in the direction of the door, lest all eyes be turned upon him. To his embarrassment he began to perspire. He pretended to be standing motionless, but all the time he was imperceptibly scuffling sideways so that, centimeter by centimeter, he could edge up to the door with no one being the wiser. But oh no, one old acquaintance, a classmate from secondary school, stopped to chat: that's all he needed! He answered the man distractedly, very nearly offending him. Alone once more, he breathed a sigh of relief and calculated his distance to the door. At length he escaped outside and rushed home; it was not yet midnight.

On his way home, he once again started thinking about Johanka. He slowed his pace and began to think through what he would say to her. With unaccustomed ease, long, powerful, dignified sentences came together, a complete discourse of stern judgment and ultimate mercy. Yes, mercy, because in the end he would forgive her. He would not turn her out into the streets. Johanka would weep and implore, then promise to mend her ways; he would listen in silence, unmoved, and at last he would say to her solemnly: Johanka, I will give you a chance to make amends for your ingratitude. Be honest and loyal; I ask no more of you. I am an old man and do not wish to be cruel.

He was so excited that before he realized it he was already home unlocking the door. A light was still burning in the kitchen. Ever so briefly he glanced through the curtains into the kitchen, and good heavens! What's that? Johanka, her face red and swollen with tears, was dashing about the kitchen and tossing her things into a trunk. He was terribly alarmed. Why the trunk? He tiptoed to his room, confused, distressed, dumbfounded. Was Johanka going away?

There on the table in his room lay all the things she had stolen from him. He touched each one, but he no longer took even the slightest joy from doing this. I see, he said to himself, Johanka has discovered that I've found her guilty of theft, and she expects to be dismissed on an hour's notice; that's why she's packing. Very well, I'll leave her with that idea ... until tomorrow, that'll teach her a lesson; yes, I'll talk with her in the morning. But perhaps ... perhaps even now she's coming to apologize! She'll burst into tears before me, fall on her knees, that sort of thing. Very well, Johanka, I don't wish to be cruel; you may stay.

He sat, still dressed in his evening clothes, to await developments. There was silence, unbroken silence in the house; he heard every step Johanka took in the kitchen, heard the angry slamming of the trunk lid, then silence. What was that? He sprang up in alarm and listened: a horrible, drawn-out howl, something not quite human, which trailed off into a series of hysterical sobs, followed by the sound of knees thumping to the floor and a thin wail. Johanka was weeping. He had, it's true, been prepared for something, but this was unexpected. He stood, his heart pounding, and listened to what was happening on the other side of the kitchen wall. Nothing, only weeping. She'll pull herself together and come asking for forgiveness.

He walked up and down the room to stiffen his resolve, but Johanka did not come. At intervals he stopped and listened; her weeping went on and on, relentlessly, uniformly, like howling. Such horrible despair was distressing to him. I will go to her, he decided, and I will say to her, "Let this be a lesson to you, Johanka. Stop crying and I'll forget all about it, but you must behave properly in the future."

Suddenly he heard forceful footsteps, the door crashed open, and there on the threshold stood Johanka, howling; it was dreadful to see her face so swollen with tears.

"Johanka," he gasped.

"How have I ... deserved ... this?" Johanka squeezed out the words. "Instead of appreciation ... As if I was a thief ... It's shameful!"

"But Johanka," he cried in alarm, "you've taken my things – all these things, look at them! Did you take them or not?"

But Johanka didn't hear. "What I have to put up with ... It's shameful! Rummaging through my cupboard like ... as if ... some kind of gypsy! To shame me so, me...! Sir shouldn't do such a thing ... You have no right to ... to insult me ... I'd never ... not to my dying day ... I'd never expect this to my dying day! Am I a thief, then? Me, me, some kind of thief?" she shrieked vehemently, in pain. "Am I some kind of thief? Me, from such a family? I never expected this, never, and ... never, ever deserved it!"

"But ... Johanka," he said, having cooled down somewhat, "just use your common sense: how did these things get into your cupboard? Is this yours or mine? Tell me, my good woman, is this yours?"

"I don't want to hear any of this," Johanka sobbed. "Lord God Almighty, the shame of it! ... As if I was ... a gypsy! ...

Rummaging through my cupboard ... This very minute," she shrieked, horribly agitated, "right this very minute I'm leaving. I'm not staying here till morning! No ... no..."

"But look here," he said, alarmed, "I don't want to turn you out. You will stay on, Johanka. As for what's happened, well, God save us from anything worse ... I haven't said a word to you about it. So stop crying!"

"Hire somebody else," said Johanka, choking on her tears. "I won't stay here till morning. As if a person was a ... a dog ... who'd put up with anything ... I won't," she burst out in despair, "not if you paid me thousands! I'd as soon spend the night on the sidewalk!"

"But why, Johanka?" he responded, baffled. "Have I hurt your feelings? Surely you can't deny that you..."

"No, you didn't hurt my feelings," Johanka cried in even more wounded tones. "It's not about hurting my feelings ... it's about rummaging in my cupboard ... like I was a thief! As if it was nothing ... What I have to put up with ... Nobody ever did anything like that to me ... it's shameful... I'm not ... I'm not some kind of tramp," she shrieked through a convulsive burst of tears, and then all at once she stormed out, banging the door behind her.

He was utterly confounded. This, a scene of repentance? What's going on? She steals like a jackdaw, no doubt of that, but now she's offended because I've caught her out; she's not in the least ashamed of being a thief, but when that's what she's called, she's hurt, as if I'm being cruel and petty ... Is the woman out of her mind?

But gradually he felt more and more sorry for her. You see, he told himself, everyone has a weakness, but you can't offend anyone more than when you discover it. How incredibly, morally sensitive we are about our faults! And how painfully and brittly delicate we are about our crimes! Just put your finger on someone's secret vice, and you'll hear nothing but shrieks of pain and indignation! Don't you see that in judging an offender, you're judging someone who feels offended?

From the kitchen came the sound of tears muffled by a down comforter. He wanted to go in, but the door was locked; he stood by it and tried persuasion, reproach, and consolation, but he was answered by nothing but louder tears. He went back to his room, grieving in helpless sympathy. There on the table lay the stolen articles: beautiful new shirts, a quantity of linen, mementos, and God knows what else. He stroked them with his finger, and they felt sad and full of sorrow.

Insulted

VOJTECH WAS SLEEPING SOUNDLY (on a November night, bed is a good place for a man to be) when suddenly someone knocked on his window with a stick. There was still a moment for the sleeper to finish his dream, in which the knocking played a decisive but confusing role, and then he woke. Again and then again! The sleeper pulled his eiderdown over his ears and resolved not to hear. The stick, however, drummed yet again against the glass, in a belligerent, peremptory manner. Vojtech bounded from his bed, opened the window, and saw on the pavement below a man whose coat had its collar turned up.

"What do you want?" he shouted, injecting into his voice the utmost irritation.

"Make me a cup of tea," answered a hoarse voice from below.

The sleeper, recognizing his brother, was now fully awake. The bitter cold of the night gripped his chest. "Wait a minute," he called down, then he turned on the light and hurriedly began to dress. While dressing, it occurred to him for the first time that he hadn't spoken to his brother for two years, since they'd quarreled over a legacy. He was so overcome with surprise by his brother's coming that he forgot to put on his shoes. He sat there, shoe in hand, shaking his head. Why had his brother come? Evidently something had happened to him, he decided, and threw on some clothes and rushed back to the window. But his brother was no longer standing there, he was walking away and had already reached the corner; perhaps he had found the wait too long. Vojtech rushed out into the hallway, opened the front door, and ran after him.

His brother was walking away at a rapid pace, without looking back. "Karel," Vojtech shouted as he ran; he was certain his brother heard him, but his brother wouldn't stop or even slacken his pace. So he ran full speed, calling excitedly, "Karel, what are you doing, Karel? ... Wait!"

Karel kept walking very fast. Vojtech stopped and stood there, shivering with cold, not fully dressed, dumbfounded. For the first time he realized that it was raining. Karel kept walking on, and then suddenly turned and came back just as fast.

For a moment Vojtech could not for the life of him think what to say to his brother. They hadn't been on speaking terms for two years. His brother was obstinate man. Yet there he stood, eyes flashing, biting his lip...

"So you won't give me a cup of tea." Karel, sullen and indignant, broke the silence.

"Of course I will, with pleasure," Vojtech gasped, relieved. "I only needed a moment to – Come back right away and I'll make you some."

"And yet..." Karel said bitterly.

In his eagerness, Vojtech's words came pouring out: "But good heavens. In any case ... you could have come long before this. Right away I'll – anything you like – If you want something to eat – I'd be glad any old time, just say the word."

"Thank you, just a cup of tea."

"I've got some bacon from Moravia, how about that? Or an egg – I don't even know what time it is! Karel, it's been ages since we've seen each other, hasn't it? Would you like some wine?"

"No."

"Whatever you'd like, just say the word. Well then, you see ... Careful, there's a step here!"

"I know."

At last Vojtech got him home. He laughed, chattered, offered this and that, made excuses – "An old bachelor, you know" – located some smoking supplies and cleared off a chair or two, hardly noticing that he was doing all the talking, but all the while, watchful, troubled, searching, he couldn't shake the thought that something must have happened to his brother.

Karel sat, frowning and preoccupied. An oppressive silence settled in. Then Vojtech asked, "Has anything happened to you?"

"No, nothing."

Vojtech shook his head. He hardly recognized his brother in such a state. He was reeking of wine and women. And yet he was a married man, he had a young wife, modest and pretty, mild as a lamb. For years he had sat at home, a prudent authoritarian, a domestic machine, a paragon of domestic virtues; strict, methodical, precise, and with an inordinately high opinion of himself. Once he had been seriously ill, and ever since that time he had instituted an amazingly hygienic, routine-oriented life, as if life itself could be redeemed day in, day out by orderliness and self-control. And now here he was, scowling, his sobriety clouded, like a man just awakening after making a night of it; here he was with an indescribable expression, as if straining, cruelly and with difficulty, to swallow something evil. It was obvious that something atrocious was going on inside him.

It was three o'clock in the morning. Vojtech clapped his hand to his forehead. "Good heavens, the tea!" he remembered, and with housewifely zeal he rushed off into the kitchen. He suddenly felt cold and, wrapping himself in a blanket like a granny, he boiled water over the blue flame of the burner, quite pleased to be occupied with something that required no thought. Setting out cups and sugar, he was calmed by the familiar clink of the tea set. He looked into the other room through a chink in the door, and there stood his brother, at the open window, as if he were listening to the roar of the Vltava's weirs, a vast yet steady voice that like a veil obscured the chill patter of the rain.

"Aren't you cold?" Vojtech asked anxiously.

"No."

Vojtech stood at the door, feeling sad and tense. Here on the one side, a quiet, snug lair, just now brought to life by the cheerful wheeze of the burner, ah, a dear little lair, a warm drink, the joy of being at home, the pleasure of being hospitable; and there on the other side, a wide-open window filled with the majestic voice of the river and the darkness – for perhaps the night itself is rolling over the Vltava weirs, such is its roar – and at the window a tall man is planted, oddly unfamiliar, oddly disturbed: your own brother, whom you don't even recognize. Vojtech stood in the doorway as though on the boundary line between two worlds: his own familiar world and his brother's unfamiliar one, which at that moment seemed uncommonly large and frightening. But he knew he would be initiated into it, that his brother had come to tell him something extremely important; he was afraid of this, downright scared, as he listened alertly, with microphonic attention, to the hissing of the burner and the vast roar of the river.

With motherly concern, Vojtech set the steaming tea on the table and said, "Now tell me whether you'd like something to eat." Before his brother knew it, he was back with bacon and crackers, urging his brother to eat, bustling about; his behavior was altogether feminine, like a kindly, solicitous aunt. Karel merely sipped at his tea and then, it seemed, forgot his thirst. "You see," he began, and then he stopped. He sat there with his face buried in his hands; he'd already forgotten what he'd wanted to say.

Suddenly he rose. "Listen, Vojto," he began, "I wanted to tell you ... that our quarrel was idiotic. Please don't think that the money was important to me. Perhaps this is what you thought. It doesn't matter to me, but it's not true. I only wanted things to be managed in an orderly way, and then ... I don't care this much about money," he shouted, snapping his fingers.

"Not this much. Not about money or anything else. I'll get by without any of it."

Vojtech's apprehensions thawed, outright melted away. Deeply moved, he burst into assurances that he hadn't thought about the quarrel for ages, that they'd both been at fault ... Karel didn't listen to him. "That's enough," he said, "I don't want to talk about it, and it's quite beside the point anyway. I only wanted ... to ask you," the words fells from his lips hesitantly, "to do something for me: to let my wife know that I've left the ministry."

"But why ... why?" Vojtech cried out in amazement. "Do you mean you're not going back to her?"

"Not just now, you understand? And perhaps not at all ... besides, it doesn't matter. She can go to her parents if she's lonely. All I want is peace and quiet. There's something I need to do, and I have this plan ... The details aren't important. The main thing is that I must be alone, do you understand?"

"I don't understand a thing. What happened at your office?"

"Nothing, it's idiotic. What happened there, what will happen there makes no difference to me at all! You don't think it bothers me, do you?"

"What is bothering you, then?"

"Nothing. It's entirely beside the point. I don't even think about it anymore. On the contrary, I'm happy, very happy, Vojto." And then suddenly, mysteriously, he turned to Vojtech: "Please, tell me the truth, be candid with me: Do you think I'm cut out to be a ministry official? What do you think?"

"I d-d-don't know," stammered Vojtech.

"What I mean is, knowing me at least a little from days gone by, do you think it could ever be enough for me? That I could be satisfied with it? Do I not have the right or should I not feel the ... need to live a completely different kind of life? Is that what you really think?"

"No," said Vojtech, reluctant and uncertain, trying to

comprehend with a single glance the whole of his brother's routine, serene, and circumscribed life, a life he'd sometimes envied, but a life in which he had never taken a close interest.

"Let's say that perhaps it looked that way," Karel continued. "Or that it was slumbering in me. You see, I myself never even knew, but now, Vojto, I know very well."

"But what is it that is slumbering in you?"

"Never mind." Karel brushed the subject aside and became lost in thought.

Vojtech waited a bit before speaking again. "Listen, Karel, something has happened to you, you're angry or hurt and ... and you're trying to convince yourself of something. First of all, tell me what happened to you. Perhaps it can be put right. Certainly it can. And as for your not going back to your wife or to your office, that's nonsense. You can't really be serious ... are you listening?"

Karel stood up and laughed. "That's enough," he said, and he began pacing the room. For the first time he looked around, stopped in front of pictures, noticed the objects placed here and there. – "Poor old Vojto," he jeered, "so this is where you live? All alone? And you have room enough here to live your whole life? Your whole life? Look, suppose you got married. Just like me! Suppose you had a nice wife. Someone to wait on you as if you were a tyrannical child. To make you her little boy because she has no children and is afraid of childbirth. As if you lived in a nest of pillows – like me! Why, you don't know what happiness is!"

"You're not being fair to your wife," Vojtech protested.

"Of course I'm being unfair," Karel retorted. "And more than that: I'm tired of her. Sick and tired of her. You can tell her that, but tell her also that I know how unfair I'm being. Tell her that she's been the model of an official's wife. Oh, God, it's an absolute crime! Think of it, she's been waiting for me all night! All night she's been stoking the fire, looking at the thermometer, setting the table and waiting. Just imagine, she doesn't suspect a thing yet. She's waiting even now, she's horrified, she's sitting on the bed, unable to understand ... Until in the morning you arrive and say, 'Madam, your husband has run away.'"

"I won't say that!"

"You must: 'He ran away because he became loathsome to himself. He became terribly tired of all he knew about himself. Just think, madam, suddenly he found in himself a soul he'd never known before, a worse soul, strange and furious, and he wants to make a fresh start with it. He cannot sleep with you any longer because your husband was a completely different person; he was a domestic fool, who drank warm beer and was loved by you!' Just tell her that, Vojto, you understand? Tell her, 'Madam, he hates warm beer, he even hates you, because last night he drank chilled wine and burned with desire and was unfaithful to you; he found a prostitute and he'll go back to her.' ... Oh, Vojto." Karel changed suddenly from official dictation to an urgent whisper. "It was awful at this girl's. If you could have seen the poverty! Good God, such wretched conditions! Her feet were soaking wet and cold as ice; it was impossible to warm them. I must go back there again because of that poverty, that misery. If you could see how she lives! It can't be remedied by charity, she drinks it all away. But someone should be with her..."

"Karel!" said Vojtech.

"Stop! Not a word," Karel protested. "It isn't only that. That's beside the point, really; at first I didn't even think about women. But tell me, Vojto, tell me if a man can return to his pillows and draperies after seeing such misery. You know what it's like at our place, Vojto; I could suffocate in it, out of shame and disgust. But that, of course, my wife couldn't understand. I know she's nice; please don't say a word, at least about that. I didn't intend to begin with this at all; it's only an example, and it didn't happen until afterwards."

"After what?"

"After I'd made a decision. Wait, you still don't know anything about it. It all began quite differently, it began ... while I was still an official. In short, in short, there was a row at the office – And I," Karel was so upset, he pounded his fist down on the table, "I was in the right, and that's an end to it!"

"What sort of row?" Vojtech cautiously asked.

"It was nothing, idiocy. Nothing worth talking about. Just the impetus. But when a man feels as if he's been trampled on and cannot, cannot defend himself ... As if you were garbage. So I stayed at work and went through the books and files, and they showed that I was obviously in the right. Someone else had made the error, but who? It's odd how little it matters to me now, but at the time I was writhing like a worm and had made up my mind to kill myself."

"Karel!" Vojtech shouted.

"You – you be quiet," Karel commanded like a drunk, pointing at him a trembling finger, "you're like that, too. I was wandering the streets the entire evening, because I didn't want to go home. I had repudiated myself. I was exhausted and I just wanted to go and get drunk. I came across a wine cellar, a disreputable place, I'd never seen anything like it: music and women and so much squalor – shockingly squalid. I've forgotten now who was sitting there with me; one girl had horrible fingers covered with sores, her nails were falling off; is that a symptom of syphilis, do you know?"

"Why do you ask?"

"Because she kept drinking from my glass – I couldn't stop her – but it doesn't matter anymore. Then there was a man I was talking to the entire evening; I don't know who he was. It seemed to me that they'd all come there just as I had, the clientele as well as the girls, all of them; that perhaps they too wanted to kill themselves because they were unhappy, and that's why they were there. It seemed to me that I had something in common with them, but in another, deeper way than with, say, my colleagues at the office; that I might suddenly start selling matches, and be filthy and old, and take the place of the matchseller there, or that my nails too might drop off painfully, that I too might become a prostitute or steal, just as they do every night. Imagine, Vojto: I got the idea that, while I was sitting there, the end of the world was happening outside and that nothing was left but that wine cellar and the people in it: whores, drunkards, street musicians, thieves, and sick people, and that this was humanity now. There were no more churches or palaces, no more philosophy or art, no glory, no nations, just that score of outcasts. Can you imagine such a thing?"

"Tell me more."

"There's nothing more. I simply thought about what I would do in a situation like that. What, for example, should I do with my documents, my position, and my worldly wisdom? None of these things would bring pleasure to any one of them, nor give them a realistic picture of a man's excellence, or his rejection; they wouldn't be an example or a picture of anything. If I were to play music in the streets, or weep, it would be a hundred or a thousand times better, do you understand?"

"Yes."

"So you see, Vojtech, that's why I've come to you, because I knew you'd understand how a new light had been thrown on my entire life. The life I'd been living was useless. It was of no value even to me, even to me. Perhaps it was of some use, possibly to the state, but the state is only a formality ... for example, the state is the tax on wine, but it's not the wine itself, nor a wine cellar, nor a mangy drunkard, nor a sickly barmaid; these are *facts*, you understand? A man must go by the facts, not merely lay down rules ... In short, I was suddenly disgusted with it all. It's true, Vojto, an official is a man who obeys and forces other people to obey, and that's all he does. A higher official, such as I was, has no idea whether people are sick or whatever. Disease, poverty, anything that disgusts, must be seen;

otherwise, you know nothing. But even if all you do is see it
and go on seeing it and nothing more, even then you're doing
a great service to mankind; it makes you unhappy, crazed, and
sick, and that is a great deal, far more than when you sit,
healthy and happy, among your pillows. That's how it is."

It was infinitely pleasant for Vojtech to sit and listen. All
bundled up, knees under his chin, huddled under a woolen
coverlet, he was like a child who is as much charmed by a
speaker's voice and gestures as by his words. "More," he said.

"More," Karel pondered. "What more is there? When I
decided I would never go back to the office again, it took an
enormous weight off my shoulders. My desire to kill myself had
already passed. On the contrary, I saw now that I should begin
afresh, that this was the start of a new life. That, I can tell you,
was such an amazing feeling, life had never seemed so beautiful
to me. I walked through the city again, not thinking at all about
what I would do, but all around me and even behind the walls
of the houses, I sensed something absolutely new. And precisely
because I found it so beautiful, I realized that I had arrived at
something both magnificent and true. You know, Vojtech,
inspiration is the greatest happiness of all. It can't be expressed
in words; rather, it's as if you were talking with God, or as if
the whole world, earth and stars and all humanity, yes, even
past generations, were all thinking your thoughts with you.
That's the kind of happiness this is. Then I met that girl and she
invited me home; I went so that I could determine, if possible,
whether life's amazing, superhuman beauty could survive even
in such ... such horrible conditions. And Vojto, would you
believe it? The farther I walked, the freer I felt. And when I saw
the misery in which she lived, it was as if I grew wings. If today
I saw all the appalling misery in the world, I would be still
happier and more certain of myself. There are an infinite
number of things I must learn, because this is what makes one
free. Are you asleep?"

"No."

"The more misery one sees, the more one has in common with the world. I have found a sense of commonality, of fellowship: it isn't sympathy at all, it's enlightenment and exaltation; it's not pity, but euphoria. In this state – " (thus he preached, standing with one arm outstretched; drunkenness, previously overcome by agitation, gripped him again with even greater force) – "you see each person's pain and discover each person's sickness and degeneracy, and feel them to be your own. You yourself are poor and miserable, a thief and a prostitute, a person drunk or in despair; you are what you see. And you long to bear all misery, every disease, to take all rejection upon yourself; you crave and thirst for this, in order to be sated. You will not give alms to the poor, because you do not right old wrongs; rather you will be poor yourself, in order to set things right you must be just as poor. You must be sick, drunken, goaded, insulted, muddied, degenerate. You must reach the pinnacle. You must reach the absolute pinnacle. You already know enough; forget it all, now you must learn. But, Vojto," he suddenly turned and said to his brother, with unusual fondness, "you'd like to go to sleep, wouldn't you?"

"No, not at all," Vojtech assured him.

"Go lie down, there's something I need to write. Go to sleep, please, you'd only be in the way."

"No, Karel," said Vojtech, "I won't sleep. But I will lie down, in order to keep out of your way; but afterwards I have something to tell you."

"All right, but do go to sleep," Karel repeated, seating himself at the table and burying his head in his hands.

Stretched out on the bed, Vojtech thought about what he would say to his brother. He was puzzled and sad; he searched for some especially kind words, words similar to a beaming smile. Considerate words, like those we say to an invalid. Something by which he could both cheer him up and repay him.

His eyes half closed, he observed his brother, bent over the table as if he were studying. He had always studied hard and so tenaciously. He had always had passionate yearnings, which he overcame by studying. He was so ambitious and headstrong. A hard drinker when young, who one day had altogether stopped drinking because he had made up his mind to. And he also made up his mind to get up at five o'clock in the morning. He would get up and study while Vojtech, hedonistic and warmth-loving as a cat, snoozed in his little corner. "Vojto, Vojto, get up, it's already seven o'clock." No sound from Vojtech, as if he hadn't heard, but all the time he would be listening to the scratch of pen on paper, delighted to have a living creature so close. Not for anything in the world would he have opened his eyes. He didn't want to interrupt his dream, but it wasn't really a dream (Vojtech smiled to himself), it actually happened to me when I was about fifteen: some seventeen-year-olds, Karel's classmates, take me to a wine cellar – wait a minute, it was Kislingr, and Dostalek too, he's dead now ... Then Vojtech hears a woman who usually sings on street corners: "And I am Esmeralda, true daughter of the south, Esmeralda, Esmeralda..." He's enjoying it, but he's afraid they'll kick him out; he makes himself small as he can, so no one will see him. He seeks shelter at a table and just watches the girl who brings around the wine. Now, with arms upraised, she's smoothing her hair and singing; now she's speaking to someone, bending down so that her face is close to his, one knee on a chair, look, below the other knee a red garter. Vojtech doesn't know which way to turn his eyes, he's ashamed of them, he is jealous and he watches ... And now she sees me, my God! She comes straight over to him, swaying a little; she leans right across the table, she looks at him from so close, with her strange, flashing pupils, hums a love song, and softly, sweetly, she laughs. Vojtech feels her moist breath on his lips and is nearly weeping with love and shame. He would like to say something, but he doesn't know what to say, nor does she, and so she merely whispers her love song and, with her luminous gaze, looks into his eyes from up so close. What does she want of me? Why doesn't she speak? Why, there aren't any boys here, but there's Karel, sitting and writing on a sheet of paper and saying to himself: you must study now. But Vojtech pretends not to hear; study as much as you like, he thinks, but now let me sleep.

When Vojtech awoke, it was broad daylight. He was astonished to find himself lying in bed half-dressed, then he began to remember and looked for Karel. Karel was asleep on the sofa. He looked worn, painfully exhausted, and he seemed older. Then quietly, so as not to wake him, Vojtech looked for what he had written during the night. He found a letter in a sealed envelope, tore it open, and read:

Honorable Minister:
Due to illness, I resign my position and request my release without pension.
K. N., former counselor

Vojtech shook his head and searched elsewhere. In the wastepaper basket were several crumpled, crossed-out, and torn sheets of paper. He smoothed them out and read:

Dear Sir,
Kindly compare the file which was taken from me yesterday with the appended document B3, file M-XXIII, and with the dictation of the Minister therein, and also with the copy of the letter of 17th September in same, which will prove that the erroneous decision was not my fault, for I obtained false material from the transcript. You will see for yourself, despite your youth, that the Minister unjustly...

At this point the letter was crossed out and crumpled, evidently in anger. The next sheet appeared to contain the beginning of an essay of sorts; there was only: If you wish to become a philosopher, you must...

But this sheet, too, was crumpled and torn, perhaps at the end of long, wakeful hours.

Vojtech carefully gathered together the pathetic sheets and, trembling with sorrow, he looked down at his sleeping brother. See, he is already gray at the temples, he is swollen about the eyes and seems ill. Vojtech scrutinized him carefully, then quietly finished dressing, locked the door behind him, and hurried to his brother's office.

He knew some people there, and it was easy for him to learn what had happened the previous day. In the afternoon the Minister had burst into the office, almost beside himself with rage. This is disgraceful, he bellowed from the doorway, whoever did this is either a fool or a scoundrel. Admittedly, he did not say it in precisely these words, but he hinted at something even worse. And who is supposed to have done this? he shouted, waving the draft of a document. Everyone was shaking with fear. Then Karel said, "That's mine," and would have liked to defend himself, but the Minister shouted, "Silence, sir!" and tore up the document and threw it on the desk of the youngest clerk in the office, his favorite. "Fix it!" And then he slammed the door behind him.

Everyone sat there, frozen in their places. Karel, pale and acting mechanistically, like a puppet, closed his desk and departed without a word. At five o'clock he returned and worked after everyone else went home. Not one of the others believed that he could have made such an error, but he didn't want to talk to anyone.

Almost by sheer force, Vojtech obtained access to the Minister, a terrifying, explosive man, and after half an hour he appeared in the doorway, crimson, exhausted, but with the light of victory in his eyes. The Minister himself accompanied him to the door in order to shake his hand once more. Vojtech flew home, and he found Karel sitting despondently on the sofa, limp with fatigue and enveloped in a circle of thought.

"Karel," he announced triumphantly, "you're to go see the Minister."

"I'm not going," said Karel.

"You'll go, because ... because he wants to apologize to you; that is, he asks that you come so that he can express his regret and – – his confidence in you. And his respect for you." Vojtech hastily recalled the words he had prepared beforehand.

"Why did you go there?" Karel asked. "It's useless anyway, I don't want to and – I want peace and quiet, Vojto. It's better for me that way. Leave me alone. Please. I have some immensely more important things to do right now..."

There was a disharmonious silence. Vojtech, in despair, bit his nails. At last, he said, "Then what is it you're going to do now? Tell me that."

"I don't know," Karel reluctantly said, and he began to pace the room.

Someone rang the bell. It was a chauffeur. "The Minister has sent his car for the Counsellor," he announced at the door.

Karel gave a start. Suspiciously, he searched his brother's eyes to see if he were by any chance playing a trick on him; he saw, however, only artless surprise.

Then something absurdly emotional flooded through him, the sort of feeling that overpowers a man when he receives some small, unexpected trifle. Tears came into his eyes; he flushed and turned to the window. Right outside the window gleamed the polished fittings of a splendid car.

"Well, then," he said, hesitantly. "I'll go."

He suddenly began to hurry, and Vojtech helped him with such elaborate and muddled haste that they scarcely had time to tell each other goodbye.

When Vojtech stepped to the window, the street was already empty. Because he felt sad and a bit lonely, he went off to announce to Karel's wife that her husband was coming back to her.

The Tribunal

THE TRIAL WAS HELD in a small train station. The man they brought in had been seized just as he delivered the final blow. He was young, pallid, drenched in a sweat of terror; blood was streaming from his lips, split open by the butt of a rifle, and he was smearing it over his face with horrendously gore-spattered hands, lacerated to the bone. He was a hideous, sickening sight; his entire body shook, he was filthy, wretched, and vile, all but inhuman.

The presiding officer questioned him. The man did not respond, not even to give his name. He merely cast his eyes about wildly, in a frenzy of anguish and hostility. Then some soldiers testified, loudly, with vindictive zeal. The case was perfectly clear: the man had done in a wounded soldier and stripped off his wristwatch. The presiding officer drummed his fingers on the desk where, only the day before, a telegraph key had clattered; there were no further questions. "In accordance with military law," the officer said, "I sentence this man to the firing squad. Take him away!" — The man had not grasped a single word; he allowed himself to be taken away, snuffling and wiping his lips with his blood-smeared hands. The trial was over.

The presiding officer unbuckled his saber and went outside the station for a breath of air. It was a moonlit night. In the marble light it seemed as if everything had been ossified. White road, white trees, pale meadows stretching as far as the eye could see. A translucent whiteness, a crystalline yearning, an endless, petrified tension. As far as the eye could see. A pale, petrified silence as far as the ear could hear. A pale, lifeless, icily peaceful night. No star gleams, nothing to give its assent; there is nothing, nothing but this icy glare.

The officer hangs his head. In the station's waiting room, the soldiers are snoring. With these warm, hearty snores, the darkness is protesting the splendor of the moonlit night; it is breaking the silence to overcome its anguish. But over there, on the other side of the rails, is the shed where the condemned man is confined, where it is dark and silent; there, the terrifying moonlight has only a slit to work its way through.

How the man had sweated, how his anguish had made the sweat pour out! The officer recalled that he had never lowered his gaze from the man's face. All at once a bead of sweat broke out, welled up, and ran down his face, then another, and another again. It was as if his forehead were shedding tears.

Has everything become lifeless under this chill hoarfrost of light? No creature stirring anywhere, no mole squeezing its way through grass, no bird piping as proof that it lives? Are things but phantoms, is there nothing but this unearthly moonlight and this solitary man, shivering in the icy radiance?

And then suddenly the silence was broken by an immense, formidable voice, as if uttered by the moonlight itself: "There is no law."

The officer stiffened. Who says, who dares to say, there is no law? Listen, we all stand before the law; we are surrounded by the law as we are by the horizon. How could we do anything unless we were compelled? How could I hold my thirty soldiers in line, how could I command them, if there were no law? Where would I turn, if there were no law? There would be no justice; man himself could not exist without the law; nothing could exist, and the world would come crashing down!

To this the serene voice speaking through the moonlight answered: "There is no justice."

How dare you say there is no justice, the indignant officer protested. I condemned him because he killed a wounded man; I acted in the name of the law. And if there were no law, I would have acted according to my conscience and killed him on the spot; I would have dashed his brains out with my pistol, and my conscience would have been clear.

At this the infinite voice uttered: "There is no conscience!"

The presiding officer of the tribunal stood up, in order to confront this terrifying voice. Look at the platform, he passionately protested: three soldiers lie there, dead. Three young men who were alive this morning. Only this morning they were laughing and talking in their rough, cheerful voices, as if they were at play. Out of conscience and justice, you weep and you rage, you become savage and you become crazed; you sit in judgment and you strike out with fury and, yes, with compassion. And were you God Himself, you could not do otherwise, you could not do other than to say the man was right.

The voice speaking through the moonlight did not respond. The solitary man turned his gaze toward the heavens, a milky dome infused with petrified light. And then the voice said: "There is no God."

The man trembled and recoiled in fear. Surely now the smallest blade of grass, the dust on the road, surely the white stones, the very droplets of the condemned man's blood drying here on the pavement, surely these will rise up against the heavens and cry out in protest; they will defend God, they will passionately bear Him witness, at least they will make themselves heard! at least they will make their terror known! Silence, deathly silence, no sound but one of the soldiers talking in his sleep; nothing stirred. The endless landscape is petrified by the unspeaking universe.

And what of me, thought the terrified man, why is there no voice within me to make myself heard? Has no sign been given to me? Is there nothing, no one to help me?

One of the soldiers stirs, clumsily wakes up. It is midnight, the changing of the guard; muttering, coughing, a belt strap jangling, the soldier goes out on watch.

The officer breaks out of his reverie and turns. In the passageway he is greeted by the flickering glow of an oil lamp, warm, rich, intimate, and he grasps it as he would a companion and takes it with him out to the platform. Beside the tracks lie three dead bodies, three slaughtered soldiers, nothing more. The moonlight shrouds them with a strange, unearthly indifference.

The soldier is patrolling in front of the shed. Ten paces, ten paces; the tip of his bayonet glints at each turning. The sand on the platform, the rails, the white stone of the shed, everything white, dazzling, unearthly, spectral. There is nothing. There is nothing at all. Only the universe.

The officer makes his way slowly back to the office where he sat in judgment, lowers himself onto the sofa, and sets the wretched lantern on the edge of the desk. The yellow flame wavers, droops, warms itself, and the man on the sofa holds it in his unswerving gaze until his eyes fill with tears, until he falls asleep from sorrow and exhaustion.